MIDSTATION

BRIAN THOMAS BARROW

Library of Congress Control Number: 2016908360
ISBN: Hardcover   978-1-5245-0316-1
               Softcover   978-1-5245-0315-4
               eBook   978-1-5245-0314-7

Print information available on the last page.

Rev. date: 05/25/2016

To order additional copies of this book, contact:
Xlibris
1-888-795-4274
www.Xlibris.com
Orders@Xlibris.com
740140

CONTENTS

To my dear brother John and my great friend Duke.
They both left this world too soon.

ACKNOWLEDGMENTS

Many people read this story and I am grateful for all of their help and input. Jim Dugan cheerfully went over the words and pages with a fine-toothed comb. Lori Barao helped smoothing out rough patches. Jean Lemongello made sure that all the words and language fit the time period. Elizabeth Burton made certain that the description of the Gold Rush, Alaska, and the Yukon were historically accurate.

I have additional thanks for Mark Barao, Tim Grud, Dietmar Fahrun, Jeff Jacobsen, Tim and Amy Kenny, Vicki Scallo, Allison Thompson, and Billy Sample.

CHAPTER ONE

---·-❋·-·---

Into the Cold

T he sunlight was fading quickly from the sky, and a whispering wind was rustling through the tall snow-burdened trees. The setting sun stroked the feathery dust of snow that drifted down, and although it created a fiery orange glow, it was cold, and I was chilled to the bone. I had never experienced the frosty cold of snow because I was raised in the warmth of a sprawling country estate in Southern California. I wasn't enthused to be trotting along this frigid path, unaware of where the hell I was going, but I would follow my master wherever he went, and I always trusted that he knew what was best.

I am a French Bulldog, and I am the voice that is authoring this story. I know my master is an established, award-winning writer, but the most compelling and redeeming parts of this story would never have happened if it weren't for my keen instincts.

I have no business being in this frigid northland. I was bred to crush the necks of rodents. I am stronger, faster, and smarter than rats, mice, and rabbits. I am also smarter than people realize. Just because I can't speak the language doesn't mean I can't understand every word that is spoken around me.

I may not be a sled puller, but my new northland cabin will be free of vermin, I can promise you that. Also, I have great vision, acute hearing, and a remarkable sense of smell. All of which, along with my keen instincts for human behavior, will be crucial to the events of this tale.

I felt kind of guilty, because I spent most of this journey under a blanket on top of a sled, and when I did trot along unencumbered, there were ten very overworked dogs pulling a burgeoning sled containing my master's belongings, as well as my master and a man I had just met, who was guiding us along our course.

I was overwhelmed by the power and determination of these dogs, and I was amazed at how they made that enormous sled slide so easily through the snow. The gentle slipping sound of the rails of the sled belied the strength and force it took to carry the formidable weight, and that made it easier to hear the rhythm of the forty mighty paws pounding into the frozen ground to pull it.

I had just removed myself from the warmth of my blanket atop the sled because I wanted to listen in on an important conversation. The man I had just met, Jan Ericsson, was talking to my master. His voice was not loud, but it was amazing how I could hear him over the wind and the sound of the sled slashing through the snow. He was explaining the dangerous nature of living in the wilderness, and everything he said was making sense to me. Jan Ericsson was a very experienced sledder from Dawson City. He had guided hundreds of gold-seeking fortune hunters all through the deadly, frosty Alaskan tundra.

I listened to every piece of information that the knowledgeable guide was providing, because my master was not experienced in the deadly ways of the northland, and frankly, despite my faith in Thomas Strong's judgment, I was more than a little worried as we were traveling into this frosty desolation.

This was the winter of 1898. So many people had been captivated by the sense of adventure and the pursuit of instant wealth in what history now calls the Alaskan Gold rush. My master was a wealthy, learned man, and he was not embarking on this journey in pursuit of gold-rush fortune. Thomas Strong was my provider and the man I depended on. Like his name, he was strong, and he had intelligence and wit and usually displayed common sense. At this moment, I felt he was being a bit rambunctious. Yet still, he was my master and caretaker, and I was his best friend and loyal servant.

My master was not in pursuit of the wealth of gold. He was in pursuit of the unique and compelling stories that made people risk life and limb in the frigid northland, chasing the dream of quick wealth by gold.

Thomas Strong made his name and considerable wealth with black and white, with black ink quill of pens upon white paper. He was a respected journalist that had traveled the world for *American* magazine, writing features about famous people, captains of industry, and creators of history.

I loved my master with all my heart, but I knew I was third place in his heart for most of my life. He had a wonderful wife and precious daughter that certainly should have been foremost in his heart and mind. Tragically, I became number one in his heart, and we were traveling on this silvery, snowy, frigid path because his beloved wife and daughter were suddenly taken away from him in a sudden and terrible accident.

I never knew the details of what happened to the family he cherished, but I knew his life was changed forever. The happy, creative, intelligent man I had known turned into a sullen, depressed, sad man with little motivation.

I felt bad for my master, and I felt worse because he could sense my sympathy for him. Because of his success and financial security, he didn't really have to go anywhere or have to do anything to make a living and provide for us, but Thomas Strong needed something to shake himself back into creativity and happiness.

I think I provided comfort to him, like a good dog should do for his master. Thomas Strong never expected anything from me, and I never expected anything from him. We always assumed the best of each other, and I knew that we both had a genuine understanding of the essentials of the master-and-dog relationship.

Thomas Strong's parents, Earnest and Emily Strong, migrated to California in 1882. They left what they considered a boring life in Baltimore, Maryland, for the new opportunities developing on the West Coast.

Earnest Strong was a sailor who spent much time on many piers, and he had developed shipbuilding skills along the way, and there were many piers and boats to be built in California. Emily Strong was a schoolteacher, and she knew that there would be many opportunities to find work in education in the blossoming state of California.

Earnest and Emily Strong settled on the land that was now the home of my master and me. Earnest spent much time away from home, building piers and boats and showing novice sailors how to navigate the sea. Emily taught many children inside their own home and did not have much time to spend with her son, Thomas. Their boy did seem much smarter than most of the children his age.

As a boy, Thomas Strong spent a lot of time on his own. He read books that often made him smile a quiet smile, and he seemed content. He enjoyed reading, which made him want to try writing as well. As a ten-year-old boy, he wrote a story about loving parents that gave a boy a puppy for his birthday. Emily Strong read the words on the pages and cried, because perhaps the story implied that she and her husband, Earnest, had in some way neglected their son.

The very next day, Thomas Strong was awakened by a licking sensation on his nose. When his eyes opened, his heart opened as well, to welcome his excited puppy. His new best friend was a shiny black poodle with eyes almost bigger than his entire face. The boy's joy was incalculable, and the happiness on the faces of Earnest and Emily Strong represented the satisfaction of a good parental decision.

"Mommy, Daddy, thank you so much!" yelped Thomas Strong.

"You are welcome, son."

"We love you, son!"

"Mommy, Daddy, what should I name him?"

"Think about it, son, and you will come up with something," offered his father.

"Thomas, you are the writer, and I know you will come up with the perfect name," assured his mother.

Thomas Strong hugged that puppy all day. He played with him, looked deep into his dark eyes, and thought about any name that might be best for his new best friend. It was very late, and he was still awake in bed, hugging his precious companion. Thomas Strong went to his bedroom window, carrying his new pal, and he looked up into a very dark sky with a new moon. At that moment, the grandfather clock in the house struck twelve. Thomas Strong looked at his little black puppy and the dark sky, and as he listened to the twelve chimes of the clock ring off, he knew the name of his dog.

"I am going to call you Midnight," whispered Thomas Strong to his tired puppy, and the new best friends headed off to a great night of dreams and a life of happiness together.

After ten years of a wonderful friendship, Thomas Strong had to leave his best friend, Midnight, behind to pursue his college education. He was heading off to Northwestern University to study English, creative writing, and journalism.

The young student returned home for the holidays and summer breaks to be with his family and his best friend, Midnight. When he came home for the holidays during his junior year, the house was quiet, but Earnest and Emily Strong were even more silent. Thomas Strong's best friend, his dog, Midnight, had died of old age while he was away pursuing knowledge and education.

The young man that was Thomas Strong hated the fact that he was not there for his friend, Midnight, at the time of his demise. I think he felt some sort of guilt that was unnecessary. As his career developed, and he married and had a daughter, he struggled with leaving his family to travel and do his job as a writer.

One day, while returning from a lengthy trip away from his family, Thomas Strong felt the need to bring a best friend home to his daughter, much like his parents had done for him when he was a lonely boy. I was the most fortunate dog to be his daughter's best friend, and I was grateful to be part of this family. I loved his wife and daughter, but I can assure this: when Thomas Strong left on a trip for work, I was the one that missed him the most.

When he was happy, my master would take me out into the grassy hills of his sundrenched California estate, and he would run me around and laugh about how he could make me chase anything he would toss into the sky. After running me into a tired state of contented exhaustion, we would retire to his cozy study and a warm glowing fire. He would sit in his old worn-out leather chair with me at his feet. He would relax and sip aged and mellowed brandy, while perhaps collecting his thoughts about what to write. The scent of the brandy, combined with warmth and glow of the fire, always coerced me into a relaxed slumber. Soon I would awake to the familiar scratching sound of pen on paper, and I would groggily snuggle closer to his feet. The soft, rhythmic flow of his quill pen on the pages carried me back into a restful, peaceful sleep. Those days were the happiest days of my life, and I could also sense the contentment of my provider and master. Now, thoughts of the whisper of pen on paper and the tangerine glow of a fire were being replaced by howling wind and impending darkness.

I wanted desperately for this frigid marathon to end, and I could sense my master was having second thoughts about this journey. Clearly, I sensed the doubtful worries of my master above the cries of the yelping dogs and whistling winds. Thankfully, an image of a simple, rustic dwelling appeared through an opening upon a small snow-burdened rise. There was joy and a cheerful yell from Jan Ericsson, because this was apparently our destination.

CHAPTER TWO

———— ❊ ————

The Cabin

As the dogs pulled the sled near what appeared to be a very sturdily constructed log cabin, our guide seemed pleased at the condition of our newly found sanctuary.

"The place looks great. You are going to love it here, Thomas!" yelled Jan Ericsson.

As we got close to what would be my new home, the hardworking dogs suddenly slowed and pulled to a halt in an open area about one hundred feet east and downhill to the cabin. These worker dogs impressed me. They had been here many times before, and they willingly went to an area that provided them with a place to be secured and tied down. Again, I need to emphasize how much these dogs amazed me. They were happy to sleep in a place that would allow them the comfort of a deep hole in the snow, with the promise of some fish or jerky in the morning. The sled dogs had earned my respect, and I felt guilty about strolling into a secure habitat with walls, a roof, and the warmth of a fireplace.

As we entered the cabin, Jan Ericsson moved quickly but spoke slowly and clearly. He immediately explained the importance of tending a fire, as he began creating flames in the fireplace.

"A raging fire is a waste of wood, but a slow-burning fire warms just as good," advised Jan Ericsson.

As my master and I huddled in darkness, Ericsson lit two lanterns, one on each side of the room. As the lanterns provided flickering light, our new fire quickly established a heat source. As Jan Ericsson nurtured the welcomed flames of warmth, my master and I surveyed our new residence. I could tell immediately that my master and I had the same first impression. We had both feared a difficult existence in the northland, but this remote dwelling was a well-designed and cozy fortress.

Jan Ericsson explained that he and a few of his hunter friends built the cabin in the summer of 1896. It was only a day and a half sled ride from Dawson City, and caribou, elk, and moose were plentiful in the area. They planned on building a simple structure, but after they found gold dust in a stream 200 yards to the east, they figured it best to construct a place that would be more comfortable for long-term residence while also providing security for what they assumed would be sudden fortune.

As it turned out, the builders of my new home were frustrated by limited success in the mining business, and they soon learned that they were about six hundred miles south from the prolific gold harvest. All but one of the hunters went north, caught up in the frenzy of the gold rush. Our guide, Jan Ericsson, was the one man that did not go into wild pursuit of golden treasure. He returned to Dawson City and was making a fine living guiding zealous gold rushers to this very cabin, the first leg of a long journey into ferocious frigidness.

American magazine was so desperate to rejuvenate their most prolific writer that they agreed to buy this cabin for him. The editors all agreed Thomas Strong's idea to detail the triumphs and tragedies of gold rushers would be compelling reading. The magazine would have done anything to have the productivity of the pen of Thomas Strong once again filling the pages of their publication, but the editors at *American* magazine also had a genuine concern for the happiness of such a valued friend.

The cabin was a very impressively crafted structure, and being so far from any human community, most everything had been constructed with resources at hand. There was a magnificent stone-and-mortar fireplace that was the centerpiece of the room. It was four feet deep and had three stone shelves jutting out from the interior walls, which served as cooking platforms amidst the warming fire.

There was an open area in front of the fireplace that featured two bearskins in the middle of the room, lying before the fire. There were two wonderfully crafted rugs, and upon each of the rugs were masterfully crafted rocking chairs. Two large tables, surrounded with benches, rested in the middle of the room. There were two sets of double-deck bunks on the wall across the fireplace, as well as another pair against the two walls on each side, which was good enough to accommodate twelve weary travelers. To the left side of the wall farthest from the fireplace, there was a small galley that jutted out from the structure. There were pantry-like shelves for storage of sugar and coffee, and a large table for food preparation and animal butchering. At the far end of the pantry, there was a small door that opened into a covered woodpile, where meat could also be hung. Just beyond the woodpile was a sturdy outhouse that featured a comfortable wooden seat hovering over a very deep hole, and it also had an iron bucket, which could be filled with coals to provide some warmth. Most importantly, inside the cabin, opposite the fire, was a table and chair suitable for writing and also observing whatever went on in the cabin. That was a great feature for Thomas Strong, the writer and observer.

After familiarizing myself with my new surroundings, I found myself nestling at the feet of my master, as he rocked away in one of the fireside rocking chairs. Slowly, my eyes began to close, and then I felt a cold draft and turned to see Jan Ericsson's back as he exited quickly through the door. He was going to tend to his dogs. Again, I was amazed. Those hardworking dogs would be spending the night in the ungodly frigidness of icy darkness, and I had the comfort of a rug, warm flames, and the love of my master.

I woke from a lovely slumber to the scent of coffee and the voices of my master and Jan Ericsson in the midst of what seemed like a significant conversation.

"Thomas, I am happy to let you stay here. I think your idea to write about the hopes and dreams and trials and tribulations of the gold rushers will be compelling reading," said Ericsson, and then he continued in a tone that grew increasingly stern.

"I will bring travelers up from Dawson City, and the people I guide to this cabin will be well informed, well prepared, and have sufficient supplies for the journey north. These people will be hopeful and happy to spend one last night in the warmth of a roofed dwelling."

"I am sure these travelers will be happy and grateful to see me and my best friend, Stanley," interjected my master.

"Yes, they will, but there might be others that stop here without my knowledge or your permission."

"I understand the nature of desperation."

"Most of the people that stop here on their own will be fine, but promise me to make sure of one thing."

"Okay . . . what?"

"You are a journalist. You are a smart and an observant man. When people stop here on their way north, and you talk to them about their hopes and aspirations, look into their eyes. Most of the travelers that stop here on the way up north will certainly remember where this cabin is, and they will be cold and desperate and looking forward to stopping here on the long journey home."

"Yeah, sure, that is what I am hoping for. The whole story, from the beginning to the end of the journey."

"Just remember to look into their eyes when they return. The freezing cold, howling wind, and constant darkness of the Yukon can suck the soul from a man."

"I know that hollow look in a man's eyes. I have seen it in the mirror every day since my wife and daughter were taken from me. Don't worry about me. The people that come through the door into this cabin with bad intentions will be greeted by a man that is unafraid and capable to defend himself."

"I have a good feeling about you, Thomas. I can't wait to read your stories. I am so proud that I will be delivering your words down to the wire in Dawson City."

"I have a good feeling about the people I am going to meet. Don't worry about Stanley and I. As long as you keep bringing supplies and travelers from Dawson City, I promise to write a glowing story about your skills and dedication to the safety of northland travel," Thomas Strong said with a chuckle.

"Very funny! Just take care of yourself, Thomas. Every time I bring a group headed north, I will return south to Dawson City with your stories from previous travelers. I promise to bring you supplies and take good care of your stories, so you just take care of Shorty."

I liked Jan Ericsson, but I growled at him when he called me Shorty. With that said, Jan Ericsson opened the door, hooked up his dogs to a sled that was now much lighter, and departed south toward Dawson City. I was a bit nervous that our knowledgeable lifeline was sledding away. I was, however, happy to have my master to myself, but I was still upset that Jan Ericsson had called me Shorty.

CHAPTER THREE

I Am Stanley

My name is Stanley. That is my name, and I am proud of it, and I don't like people calling me other names. I hate being called cute, insulting monikers, like pooch, or booby, and I don't like being called Stan.

I am named Stanley because my master went to a banquet in Montreal in 1893 to interview the owner of a hockey team that won a significant championship. Montreal HC they were called. Great name. HC stands for Hockey Club. Even a dog like me can figure that one out. Anyway, the trophy was a silver bowl, named after Lord Stanley of Preston, who, at that time, was the General Governor of Canada. My master had interviewed the Governor, and he liked hockey. He could have named me HC or Preston, or Governor, but he named me Stanley. I like my name, and I love hearing my master, Thomas Strong, call it out to me.

"Here, Stanley."

"Oh, Stanley."

I especially liked it when my master, Thomas Strong, stretched out the last syllable of my name in a funny-sounding screech, "Stanleeeeeeeeey."

One day, a few months after the horrific loss of his loved ones, my master and I went for a long walk. It seemed he might be getting through his horrible pain. He had a little more jump and quickness in his step, and I was hoping he would be on the way to being happy again.

Upon our return from our pleasant walk, my master and I returned to find two men, both unfamiliar to me, sitting on the porch, my porch, and I was immediately turned from peaceful happiness into angry defensiveness. I leaped at the two strangers with grit and growl. They were too close to the door of my master's home.

I leaped at the two trespassers with zeal and zest, but I was swatted away with ease and laughter. My anger grew but started to subside when my master was soon hugging and laughing with the strangers. I calmed down more when I heard the name-calling and laughter.

"Good to see you, Writer Boy!"

"Hey, Loser!"

"Hey, Thomas!"

"Great to see you, Bullman!"

Thankfully, Loser and Bullman were old friends of my master, Writer Boy. They knew my master even before I was born, and I suddenly sensed the strength in the bonds they had together. They embraced and cackled with joyful laughter that warmed my heart. After they were done hugging one another, they played with me and gave me a sense of their good nature. I was thrilled to see the smiles and laughs from my master. He had a light heart for the first time since his horrific loss.

"I am so sorry, Thomas, for everything," said Bullman in a sympathetic tone.

"We felt we needed to come for a visit, Thomas," continued Loser.

These two men had traveled a long way to support a suffering friend, and I respected them instantly. It was obvious that these men shared a durable bond. They were more than friends.

Loser was one of the captains of industry that my master had met, interviewed, and written a glowing feature about for *American* magazine. Louis Bostock was not a loser. He never lost at anything but poker. His face was too honest for five-card stud, but his sincere features and genuine nature allowed him to broker the trust of everyone that ventured into business with him. He was a diverse man with ability to analyze any type of business and turn problems into profits. Unfortunately, Bostock's unmatched ability to analyze business ledgers was forlornly equaled by his failure to comprehend the mystery of the fairer sex, and he had three ex-wives to prove it.

John Foreman was the Bullman. He was a cattle rancher from a remote area in northern Montana. He was a very strong man, not overly big or imposing, but just as Bostock had honesty written upon his face, the sturdy nature of Foreman was immediately apparent.

Foreman was fortunate to own some of the most perfect land to raise cattle in North America. He had a reputation for bringing some of the best beef to market, but his route to the railroad was long and treacherous. His cattle were worth more per pound than most ranchers', but he lost many cattle along the drive due to a long, arduous route around three enormous neighboring estates.

Foreman had read the article about Louis Bostock that my master had written for *American* magazine. There was a brief mention in that article that Bostock enjoyed the great outdoors, so Foreman whimsically penned a letter seeking business advice in exchange for some professional guided time in Big Sky country. More than anything else, Foreman's letter was a way to release and vent his frustrations.

Bostock received the letter from Foreman at an auspicious time for both men. The business genius had just weathered his third divorce and needed time in the open country, and Foreman's problem seemed an enjoyable problem to solve. Bostock immediately started to pack for a trip to Montana, ready to tackle a new challenge and take in some of the most beautiful country in North America.

Upon his arrival, Foreman, the cattle rancher and tour guide, wanted to show Bostock, the business genius, his appreciation for making the trip. He suggested a horseback ride into a steady upgrade that would be the perfect vantage point for a Montana sunset. The ride would be followed by an evening in his enormous, rustic, picturesque ranch, complete with a raging fire and an unforgettable meal that his wife, Dorothy, would prepare.

Bostock surprised Foreman with a request to skip the horses and go right to the fire and the meal. Foreman's wife, Dorothy, seemed to struggle with the change of the schedule, which was unusual, because she was a strong woman that normally could withstand a Montana hailstorm. Still, Dorothy and Bullman were thrilled with the direct and sincere approach of their enthusiastic guest.

Bostock had already examined the geography of Foreman's situation and suggested trying to purchase a small route of land that passed directly through all three of his neighboring estates. He said it would be minimally invasive to all and would cut Foreman's herding time in half. To Foreman, that meant it would cut his costs for labor and supplies in half.

The next day, Bostock and Foreman did take a ride on horseback, but it wasn't to see a sunset. It was to talk to the owner of the nearest of Foreman's neighboring estates. Bostock's sincere demeanor and honest face helped broker a mutually beneficial agreement, which would soon be presented to, and accepted by, the two other neighboring estates.

With the new, shorter route in place, the next time Foreman brought his cattle to market, the herd was both larger and healthier and sold for a much higher price than he had ever received before. The next season, Foreman invited Bostock back for a week in Big Sky country to thank him for his newly thriving business, and again Bostock surprised him with another massive opportunity for capital gains.

Another rancher with a large cattle property both north and adjacent to Foreman's estate also wanted a quicker route to market. Bostock negotiated a fee for a pass through Foreman's superior route, and three other ranches north of Foreman soon followed suit. Suddenly, Foreman was not only a successful cattle rancher, but he was a highly paid toll keeper for all the ranchers around his estate.

Foreman went from being a struggling cattle rancher to the most successful business story in the rugged country of early Montana. Foreman's sudden success was the type of American dream tale that *American* magazine made their goal to provide to hopeful readers. They sent the best writer they had to capture this wonderful story that combined the business acumen of Louis Bostock and the rugged labor of John Foreman.

Thomas Strong had previous knowledge of the golden business touch of Louis Bostock but had never been to Montana, and he knew little of the cattle ranching business in which Foreman had recently risen to prominence. Louis Bostock was enjoying his time in

Montana with his new friend John Foreman, and he was thrilled that Bullman's recent success would be documented in *American* magazine by the great Thomas Strong.

Sadly, unlike when Bostock had arrived for the first time two years earlier, there was dimness in what had always been a joyous and vibrant atmosphere. Thomas Strong, the writer, showed up to pen a story about a wonderful business relationship and a unique friendship, but upon his arrival, he was confronted with a more tragic and tearful tale. John Foreman's wife, Dorothy, was in failing health.

When Bostock had first visited two years earlier, Dorothy seemed strong, but she appeared to be struggling to hide symptoms of illness. Now, as Bostock, Foreman, and Dorothy met the writer Thomas Strong at the door, it was obvious to the author that his happy story was going to have a sad ending.

Dorothy Foreman was a strong, durable, and vibrant woman who could not hide her inevitable demise. She was such an amazing pillar of friendliness and an attentive host, but the joyful story of business success emerged into something quite solemn. It was no longer about wealth or money, but now about love and devotion.

Thomas Strong; Foreman, the cattle rancher; and Bostock, the business genius, gathered by a fire after Dorothy had retired for the night. As a hollow wind whispered outside Foreman's glorious ranch, and a glowing fire crackled that provided sepia-tone warmth inside, three very different men bonded in a rare and unique way.

As the flickering flames showered the room, Foreman expressed regret that Bostock and my master had traveled such a long way to tell his story of business success, and now so quickly, his wife's deteriorating health made that so insignificant to him.

Foreman told stories of his love for Dorothy and how he spent the early years of their marriage building a business and, more importantly, building a life together. My master was an understanding and sympathetic ear, and all the while, he was thinking of his lovely wife and child that he had at his home in California. Meanwhile, Bostock, who was the champion of business and had many failed relationships, listened and learned about the meaning of devotion.

The three very different men talked, conjectured, and revealed things about one another that seemed perhaps awkward at times. Their discussions garnered an amazing familiarity and closeness, and that was when the nicknames Bullman, Loser, and Writer Boy were born. Their lengthy conversation was punctuated by a sliver of the rising sun, a new day in cattle country.

Foreman gathered himself as the sunrise sneaked into the conversation, and he took his guests outside, walking to a vantage point that would provide a glorious view that could not be described by words or captured by pictures. Again, the three men bonded, but now in silence, not by words.

The new-day sun strolled over a distant hill, and its warmth created a smoky mist that rose and then so quickly disappeared. It was a gloriously majestic moment. As the three men strolled back to Foreman's ranch, nothing was said, but it was evident that friendship between all three would be enduring.

Upon returning to the ranch, there was an eerie stillness. Foreman quickly noticed the absence of the aroma of coffee brewing, and there was a chill in his home that was unfamiliar. The fire was unattended, and when Foreman looked toward my master and Bostock, they both sensed the worst.

Dorothy was buried at sunset that very same day, and three very successful, powerful, and proud men were not at all ashamed to cry and sob out loud above her grave. They would be friends, more than friends, for a lifetime. When my master finally left Foreman's ranch a week later, he felt guilty to be going home to his loving wife and daughter.

The article that Thomas Strong wrote for *American* magazine perfunctorily mentioned the story of business success of Bostock and Foreman, but when the tale twisted and extolled that there is no joy in success when loved ones are lost, readers wept, and my master was awarded the Pearson Award for journalistic excellence. He did not attend the awards ceremony, but he did make sure the small gold statue was shipped to Foreman's ranch in Montana.

Bostock and Foreman had visited my master because they were worried about him after his terrible loss. They arrived and made him feel better, even rejuvenated. They all laughed, ate, drank, and reminisced for days. I don't think Loser and Bullman knew this, but their visit awoke my master's soul and is the reason why I am a northland resident.

CHAPTER FOUR

Here They Come

After Jan Ericsson had left me and my master to ourselves in the cabin, we spent a couple of funny days getting acquainted with our new surroundings. Have you ever seen a dog when he enters an unfamiliar dwelling? Our curious nature makes us roam around, sniffing everything, until we get comfortable with our new environment. I was done sniffing, scratching, and searching after two hours. My master had his head up the chimney, evaluated the woodpile and property, inspected the roof, made sure the latches of the door were secure, and did a general cleanup of our somewhat musty surroundings. It was funny watching him try to figure everything out.

Our first night alone in the cabin, I felt so happy to have my master all to myself. He made a fire that crackled and glowed and made our cabin the warmest place in Alaska.

"Slow and steady," we both remembered Jan Ericsson saying at the same time, and we smiled at each other.

The fire settled to a glowing burn, and my master, Thomas Strong, cooked our first meal in our new home. In a cast iron pot, my master seared big chunks of bacon and then slowly heated some beans. Our new home felt so cozy, especially because I could hear the wind howling outside just a bit louder than the fire crackling inside. I had an instant sense of comfort. The fire flickered throughout the room, and the warmth it provided made me feel secure even as the wind whipped through the trees outside. We ate bacon and beans, and later, as my master rocked away in a chair by the fire, I dozed at his feet, occasionally passing wind, which always made him laugh.

I woke in the middle of the night to a noise that was not of recent memory yet was still familiar. It was a sound that had always brought warmth to my heart. My master was scratching his quill pen on paper, perhaps describing his new surroundings, and I looked up and saw happiness and contentment in his face.

The next morning, we went outside for a while. I knew what my master was doing. He wanted me to get used to the cold. I was thinking that nobody can get used to this cold, but I did agree I should build up some tolerance to this frigid climate. We inspected the outhouse and stared in amazement at some enormous trees, wondering how they ever grew so tall. We made our way to investigate the old mine that never did produce any gold, and as we finally worked our way back to the cabin, I learned how to walk softly on the top of the snow so as not to fall in legs deep. This is important for a dog, so you can pee and poop without freezing important body parts.

When we got back to the cabin, my master and I were both chilled and tired. We both knew that we needed to know our limits spending time in the cold. Suddenly, my master beckoned me. He had pulled one of the bearskin rugs very close to the fireplace, and I knew we were going to snuggle and take a lazy afternoon nap in our northland cabin. As I nodded off, my last thought was that this trip into the northland might not have been such a bad idea.

Soon I was rustled by the sounds of the arrival of our very first visitors, well before my master had awakened. Thomas Strong, the award-winning journalist, needed me to alert him that his first subjects were sledding toward our cabin. I licked his nose and tugged on his shirt, and sluggishly, he became aware that visitors were upon us. He looked at me with gratitude for waking him, and he knew my instincts and senses would always be important in this desolate landscape.

My master opened the door and welcomed into the cabin a sledder guide named Payuk. He was a very experienced sledder and guide who happily called Dawson City home. His vast experience made him skilled at the most important thing a guide needs to do well. Payuk knew how to choose good and safe clients and those who wouldn't cause risk to his existence.

My master had never met Payuk, but Jan Ericsson had raved about his skills in the wilderness. Payuk, the sledder guide, looked at me and smiled. I liked him. He was a good first guest, I could tell.

Payuk explained to my master that he was guiding two men, and they were outside securing a twelve-dog sled team. They would be inside shortly, and he felt confident about this journey. Payuk mentioned Jan Ericsson and handed my master a bottle of whiskey.

That bottle of whiskey would end up being sipped in front of a glowing fire by my master, the sledder guide Payuk, and our first two gold-rushing visitors, Wolfgang and Dietmar Fahrun, twin brothers of German descent. I would like to say that I liked instantly, but it took a few minutes and a few insults for me to warm up to them. When the Fahrun twins entered the cabin, they simultaneously made negative remarks upon seeing me.

"What little sled did he pull to get here?" said Wolfgang as he chuckled while removing his layers of wool and skins.

"How come the tough little guy didn't bark when we pushed in the door?" asked Dietmar.

I probably would have preferred a little pat on the head for a welcome greeting, but I could tell the Fahrun twins were just having fun with me.

"You are our first guests, and he likes you," my master replied, but I wished he had explained better to the Fahrun brothers that I have an instinct when it comes to the nature of people.

It was exciting to have a fire crackling, voices bellowing, along with the sound of healthy chuckling and laughter in the air, and most importantly, my master was smiling. He was so enthused with our first guests, and he quickly went to work, getting the story that brought them to our cabin.

"I have been told that Payuk is a great guide with incredible instincts," said Thomas Strong, the writer. "He has great confidence in your successful return," he continued.

"Thomas, we are wealthy men, but we are in search of the riches of adventure," stated Wolfgang.

"We are not desperate for the money and spoils of gold," said Dietmar. "We know of your desire to tell the stories of gold rushers, and since we are your first visitors, we promise to be first to return with either gold or a golden story."

The brothers certainly were not in need of the instant riches of the gold rush. Wolfgang and Dietmar were the twin sons of wealthy parents, Bernhard and Andrea Fahrun.

Bernhard and Andrea Fahrun came to America as teenagers in love, chased their adventures to California, and then were forced to stop moving around when, in San Francisco, Andrea became pregnant. Bernhard Fahrun was a skilled woodworker, and he knew he could design quality furniture for the growing city of San Francisco. So Fahrun Furniture was born, and a few months later, Dietmar and Wolfgang were also born.

Fahrun Furniture became famous for quality custom furniture, and the business flourished and grew. The twin boys grew as quickly as the business, and at the age of twenty, both boys realized they didn't want to follow into the furniture business of their parents.

They wanted an adventure like their parents experienced when they came to America. Bernhard and Andrea Fahrun understood their twin sons' ambitions and, thus, encouraged them as they went on their way to Alaska in search of adventure and, perhaps, gold. Unlike most rushers, however, Wolfgang and Dietmar Fahrun departed toward Alaska with plenty of cash in their pockets, which was probably why Payuk was such a happy guide.

Wolfgang and Dietmar were such pleasant guests. They were excited about their impending adventure and were happy to explain why two wealthy young men would risk life and limb in the frigid north. My master, the writer, seemed thrilled to soak up the thoughts, hopes, and desires of these two interesting young men.

In the morning, Payuk, Wolfgang, and Dietmar went out to harness the dogs and get moving on the trails headed north. My master was still sleeping, and I heard the dog harnesses snapping. I thought they were gone, but then the door quickly opened, and Payuk entered, came toward me, and put a cold sardine in my mouth.

"I will see you again, Stanley," he whispered.

He left before I ate my sardine, but I knew I liked him. I remember thinking that the Fahrun brothers were lucky to have him as a guide. I had a good feeling about our first visitors, and I was confident that I would see them again.

My master awoke, disappointed that he didn't have the chance to bid farewell and good luck to our first visitors, but he smelled the sardine on my breath and sensed my contentment, and he knew that I had a chance to say good-bye and wish good luck to Payuk and the Fahrun twins.

CHAPTER FIVE

---◆◆◆---

Hopes and Dreams

There was a warm, consistent sound within our dwelling that often drowned out the noise of the wind and rustling of the heavy snow burgeoning upon the pine trees. In our fireplace, the crackling of flames scorching wood and the consistent toasty tone it created was a welcome feeling of comfort. The continuous sounds and warmth of the fire were like the indescribable colors of a picturesque sunset being allowed to sing a sweet melody. I love the combination of the welcoming warmth, toasty glow, and snapping sound of a fire more than anything, especially when I am nestled at the feet of my master.

One thing that was consistent with all the arrivals of our visiting gold rushers was that I was aware of them approaching our cabin well before my master knew they were nearby. My master is a great writer, but I have a great sense of smell, excellent hearing, and much better instincts.

In the next couple of weeks, we would have a number of visitors in the cabin. One particularly interesting group of travelers sought shelter in the comfort of our dwelling. It was a unique foursome composed of two married couples, and they were not accompanied by a guide. They were interesting and curious to me right away, because the two men entered the cabin first, while the women tended to the dogs in the cold outside.

23

I was sitting in front of the cabin door before the two men knocked and asked for entry. My master would eventually become accustomed to me in this position, poised at the door to greet new travelers.

As Jack Winston and Ted Bagley entered the cabin, I instantly had a bad feeling that was colder than the rush of the wintery briskness breezing in through the open door. They were gold rushers, briefly stopping here with us, before making the difficult journey into the northland. I was not confident in their success.

Outside, I heard two women sternly issuing orders to dogs. Meanwhile, inside, Thomas Strong began conducting a conversation that was casual but would give him the constructive fibers to weave together the fabric of this group's interesting tale.

"Greeting, gentlemen, welcome, I am Thomas, Thomas Strong. Are you okay? Do you need any help securing your team outside?"

"No, thanks, Tom, we are just happy to be here," said Jack Winston.

"Our wives are outside tending to our sled team. We should be out there, but the dogs deal with our wives better than they do with us," yukked Ted Bagley.

"Well, that is my boy, Stanley, and that is the fire!" said my master.

"Great to be inside. Warm and out of the elements!" bellowed Jack.

"How did you know about this place?"

"Jan Ericsson from Dawson City sent us your way. He told us that you would keep us warm for a night if we spilled our guts about our hopes and dreams," chuckled Jack.

"Cute dog, he reminds me of my wife," snickered Ted.

The chuckling and snickering immediately stopped as Jack's wife, Maureen, and Ted's wife, Mandy, pushed open the door and instantly started barking orders at their husbands, who were content to be warming by the fire. The two women entered with cold air cascading off their bodies, but there was heat, fire, and sarcasm in the remarks spewing from their mouths.

"Are you warm yet?"

"Comfy?"

"Welcome, ladies. Welcome, ladies," my master implored in a surprisingly successful effort to ease the angst of the agitated wives.

After my master welcomed the two women, they both collected their bearings and cooled down as they warmed up, and then they were quite polite. I liked both women right off, but I wasn't sure why these fiery, tough women would be with guys more concerned with huddling by my fire.

"I'm sorry about our rude entrance, Mr. Strong," said Maureen.

"We have been so looking forward to meeting you," ushered Mandy.

"We both have read many of your stories in *American* magazine," said Maureen.

"Jan Ericsson told us that you would be telling tales of journeys like ours. I beg you to be gracious when describing the two lumps overheating over there in front of your fire," asserted Mandy.

Then simultaneously, the two hardworking wives immediately began acting like most women act when they meet me, yours truly, for the first time.

"Heeeeee's sooooooo cute!" Maureen and Mandy both screeched at the same time.

I enjoyed the way that Maureen and Mandy quickly rustled with me, and I was happy to meet their acquaintance. They petted, rubbed, and scratched me with such exuberance that I forgot that there were three other people in the room. I could feel the cold air coming off their icy coats, but at the same time, their attentiveness brought me warmth, and I began to think about the glorious warmth of the coast of California.

As Maureen and Mandy settled into the toasty air of our cabin, the chill of their attitude toward their husbands seemed to melt away quickly. It was quite clear that Jack and Maureen Winston cared deeply about each other. Ted and Mandy Bagley also seemed connected in a complete and deep manner, which made me feel troubled about my negative instincts about their journey into the frigidness of the Yukon gold rush.

I tabled the worry of my instincts, as the fire roared and crackled. The flames provided a flickering orange glow that made Maureen and Mandy look so beautiful and the rest of us men in the cabin look rusty and tired. Jack, Maureen, Ted, and Mandy captivated our cabin with stories that brought smiles and laughter to the writer and me in the room. The obvious excitement spilling from our new guests about their journey northward was contagious.

The Winstons and the Bagleys warmed by the fire, and Thomas Strong soaked in all the details of their lives as quickly as our guests soaked up the heat from the burning wood in the fireplace. The two couples were friends since childhood, growing up in a small town called Delbarton, a fishing community on the shores of Lake Michigan, and they were the products of a relatively wealthy background. Their parents were successful businesspeople working in the ports of Lake Michigan, shipping products in and out of the blossoming Great Lakes area.

Jack and Maureen Winston and Ted and Mandy Bagley were impressed with the success of their parents, but similar to our first guests, the Fahrun twins, they wanted to venture out and achieve happiness on their own. The two couples married on the same day, together, before they headed west, toward the promise and sunshine of California.

Maureen Winston and Mandy Bagley did most of the talking for a long while. The sound of the voices of women telling stories was soothing and relaxing. But when the stanzas of the tales were important to the storyteller, it kept me alert and attentive.

I am a dog, so by nature, I am a good listener. I hear better than the average man, but the prolific writer Thomas Strong listens, hears, and understands what people are saying better than anyone.

"It took a while for us to get to California, but we knew what we were going to do by the time we got there," allowed Maureen.

"A small hotel seemed like a business we could be successful at," offered Mandy.

"Our parents were always dealing with new and different people in their business," said Jack as he rose and moved away from the fire for the first time since he entered the cabin.

"We liked the idea of a small hotel because we could fish, farm, cook, and clean with just the four of us doing everything," delivered Ted.

"Yeah, just the four of us doing everything!" chuckled Maureen.

"Two guys drinking and having fun and us women doing all the work! Damn right, the four of us doing everything," exclaimed Mandy in a very sarcastic manner.

There was laughter in the cabin following the snappy comments of the two women. My canine instincts were correct. The women were in charge of this group of travelers, and as I watched and listened to my master conversing and interacting with the two northbound couples, I could tell he had concluded the same.

Soon the storytelling came to an end, and the evening needed to come to a close. Jack and Ted headed for two bunks closest to the fire. My master, in his chair, was slipping into a happy slumber, complete with a crooked smile of contentment. Maureen and Mandy were too diligent and not yet ready for sleep.

Maureen went to the woodpile, grabbed a few pieces of dry lumber, and arranged them in the fireplace in a manner that would provide a slow burn throughout the night. Meanwhile, Mandy gently placed a heavy blanket upon the gracious host, Thomas Strong, and then proceeded to push his chair just a little bit closer to the warmth of the fire.

Then Maureen and Mandy started pulling one of the bearskin rugs that was directly in front of the fireplace, toward the chilliness of the front door of the cabin. As a dog that enjoys a cozy rug and comfy fire, I was a bit confused with this, since I was nestled upon that bearskin sliding toward the door. I was not upset for long, as Maureen placed me onto a wool blanket at the feet of my master, just close enough to the fire to keep me toasty for a wondrous night of dog dreams.

Before I fell into my dreamy slumber, I realized why Maureen and Mandy moved the rug closer to the door. They would sleep comfortably for a while, and then the cold draft near the door would wake them up early, and they would begin their day that much sooner.

As they had planned, Maureen and Mandy woke quickly with the chilly bluster of frigid air seeping through the cabin door. I watched as they considerately moved gently and quietly about the cabin. They added more wood to the fire and began to brew some coffee. I think they planned to leave our cabin without waking my master, but Thomas Strong loved his coffee, and he got a whiff of the sultry aroma. As he stood up quickly, he stepped on my paw. I yelped, a high-pitched howl that I was not proud of, startling the early-rising women and rustling the two men dreaming with content in their toasty bunks next to the fire.

"Sorry, my boy, Stanley," moaned my master in a half-conscious belch.

Maureen and Mandy raced to my rescue, making sure I was not badly injured. I immediately realized that my injury was insignificant, but I was dizzied with joy from the overwhelming concern of my two women friends. At the very least, the excitement had rustled Jack and Ted from their toasty bunks. The two men rose, sipped coffee, and put on their skins and coats, as their wives went outside to ready the sled team.

The women came back into the cabin one final time to collect their husbands. Everyone hugged and said good-bye. I felt bad because I was worried that some people in this party would not be coming back. Maureen and Mandy hugged me and rubbed my nose, but I made sure to lick the foreheads of Jack and Ted right before they left the cabin.

CHAPTER SIX

---·❋·---

A Warm Cabin They Will Find!

Our next visitors arrived late in the evening of the same day that the Winstons and Bagleys had departed northward. Francis Krause knocked on our cabin door and then waited for the hinges to creak and our dwelling door to be opened by my master. This would be rare that such patience was exhibited by anyone before entering the warmth of our toasty cabin.

"Hello, sir, welcome," greeted the host of the cabin. "I am Thomas Strong, and this is my guard dog, Stanley," said my master as he glanced at me and chuckled lightly.

"I am glad to be here. Both for the chance to escape the cold and for the chance to meet a master of the quill pen and paper!" bellowed Francis Krause. "My guide, Maruk, is outside securing my team," continued Francis. "Did you say that was a guard dog?" Francis queried with mocked confusion.

My master was chuckling at the comment made by Francis as the door opened and Maruk, the guide, entered the cabin. He had settled the dogs in a swift manner. It was immediately obvious that Maruk was an organized, experienced tactician, learned on how to deal with traveling into the treachery of the frigid north. I respected him right away. With a quick glance of his eyes, he offered appreciation for the shelter and acknowledged a respect for his host, and on a much lesser note, I could sense he liked me.

It was obvious that Francis knew of Thomas Strong's career, and it seemed that our new guest was quite interested in conversing with the skilled literary host. Maruk, the guide, however, needed to interrupt the pleasantries to discuss the scheduling necessary for an early departure, which would enhance their chances for a smoother and more productive trip. Maruk made sure he had captured the complete attention of Francis Krause. He did it without being rude, because his knowledge and veteran leadership commanded immediate attention.

Maruk deftly guided Francis Krause toward the roasting fire, knowing that the crackle of the burning logs would diminish the ability of my master to hear what he was saying. Francis Krause was the boss, but Maruk was telling his boss what he had done to feed and secure the sled team and what he would do during the night to make sure the dogs would be ready to work hard in the morning. He was also telling the man paying him a substantial amount of money to guide him northward something very important, something crucial.

"Drink, eat, and have a wonderful conversation with Mr. Strong. Enjoy this night with this intelligent man in front of a warm fire. Relish this evening, because it will be a long time before you will be in such comfort again," whispered Maruk, just loud enough so that I could hear his powerful message.

Francis Krause thought he had paid for a guide to weave his way northland to adventure, but he now realized he had hired a much more valuable individual. As advised, he sat down to talk with his host. But after the quick fireside chat with Maruk, Francis realized that his guide had wisdom far greater than just of sled dogs and trails.

"Mr. Strong . . ."

"Please, Francis . . . Tom."

"Okay, Tom. Thanks. I have read many of your stories in *American* magazine. You are a great storyteller."

"Nice of you to say, but the storyteller is only as good as the story beforehand."

"I think you might be in the right place for good material, Tom."

"Well, Francis, that is why I am here. I just hope the stories have happy endings."

As my master and Francis settled into an engaging conversation, Maruk quietly slid a chair closer to the cabin door and sat down. I sensed he wanted to be more quickly alerted to trouble or more aware of any problems with the dogs outside. Even though it was colder and draftier by the door, I rested my head on Maruk's still-thawing boot, because I knew he soon would be heading into treacherous territory, and I wanted him to know he had a friend.

Francis Krause definitely followed the advice of Maruk, perhaps too well, as he never stopped yammering. For the first time in the cabin, I didn't hear the whirling cold breeze or the rustle that the wind caused blowing upon the trees or the howl of cold, lonely animals. All we heard inside our tiny remote cabin was a continuous, loquacious stream of chatter exuding from the windpipe of Francis Krause.

"My parents came from Norway. I guess they liked the climate of the Great Lakes region, so they settled in an area called Mackinac. It was on the northwest side of Lake Michigan. It had flourishing forests and fertile soil for farming. There was great big-game hunting, and the fishing in the lake was bountiful."

"Sounds nice, Francis, why did your family—"

"My father built a sturdy cabin," interrupted Francis, completely disregarding my master's attempt to ask a question.

"I was just a toddler when the cabin was being constructed, but I had an older brother, Martin, who was quite helpful to my father. I was too small to help, but my father and brother built away, and they always would show me what they were doing as they went along from step to step."

"Where is your—" my master tried to inquire.

"I am here for my brother. He would have liked this adventure. Martin died two years ago. He was hunting along a frozen stream, slipped on an icy rock, and fell through crackling ice. When he smashed through the jagged ice, his torso was slashed open, and his ribs were fractured. He struggled and willed his way back to our cabin."

"What happened to . . ."

"He died of pneumonia four days later," finished Francis, and he paused for the first time in what seemed like an eternity.

Francis exhaled deeply in pause, and Maruk, my master, and I all took a shallow breath in sympathy. A very quiet moment followed. I took the silent pause as an opportunity to gaze into the eyes of everyone in the room. In the eyes of Francis was a look of bewilderment. He was lost, and I sensed that no guide could find what he was searching for. What I noticed in the eyes of my master, as well as in the eyes of Maruk, was a sense that Francis might not return to our cabin. Then there was a simultaneous yet subtle glance by Thomas Strong and me toward Maruk. We both knew Maruk would be back.

CHAPTER SEVEN

---❄---

Ericsson Delivers

My master and I had been nestled in our remote Alaskan cabin for about two months now. It surprised and amazed me how comfortably we were living and getting accustomed to our new surroundings, and to be honest, we were actually quite content and happy.

Our friend Jan Ericsson had visited us twice during our first two months. We enjoyed his visits like a child enjoys a bedtime story before being tucked into bed for the night. My master would read the words that had been carefully scratched from his quill pen to paper. He shared the stories that he had written about the travelers heading north for the very first time with our friend and trusted provider, Jan Ericsson.

My master and I equally enjoyed the fresh supplies that Jan Ericsson brought with him, and we were always curious to hear from him about what was going on in the distant world of the growing country of the United States of America.

While Jan Ericsson's dogs buried themselves in the frozen snow outside, he told us of stories of automobiles that were becoming a new and fancy source of transportation for the wealthier class. We all chuckled that the steel boxes on wheels wouldn't make it to Alaska anytime soon. There was a Spanish-American war beginning, and we couldn't even imagine a conflict as monumental as a war as we sat comfortably and cozily by the toasty fire in our cabin.

Our experienced guide was proud to be the courier that brought Thomas Strong's stories down to Dawson City, and then be sent for publication for the national audience of *American* magazine.

I think Jan Ericsson felt a unique sense of pride that he was the first person hearing the tales penned by a famous writer like Thomas Strong, and he was also thrilled that he was delivering the material from the cold, dark wilderness into civilization. When he would leave and head back to Dawson City, I would watch him smiling, with his face cutting through the wind, on his sled, behind his hustling dogs, as he remembered the tales that my master had told him and that he was now carrying for others to enjoy.

Jan Ericsson had been a great friend that provided my master and me with so much knowledge and a sense of security. He had sent many travelers north toward our cabin. He always told my master to try to read the souls of the people heading into the frozen danger of the Yukon. There had been many visitors that just stopped in for a few hours to thaw their chilled bones, and some stayed a bit longer. So far, we were lucky to have encountered only good-hearted souls.

Soon the warmth of the late spring and summer would melt the snow on the trails and soften the ice on rivers and lakes. The trails south of our cabin would be the first to become soft and slushy, making it impossible to use dog sleds to travel north from Dawson City or, for that matter, to head south to civilization.

Meanwhile, the gold rushers that had passed through our desolate area would not be able to return until the autumn brought cold winds and chilly temperatures that would once again freeze the trails, rivers, and lakes for a safe return.

"Tom, you and Stanley won't have many visitors for the next couple of months, except for maybe a bear or a moose every now and again," quipped Jan Ericsson after a nice, long sip of whiskey.

"We will be fine, Jan. I am looking forward to seeing this place with some sunlight and the pine trees without snow bending the branches," joked my master.

"Don't get too ambitious when the snow first melts, Tom. The first few days when you can see the ground, there will be a murky mud that will be difficult to move through."

"How long should we wait to go out? I know after being cooped up in this cabin for so long, my boy, Stanley, will want to go out and explore the neighborhood."

"Give it a week before you venture out. After a week, throw a big hunk of firewood out into the ground. If it doesn't splatter or make a squishing sound, you are good to go out and explore."

"I am looking forward to venturing out into the surrounding areas, and I think I'd like to pay a visit to that failed gold mine down by the stream below."

"Just don't go inside the mine, Tom. It might not be secure."

I listened to my master and our good friend Jan Ericsson chat away in front of the fireplace, and I realized this was a special night. As I alternated nestling at the feet of my master and Jan Ericsson, I knew that our reliable and trusted friend would not be returning for a long while. A dog can sense the emotions of his master and friends. We can gather a man's feelings from the tones of their voices.

I was feeling sleepy. I don't think my master was upset that I fell asleep at the feet of Jan Ericsson. As I drifted into a deep slumber, I knew I would miss our trusted friend, but I was positive I would see him again and be happy and thrilled when he returned. I dreamed of Jan Ericsson and his team of dogs sledding home, and I was also envisioning him and his team coasting smoothly into Dawson City.

My dream abruptly ended as Jan Ericsson stood up to begin his departure. I looked up at him and sensed he was trying as best as he could to prevent waking me. I think Jan Ericsson was a man that didn't like saying good-bye. I scratched his boot and gave him a subtle smile. I pretended to fall back to sleep as he moved to open the door and head south. As he left, I heard the thump of the door closing, then the rustling and yelping of the eager dogs, followed by the swishing sound of the rails of the sled gliding through the snow.

The last sound I heard before I returned to slumber was familiar and comforting. It was the sound of my master snoring relentlessly, so I returned to his feet to sleep. Our comfortable snoring session was tranquil and relaxing, but soon a period of unexpected late-season activity would surprise both of us.

We both awakened lethargically and sluggishly, feeling somewhat disoriented. Jan Ericsson had departed and left us with the sobering thought that we would probably be alone and isolated for some time. Certainly, the weather would be warmer, and my master and I looked forward to getting out of the cabin and exploring. We were anticipating a couple of months of quiet isolation, and perhaps this is why my senses might have been dulled and less alert.

In a very rare moment, my master looked toward the cabin door before I sensed anyone approaching. He headed quickly across the room before I even sprung up off the floor. My master leaped over me and opened the cabin door, and I was relieved to see a smile burst onto his face.

"What the hell are you guys doing here?" my master yelled, and then he bellowed a boisterous laugh.

I bolted quickly to peer around the door to see my master's great friends. It was Louis Bostock and John Foreman, accompanied by a guide I did not know.

"Loser!"

"Writer Boy!"

"Bullman!"

"Writer Boy!"

It was an amazing change in the mood of our cabin. My master and I were just settling in to a lengthy period of loneliness, and in a split second, we were in the company of wonderful friends. After all the excited greetings and hugs, Bullman finally noticed me.

"Hey, Tom, I am surprised to see Shorty survived the trip north." John Foreman chuckled.

I growled just a brief, friendly growl in response to the "Shorty" remark, because I knew how surprised and happy my master was to see his friends. I was also happy to see Loser and Bullman again, and our excited greetings took longer than we realized, because when we all finally settled down, the door to the cabin quickly opened again.

Into the warm and suddenly jovial dwelling entered Kituk, who was serving as the guide northward toward the Yukon for my master's two great friends. Introductions were made with Kituk, who shook his host Thomas Strong's hand very respectfully and offered a smile aimed toward my direction, which made me feel that we had already met.

I noticed immediately that Kituk had a very friendly disposition. He had brightness in his eyes and a thin, scruffy beard that suggested he was relatively young as far as Yukon tour guides go. After a brief pause from all the excitement of the unexpected arrival, my master, always the writer, repeated the first query he had yelled when he first opened the door.

"What the hell are you guys doing here?"

CHAPTER EIGHT

Include Us in Your Stories!

There was not an immediate answer to my master's question. I was wondering why these men would make the long journey to this cabin and also so late in the season. Chuckling, head scratching, and the sound of whiskey being poured into glasses were delaying the responses that were supposed to be forthcoming. I settled myself into the middle of the room, with my butt facing the fire. I wanted a good view of our guests. I had a feeling the tale of my master's friends' arrival would be an entertaining and detailed yarn, simply because Loser, Bullman, and Kituk seemed to be taking their time collecting their details and thoughts.

"Well, guys, I am so happy to see you, but seriously, what the hell are you doing here?" my master asked, with his voice cracking with emotion.

"Tom, we read your articles in *American* magazine," started Louis Bostock.

"The stories were so compelling," added John Foreman.

"But your writing brought life to the tales," Loser finished Bullman's thought.

"Seriously, Tom, we read your stories and knew this place and this life here had rekindled your spirit," offered Bullman, with a scratchy voice and salty moisture in his eyes.

"We had to come see you, Tom! We knew you were alive again," finished Loser.

My head rotated to and fro, looking at each man as they chipped in with a part of the story. Can you picture my little head, with two brown patches around my eyes, moving back and forth, and side to side, as if I were watching a tennis match?

"Hey, guys, I am glad you have been reading my work, and Stanley and I are thrilled to see you, but you shouldn't have come all this way to check my pulse!"

"I am taking your friends north, sir," Kituk, the young guide, abruptly chirped in.

"Oh, are you? Are you an experienced guide?" barked Thomas Strong. "The guides that have already been through here told me that at this time, the trip north is too risky . . . it is too late in the season. I will not let you lead my friends towards such danger!"

I actually don't remember Thomas Strong being passionately angry before. I have such fond memories of him being happy, and then I remember him being so sad. My master's anger was a new thing for me to see. He was pointing his finger in Kituk's face and was screaming at him.

"You will not take my friends—not taking them!"

"Take it easy, Tom," was Bullman's attempt to calm Writer Boy.

"Easy, Writer Boy," calmed Loser, as he stepped in between my master and Kituk.

My head was tired of twisting around, trying to keep up with the back and forth of this escalating drama, and so my eyes rested and focused upon the face of Kituk. He seemed confused, overwhelmed, and determined all at once. My master's emotions had quickly risen to a level of agitation never before seen by me or by his two great friends. This certainly confused Bullman, Loser, and me, but now I noticed disappointment and sadness forming upon the face of Kituk.

"I am so sorry, Mr. Strong. I did not come here with any intentions to upset you, and I would never let anything bad happen to your two great friends," said Kituk in a sentence interrupted with short, shallow breaths and long hesitations.

As Kituk finished his statement, my master stepped back and quickly calmed down. I knew the look on the face of Thomas Strong when the wheels of his brain started to churn into action. The writer shifted his head from side to side. Then he scratched his chin.

"How did you know my name was Strong?" asked my master.

"Mr. Strong, I know your name because I have read many of your wonderful stories," responded Kituk.

"He is a big fan, Tom," added Bullman.

"Your stories inspired me to try to become a writer," continued Kituk.

"Tom, Kituk wouldn't be here if not for me and Bullman. We wanted him to bring us here," offered Loser.

My master trusted the instincts of his two good friends, and soon a slow, settling calm came over the cabin. My master had concerns, but his happiness upon seeing his friends warming safely in the comfort of our cabin turned his trepidations into a writer's curiousness about why they were here.

Bullman, Loser, and Kituk took turns explaining how they ended up together and then ended up headed north to our cabin. Thomas Strong, the writer and host, listened and continuously paced around the cabin as the three men spoke.

John "Bullman" Foreman and Louis "Loser" Bostock had read the first stories that had traveled the lengthy distance from my master's quill pen to the pages of *American* magazine. They knew Thomas Strong, my master, and they sensed from his writing that the sad and depressed man that they were concerned about had been revitalized by this unique storytelling opportunity in our remote cabin.

The two men met in San Francisco with hopes of traveling up north to visit their friend, Thomas Strong. As Bullman and Loser cruised north on the steamship headed toward Dawson City, they marveled at the way their friend had thrown caution to the wind and changed his life so dramatically. The more they talked about the courage of their friend Writer Boy, the more they wanted to do more than just pay him a visit.

When they arrived in Dawson City, they were still hemming and hawing about what they wanted to do. The two men got a room in a hotel in the center of this newly thriving town. Mother McCreary's was the name of the hotel, and it was a bustling establishment that only had one rule to be followed by all guests: "No whining allowed!"

After settling in, they went downstairs to have a few drinks and a steak dinner at the restaurant. As they ate, they discussed their journey and tried to figure out their plans and what they would do when they surprised their friend Thomas Strong. The two men were well out of their normal comfort zone, and most importantly, they knew a sled team would need to be procured for the trip north. They also had a bit of trepidation about how they would guide the dogs north, since Bullman had only guided cattle and Loser had only ushered wives to divorce court.

Working in the hotel that night was a nineteen-year-old boy that dreamed of becoming a writing student at one of the numbers of growing universities in the blossoming state of California. As he cleaned tables and swept the floors, he couldn't help but overhear the conversation of the two interesting men talking about Thomas Strong. Kituk was the young man working and listening, and he felt compelled to interject himself into the conversation.

"Gentlemen, my name is Kituk. I am sorry, but I could not help overhearing your conversation. I think I could be of service to you, and perhaps you might help me."

"Well, grab us a few beers and pull up a chair, Kituk. I'm John Foreman."

"Hey, Kituk, I am Louis Bostock. How can we help each other?"

"It's nice to meet you, Mr. Foreman and Mr. Bostock. I loved the story that Thomas Strong wrote about you guys in *American* magazine. I feel like I know you guys already."

Bullman and Loser were surprised at how much young Kituk knew about them and their friend Thomas Strong. Not only had Kituk been touched by my master's article about Bullman and Loser, but he had also read so many more of Thomas Strong's award-winning stories. Since Kituk seemed to know so much about them, they sat and listened and learned as Kituk told them of his life, his ambitions, and his hopes and dreams.

Kituk was Koyukon Indian, a people native of Alaska. The Koyukons were naturally adept at survival skills in the frigid north. Hunting, trapping, and fishing in the arctic northland were prerequisites for survival for many generations and had become instinctual.

The young and charismatic Kituk explained to Bullman and Loser that as a youth, his father introduced him to the frigid danger of the northland by bringing him along on hunting and trapping excursions. Kituk described the emotions of those trips with an eloquence that captivated his listeners. The young guide expressed his admiration and respect for his father, because the men for whom his father had provided leadership and direction obviously valued his knowledge.

Kituk also explained why the trips with his father abruptly ended. While following his father and learning so much about life, death, and survival, Kituk took the time whenever and wherever he could to pencil his thoughts and feelings into a more than rudimentary journal. When Kituk's father discovered his son's writing, he was amazed and impressed by the captivating clarity of the words on the paper. He immediately ordered his son to stay at home, study, and read as many books as he could each day and then someday leave home to venture off to school.

His father continued to earn a living as a guide, and Kituk was chipping in, helping provide for his family by working at Mother McCreary's, the very same establishment that granted him the chance to meet Thomas Strong's great friends.

Kituk's story had been quite interesting to John Foreman and Louis Bostock, but the real meaning for Kituk's tale had sailed right over their heads! Kituk most certainly thought his education as a writer would get off to a rollicking start if he met a great author, one that he admired and especially one he could learn from firsthand. The two men he had just met would be able to broker an introduction with just such a renowned writer, and he was certainly qualified to guide them toward the cabin of their friend.

"Gentlemen, I have been to the cabin where your friend Thomas Strong now dwells. You want to see him again, and I want to meet him. Get your bags and gear, and let's head north first thing tomorrow."

Bullman and Loser were now comfortable that their trip north from Dawson City to visit their great friend would be much easier, because they trusted the charming young man that had offered his services. They were so impressed with the intelligence, composure, and knowledge of their new friend Kituk. The men all shook hands, and after returning to their hotel room to pack, Bullman and Loser were so confident in the success of their journey that they actually got an unexpected good night of sleep, complete with a snoring contest that kept the rest of the hotel's guest awake much of the night.

The next morning arrived much more quickly than Bullman and Loser anticipated, but they greeted the daylight and welcomed the journey north. Kituk expected a sluggish departure, but when Bullman and Loser gradually meandered from the hotel lobby, they were quickly snapped to attention by what Kituk had waiting for them.

Outside, in front of the hotel, Kituk had a complete team of tremendous dogs and a sled full of supplies that was obviously more than what was required for the journey to visit our cabin. Kituk helped Bullman and Loser load their belongings onto the sled, and they began to travel north.

Along the journey to our cabin, something became evident to Bullman and Loser, without ever speaking to Kituk. The eager young guide, with aspirations to be a writer, had loaded a sled of supplies for a trip much further north than the cabin of their friend Thomas Strong. Kituk, the aspiring writer, had the beginning of a great story. He was bringing Thomas Strong's friends up north for a visit, but Bullman and Loser realized that Kituk wanted to author his own dramatic tale. They sensed that they could be part of the first great story of a young writer's career, if they went all the way north, deep into to the Yukon.

As Kituk guided the sled team to rest outside our cabin, Bullman and Loser came to a sudden realization. The words were quick but had been thought about for a long time.

"We are going to go farther north, Kituk," barked Bullman through the frigid air.

"Take us to the excitement of the Yukon and then promise you will bring us back here again to our friend," continued Loser.

"It will be a great story to begin your writing career," offered Bullman.

"But now, we must convince our writer friend that this is a good idea," finished Loser as he and Bullman entered our cabin to the surprise of my master. Kituk was headed toward the dogs to settle them in for the night. After securing the dogs, Kituk entered our cabin, looking to secure the respect of my master.

CHAPTER NINE

---※---

Friends and Fun

My master listened to the story of how his two great friends and the young Kituk had merged their ambitions together. He was intrigued at how they managed to arrive at our doorstep. As the men settled near the fireplace, any apprehensions my master might have had with Kituk melted away as quickly as the roaring fire warmed the cold bones of our cherished guests.

Writer Boy was so happy to be with his friends. He was such an attentive host. When a glass was near empty, my master was quickly up and filling it with more scotch. If the fire started to crackle and burn just a bit slower, he rose and tossed some fresh logs on the fire.

Kituk wasn't drinking, but he was soaking in all the dialogue and enjoying the camaraderie of the evening. As Kituk watched the three friends enjoy one another's company, I watched him. He was a good-hearted soul, and I knew I could always trust him.

After a good while, the boisterous conversation of long-missed friends turned into a drunken symphony of cacophonous snoring. I considered the noise a wonderful prize of friendship, and I was so content sleeping in front of the fire. The only time I was rustled out of my slumber was when Kituk patted my head right before he rose and quietly placed a log on the fire.

In the morning, my master continued his attentiveness toward his dear friends. He quietly began to heat a pot of bacon and beans. The noise of his footsteps and the clanking of the pot he hung over the

---

fire didn't disturb his friends from their slumber. Soon, the smell of the bacon melding with the beans in the pot wafted throughout the cabin, and quickly there was a rustling sound of sluggish men rising from slumber. When the robust aroma of strong coffee came over the cabin, it was time to greet a new day and a hearty meal.

"Damn it, Writer Boy, that smells good," said Bullman in a scratchy gruffness, as he staggered to upright posture and stepped on Loser, who was slower to arise.

"Ahhh! Watch where you are stepping, you big bull bastard!" was the awakening yelp of Loser.

Kituk and I watched Writer Boy, Bullman, and Loser continue to reacquaint themselves over coffee and breakfast. The conversation was different from the boisterous and excited howling from the night before. There was a quiet discussion among these men that had such great respect for one another. I watched their faces as they expressed genuine concern for one another's well-being. Plans were made to spend the day exploring the area around the cabin. I thought that was just my master trying to delay the departure of his friends heading northward, and when I looked at the face of Kituk, I knew he agreed with me.

We all ventured out into the bright sunshine as it glared off the pristine white snow. Thomas Strong pointed out to his friends the frozen stream that, in just a few weeks, would begin to thaw and provide great opportunities to catch a wonderful fish dinner. My master's tour also displayed the abundance of trees that would turn into firewood, and he even managed to point out the old, useless mine, which was the initial reason for building the cabin in which we now resided.

I was casually plodding along on my master's tour, and getting a bit chilly, but I was easily strolling atop the snow without breaking through the thin icy crust. I looked up at Kituk and sensed concern as he walked along. I figured out why he was alarmed without him even saying a word. The sound of Kituk's footsteps had no crunch, and as he took each step, the sound of his foot hitting the snow was becoming more and more soft and slushy.

To Kituk, this was an alarm that needed to be addressed immediately. If the snow he was walking on here was already getting soft, the trip north traveling over frozen rivers and lakes would soon be even more treacherous. As we headed back to the cabin, I watched Kituk getting determined to take control.

Entering the cabin brought jocularity and laughter to my master and his friends. It seemed they would be content spending another night in the warmth of our dwelling. There would be a good meal to devour, scotch to sip, and stories to be told.

That was not going to be the case. As coats were opened and layers of garments were beginning to be removed, Kituk's stern voice halted the jovial atmosphere.

"Gentlemen, please don't get too comfortable" was the statement made by Kituk, which brought a sudden silence to the room.

"We need to make a decision, and it is a decision that must be made now," continued Kituk as he caught the eyes of my master in a concerned stare.

"The snow is already becoming soft. We need to make a crucial decision right away. The daylight provides the warmth of the sun, but the moonlit night sky provides the best travel conditions for sled dogs to work."

The usually talkative men suddenly were quiet. They focused their eyes on Kituk as he tried to impose his will on these established and successful men. I was staring up at Kituk, and I felt the sense of urgency that his message provided. Kituk had been staring at my master, but then his eyes drifted from his face and settled on Bullman and Loser.

"Gentlemen, if you want to stay here and continue to enjoy the company of the great Thomas Strong and his friend Stanley, I most certainly would understand. But if you want to travel north and have me to serve as your guide, we need to leave now."

As Kituk spoke with such decisiveness, my master, Bullman, and Loser had many thoughts swirling within their heads. Kituk had established what most adventurers call "the moment of truth." I took my time examining all the faces in the room. Many people have said that dogs can sense how people are feeling, especially when it comes to powerful, emotional thoughts. At that time, in that room, I knew exactly what everyone was thinking.

My master, Thomas Strong, felt reluctant to let his friends travel north into such dangerous conditions. He had felt worry and concern for all the travelers that had taken respite here, but these were his dear friends. I could also tell that he felt secure with the knowledge that Kituk could be trusted to look after his friends and then bring them back to the safety of our cabin in the months after the warm season.

Bullman was thinking that Kituk was right about establishing the need for departure. He had adventure in his eyes, and he wasn't worried about the potential danger of continuing north. I did sense a bit of concern from Bullman, because he was worried that maybe his friend Loser didn't want to make this journey as much as he did.

Loser was definitely less driven than Bullman to continue sledding into the unknown of the Yukon, but he didn't want to prevent his friend Bullman from doing so. I could sense that Loser trusted Kituk, and the strength of his connection to Bullman made it obvious they would not be spending another night in our cabin.

"I guess we need to be on our way," barked Loser.

"Damn right, you financial freak." Bullman laughed.

"Then get the hell out of here, you idiots!" barked Writer Boy.

"Let's go then," said Kituk.

Kituk was not concerned about Bullman and Loser, because he was certain that they would be safe under his guidance. I noticed as Kituk briefly glanced at my master, and the expression on the young guide's face reminded me of how I felt when I was just a puppy. It was a look in search of approval. It was a look that is only awarded to a person of great respect from the eyes of the looker. I gathered many feelings and emotions from the faces and body language of these men in just a few minutes, and I felt confident Thomas Strong's greatest friends would return with a great story that would provide smiles and laughter for everyone.

"You better get going, boys," ushered my master. "Kituk is right. You need to go now," continued Thomas Strong. "My good friends, you have a perfect situation. You have a great guide in Kituk, who can also record the trials and tribulations of your journey, and you have a great place here to welcome you upon your return," he finished.

"So, Writer Boy, you are kicking us out." Loser chuckled.

"I believe he is," chimed in Bullman.

"Don't let the door hit you in your backsides as you leave." Writer Boy laughed.

"I'll get the dogs ready," said Kituk as he headed toward the door.

Just before Kituk opened the cabin door, he turned to look toward the writer he admired. The eyes of the great writer and the optimistic raconteur connected with sturdy quickness. There was a certain understanding that this story most definitely would have a happy ending.

Kituk headed outside, while Bullman and Loser gathered themselves. Thomas Strong's two best friends tightened up their clothing as he poured a healthy drink for each of them, just for good luck, as they departed. The men toasted health and good fortune and then hugged one another in a scene that made me entirely too emotional. As these two special men headed toward the cabin door, they both took a brief pause to say good-bye to me.

"Take care of Writer Boy for us, Stanley," quipped Loser.

"Make sure he writes more than he drinks," offered Bullman as both men patted me on the head.

Quickly, the cabin door was open, and my master and I stepped outside to watch the departure of a dog sled heading into the darkness of the unknown. My master's friends both waved, but the last thing I noticed was the arm of Kituk throwing something toward me at the front of the cabin. He had good aim, and it landed right in front of me. It was a small piece of the fish that Kituk had fed to the sled dogs. I was so happy that he would give me such a present, and I almost saved it, but it smelled too good for me to resist, and I enjoyed devouring it quickly.

CHAPTER TEN

---※---

One More Heading North

After the departure of Kituk and my master's good friends, Thomas Strong and I settled into a slow and thoughtful day, with the expectation that we would not be welcoming any more visitors. Kituk made it very clear the night before that each passing day, as the weather warmed, it would make it more dangerous for people to leave Dawson City and travel north.

We were hoping for one more visit from our good friend Jan Ericsson. We had plenty of supplies, and the warmer weather would present other opportunities for sustenance, but another visit from Jan would give us tales to tell by the fire and stories for our friendly courier to carry back to civilization in Dawson City.

After a day of solemn thought and quiet introspection about the upcoming desolation of the warm months, my master and I settled into a productive mode. A fire was built, my master got comfortable at his writing desk, and I nestled at his feet. I heard the scratching of his pen on paper, and I knew he was writing another wonderful story. Most certainly, he would write about his surprise visit from Bullman and Loser.

Thomas Strong, the talented author, was writing productively, and the sound of his stories transitioning from his brilliant mind to his quill pen and then to paper was also useful to me. The wispy, scratching sound of quill on paper always made me float into deep slumber.

Three simultaneous noises awakened me from the midst of a glorious dog dream. It was a great dream, one that featured me chomping on a huge piece of ham and then canoodling with a pair of finely quaffed poodles. I was not happy to be rustled from that nocturnal ecstasy!

Quickly the three sounds occurred in a rhythm just like if someone said "ONE, TWO, THREE!" The fire had been burning away nicely all night long, providing the comforting orange glow and smoky warmth that I always loved. But the fire had been left unattended for some time, as my master concentrated on his work and then drifted off.

The first sound was the cracking and thumping of burning wood as it settled in the fireplace. The second sound was my master bellowing a prodigious snore, and the third was the snapping noise of my master's quill pen as it hit the floor.

It took all three distinct noises to awaken me. Now that I was awake, and my master was still sawing wood in a symphonic cacophony, I figured it best to jostle him out of his sluggish slumber and get him into a more civilized version of sleep, perhaps in a bed with a blanket.

I tugged on his foot and scratched his leg and managed to wake him without bringing him fully out of unconsciousness. I watched as my master stumbled into a bunk and groaned in a way that I wasn't sure if it was happiness or pain. As I relaxed after watching my master settle in, I moved toward a cozy spot closer to the now-dwindling fire. Just as I began to relax in hopes of returning to my dreams, my instincts propped up my ears and alerted my nose. I heard the now-familiar sound and smelled the obvious scent of a dog sled approaching.

As this team of dogs arrived outside our cabin, I was surprised at how silent they were as they began to settle in front of our dwelling. The unexpected and new arrivals were so quiet that my master didn't even stir at all from his middle-of-the-night prayer session with God.

I sat near the door in an alert position and waited as a short while passed. I stood motionless and alert as the sound of one person's footsteps became more pronounced and drew nearer to the door of the cabin.

As the door pushed open, I shuffled back a bit and used my instincts to try to determine whether I should leap at the new arrival's neck or welcome him with a bark and a face lick. I sensed the good nature of this solitary sojourner, but before I could express my friendship, my master had achieved a moderate level of consciousness and meandered toward our new guest.

"Welcome!" barked my master as he stumbled to shake our new visitor's hand. "This is my attack dog, Stanley, and since he didn't leap and try to bite into your neck, I know you must be a good soul."

Our new guest was slow to offer his first words of greeting. He seemed more concerned about making sure he removed his ice-covered coat and boots without tracking snow into our dry and cozy cabin. He was genuine, and I sensed honesty. I immediately knew he was a man of sturdy character, and I eagerly anticipated hearing his story.

In the brief time the door was open, I noticed that our most recent, and probably last traveler heading north, had a team of ten dogs and was apparently traveling by himself. Usually our visitors are so happy to be in a room with fire, booze, and food that they hugged my master and petted me furiously even before they removed their layers of protective clothing. This man took his time to remove and prop his garments by the fire to warm them, and my master held his hand out to greet him.

"My name is Tarkenton, Charles Tarkenton, and I did not want to make a mess in your home."

"You're not making a mess, and we are happy to have you. Are you by yourself?" asked my master.

"Yes, sir, just me and my dogs."

"I'm Tom, and this is my boy, Stanley. Please, sit down, relax, and enjoy the warmth of our shelter."

"So you are the writer Thomas Strong?" inquired our guest, already knowing the answer to the question as he began to thaw by the fire.

"Yes, Mr. Charles Tarkenton, I am Thomas Strong, the writer," established my master. "I presume that you've heard about me from people you met in Dawson City. Perhaps a fine man named Jan Ericsson conversed with you and sent you our way," continued my master.

"Yes, Mr. Strong, I am happy that Mr. Ericsson's guidance proved true, and I am happy to be here with you and Stanley."

"Very well then, please, just call me Tom."

"Everyone in Dawson City knows who you are. Jan Ericsson hands out copies of the *American* magazines that have been made so popular in the most recent issues due to your stories about the adventures of people heading to the north."

"I guess my friend Jan is trying to make me a celebrity."

"Actually, Tom, your writing has certainly become of national interest because of the popular series of stories in *American* magazine, but your boy, Stanley, is becoming a folk hero in Dawson City."

"And why would that be?" inquired my master as my ears perked up hearing the sound of my name.

"Well, I guess your friend Jan Ericsson told a few people about how cute Stanley was and how he seemed a bit like a fish out of water up here in the land of sled dogs."

"Stanley has adapted well up here," declared my master as he quickly came to my defense.

"Anyway, Jan described your boy, Stanley, in great detail to many of the customers at Mother McCreary's. One artistic patron drew a picture of your boy, Stanley, complete with a Beware of Dog headline that mentioned the location of this cabin. Everyone that steps up to the bar chuckles at the drawing, and seeing Stanley now, it certainly is a wonderful likeness!"

"How about that, Stanley? You are a celebrity in Dawson City," cackled my master as he rubbed my head.

"Well, Tom, I don't have any interest in being a celebrity, and you don't need to tell my story to the world."

"Mr. Tarkenton, the fact that you don't want me writing about the story that brought you here makes me more curious and more interested to hear your tale."

"Tom, the reason I am here going north is not a tale or a story for others to read. I am on a journey for my own salvation, and please call me Charles."

"I won't write anything about your journey without your approval, Charles, but please feel welcome, get warm, eat a nice meal with us, have a drink, and maybe you might just tell me a bit about why you are here," said my master in the longest sentence he ever managed toward a new visitor.

I immediately got a sense from Charles Tarkenton that he was engaging my master and me in a perfunctory nature. I don't think he wanted to talk about what his journey north was all about, but maybe his experience meeting Jan Ericsson and being with us in the toasty cabin made it seem to him that he had some sort of obligation or duty to speak. As these thoughts crossed my mind, Charles began to express himself.

"My father was a man of God, a minister, a devout Christian," began Charles. "He always told me that I would someday have a moment of truth, a moment that proved to be a reason for faith," he continued. "Then, on a day of great joy and happiness in my life, I learned of the death of my father. My emotions were scrambled, and I was very confused."

"Oh, I'm so sorry, Charles," offered my master as I fought back a tear, and the author fought back the instinct to ask what was the great moment of joy that had been interrupted by his father's death.

"My father never told me when he had his moment with God, the moment that clarified his faith, but I know it was something special, and it was just between my father and our Maker."

My master's instincts sensed something about our guest, and it seemed Charles Tarkenton was not headed north for adventure, gold, or prosperity. He was headed to the isolation of the north in search of a communion with his creator. He was hoping that the privacy offered by the frozen wilderness of the desolate Yukon would provide him with an opportunity to have his moment of truth—the moment of truth his father once had.

As Charles Tarkenton settled into the coziness of our cabin, the dialogue between the storyteller and his guest became more prolific and entertaining. The enthusiasm and the back-and-forth banter between these two intelligent men were quite compelling. The sound of my master conversing vigorously with our singular guest enthused me with an overwhelming sense of contentment. I slipped into a peaceful slumber, only to be awakened by the sound of the cabin door closing, with the early-morning departure of Charles Tarkenton.

CHAPTER ELEVEN

Evil Arrives

So far, it had been an interesting and rewarding experience, welcoming travelers as they made brief pit stops at our remote but sturdy cabin. It seemed like Charles Tarkenton would be our last guest traveling north, and once again, I began to think about what it was going to be like without the entertainment and excitement of new visitors.

Throughout the season of sledders heading north, my master began to rely on my instincts to alert him upon the arrival of parties in search of gold and adventure. Sometimes, I heard the swishing sound of the rails of the dog sled first or maybe the crunchy, rhythmic thumping of the paws of the powerful canines pounding into the snow as they were getting closer. Then there were times when I could smell the dogs and their masters as they approached. Any one of these things, or all three, I normally noticed before my master had any clue of an impending arrival.

My instinctual awareness of new visitors was quite easy for my master to notice. I had a comfy, cozy, and lazy resting place just in front of our perpetually glowing fireplace. If my senses were alerted in any manner, my master would notice the tiny twist of my ears and the subtle raising of my head.

"Hey, Stanley, who is here?" my master would always ask me, as if I had any clue.

Then I would rustle up from my comfy resting place, and the host would throw a couple of fresh logs on the fire and hang a pot of water over the flames to boil. I would always make my way to the cabin door quickly to make sure that when our new guests entered, I would impede their progress into the warmth of our cabin, just a little bit. I did this just long enough for them to shake the snow and ice from their clothing and remove their frozen boots. Charles Tarkenton was the only guest that didn't need my assistance in this area. Once I had ensured that snow and ice would not be melting all over the floors of our cabin, I did my best to make sure that our visitors felt welcome.

Almost always, there was some immediate connection between the travelers and me. I guess weary people coming inside from out of the snarling frigidness of the trail heading north would be happy to see a wolf or a grizzly bear just to get near a fire. Maybe that is why they always smiled and laughed when they first encountered me.

I was always excited and happy to welcome new guests into our cabin. I have excellent instincts when it comes to people. I am a great judge of character. In the northland, it becomes easy to judge people. It is kind of like playing cards with all the players showing their hands before wagering. Everyone knows the hands that have been dealt, so you just accept what is yours and play the game with a smile on your face.

People would enter the cabin, take a moment to catch their breath, make a jocular comment about me, and then start the process of introducing themselves. With each arrival, there would be a variation or two to the process, but it was always good people ending up having a good time, and the stories they told ushered life into my master's soul.

There was one exception.

One night there was a lazy, comfortable feeling in the cabin. It was unusually warm outside, and there was not much wind to speak of. Charles Tarkenton had departed, and we had no expectations of any more visitors. Thomas Strong had fallen asleep, and the gentle whisper of his quill pen scratching the welcoming paper had been quiet for a while. I was halfway to joining my master in an evening of slumber when my acute senses were activated.

I heard the usual sounds of a sled team approaching, and I rustled up and wobbled toward the cabin door. I waited for the familiar sounds of voices yelling orders to a sled team and harnesses being secured. I was accustomed to the common sound of sledders screaming at the dogs, followed by the hollow, crunching sound of boots pounding the snow, striding toward our cabin in hopes of an eagerly anticipated fire in the warmth of our dwelling.

On this particular evening, the typical sounds of travelers arriving were strangely interrupted. It was just a momentary stall to the typical noises of welcomed guests, but it throttled my instincts into an extreme sense of awareness.

Soon, I did hear the sound of boots crushing into the frozen snow, and I knew the travelers were getting closer. Because my instincts were on high alert, my sense of smell was remarkably keen. I smelled two men approaching our cabin, and I heard them getting closer. Then, as the door of the cabin opened, I smelled the scent of someone else, and I saw only evil in the eyes of these unwanted sojourners.

My master was slower and a bit clumsy as he tended to the fire and tried to hang water in a pot to boil. He had been rustled from a state of delirious comfort, and he was not yet aware of the potential danger of these two men, whom I had immediately considered dangerous intruders.

The door pushed open quickly, and it slammed closed even faster and harder. Two extremely imposing figures entered, and for the first time, I actually heard the floorboards of our cabin creaking. I think the sounds of the bending planks were more audible due to the strange silence in the cabin as these two men entered. The high-pitched snapping sound of the lower planks was in stark contrast to the depths of darkness in the rugged faces of these men.

"Welcome, gentlemen," greeted Thomas Strong, who still was unaware of what I had sensed immediately.

My master is a great writer and a talented observer of humanity, but he had no clue of the evil that I now sensed. I didn't bark, nor did I growl. I was aware of their hurried and nervous nature, and any antagonistic behavior on my part might have slowed them down from what I thought was going to be a quick departure. I wanted them to leave as quickly as possible.

"Hey there, Thomas Strong?" was the forced and uncomfortable inquiry offered by one of the unwelcome visitors that had just barged through the door of our usually peaceful sanctuary.

"I'm Dirk Pearson, and this is my brother, Bob."

"Welcome, boys," responded my master, not noticing my immediate dislike for the Pearson brothers.

"Jan Ericsson told us about this cabin before we left Dawson City," grumbled Dirk.

"That's great. I am glad he did. Warm up and enjoy the fire. It will be the last roof over your head for some time," my master babbled, still not noticing what was so apparent to me.

"Thanks, Tom," muttered Bob Pearson in an anxious and nervous manner.

Dirk and Bob Pearson were big men. They had big bodies, big hands, and big heads, and they were big trouble. I was starting to get agitated. I knew something was wrong outside. My master was not picking up the corrupt nature of the Pearson brothers, but I didn't want to alert him for fear of trouble.

"Hey, Tom, we just want to dry our boots and warm up for a bit. Is it safe to sit down by the fire for a short spell, or will your attack dog get us?" snickered Dirk.

"He took down an elk last week." My master chuckled.

As everyone in the room laughed but me, I noticed my master slowly noticing the bad nature of these men. I hoped the Pearson brothers were not as quick to recognize my master's awareness. I just wanted them to do what they said they wanted to do, which was just warm up and then leave.

"You built a great fire, Tom. We'll be gone before these logs are ashes," said Dirk Pearson as the brothers toasted themselves near the roaring fire.

"Yes, we need to make quick headway north," said Bob Pearson.

My master had finally noticed my agitation and that something was not right with the Pearson brothers. Then the observant and award-winning writer noticed that the latest guests had never asked him what my name was. Thomas Strong noticed how quiet I had been. My master and I caught a good look into each other's eyes as the Pearson brothers dried out by the fire. We both knew to try to stay awake and watch the Pearson brothers leave.

After a couple of hours, I was still pretending to sleep when the door closed behind them. As much as he tried to remain alert, my master wasn't pretending to snore.

I quietly and with remarkable patience listened as the Pearson brothers harnessed their dogs and pulled their team on their way northward, away from our cabin. The sound of their sled thankfully faded quickly underneath the rustle of the blustering wind whipping among the pine trees.

From the bottom of my instinctual belly, I knew there was someone that needed help. I hurriedly sprung into action. I jumped up and tried to awaken my master. He unwillingly rolled out of his fireside chair and opened the cabin door, thinking it was time for me to do my rudimentary business. I quickly sniffed the area where the travelers normally secure their sled dogs down for the night, and then I followed the scent of the most recent sled dog rails. My heart began to pound faster and harder as I picked up a faint scent of person that had never entered our cabin.

It was cold, but I felt an engine inside me built out of determination. I knew something was wrong, and I needed to help whoever was out there. I ran and slid upon the icy snow for a few hundred yards. I followed the trail to the south of our cabin left by the Pearson brothers, until it came to an area interrupted by footprints that smashed down the snow. The smell of an injured person was so strong now, and I followed a trail of blood to the edge of a steep embankment. Then my hearing took over.

There was no call for help or a scream of pain. I heard a quiet murmur muffled by snow, wind, and distance. I carefully edged toward the top of the embankment, and as I peered down, I saw what I had smelled—the scent that had been emanating off the Pearson brothers just a few hours before. My senses had correctly steered me toward an injured young girl. She was crumpled on the ground, twisted in a heap of ice and snow in a ravine thirty feet below.

I have great instincts, but at this point, I wasn't sure what I should do. I looked up the trail toward the cabin and searched for my master. I looked down at the bottom of the embankment toward the injured and freezing victim of the Pearson brothers. I was already shivering and cold, but I felt a strong need to make my way down the ravine to do whatever I could to help.

I struggled slowly and made my way down the icy slopes to find a seriously beaten and injured young girl. As I finally approached her, the moaning had stopped, and I wasn't sure if she was breathing. Her body was twisted and distorted, and her eyes, swollen and closed. I was afraid to touch her, but I finally licked her cheek to see if she was alive. A barely perceptible breath escaped her lips, and her eyes opened just enough to send me a message. I knew that message was that I was her only hope!

I darted up the steep embankment with a determination I had never known. My frozen paws somehow found traction in the ice and snow. Up the hill and back to the cabin, I raced, and as I approached the cabin, my master was outside, yelling for me. He had awakened from his slumber. I had been gone for a while, and he was worried the Pearson brothers had done something harmful to me.

I didn't have time for those emotions. I yelped at my master and then grabbed a rope from the front of the cabin between my teeth. I bolted back down the hill hurriedly, trying to help the injured girl. Thankfully, my master's instincts had kicked into high gear, and he followed my lead. The rope I dragged down the path would not have been long enough to help, and if not for Thomas Strong hauling two more long lengths of rope down the trail, my efforts would have most certainly been futile.

When my master arrived on the scene and saw the injured girl, he began to shake and tremble nervously. I was shaking, not out nervousness, but only because I was freezing my paws off! I am a French Bulldog. *French* and *freezing* might both be words that start with the letters *F* and *F*, but trust me, those words don't go together with me at all.

My master's hands were shaking, but thankfully, his mind was sharp and decisive. He made a loop in the rope that I had dragged to the scene, and then he knotted all three lengths of rope together. Again, I worked my way down the steep slope, this time pulling the looped rope between my teeth. When I arrived with the rope, there was no response from the injured girl. I licked her cheek again, but there was nothing—no response—but I was now furiously determined, and I certainly wasn't going to give up.

"Stanley, Stanley!" I heard my master yelling as I went into action.

I placed the top of the loop in the rope that my master had made just above the head of the girl and then the bottom of the loop on her waist. I grabbed her tattered coat by the collar and yanked and pulled as hard as possible. I needed to get her head above the loop in the rope. It was hard work, but I finally pulled her body far enough so that her head was resting above the loop in the rope. I then pushed the part of the loop of rope on her waist up toward her neck. I grabbed her lifeless left arm and maneuvered it through the circular opening of the rope. Her right arm was so twisted and broken, and I was afraid that I would cause her pain, but I needed to get her injured arm above the loop in that rope if we had any chance of pulling her up from the bottom of the ravine and give her any hope of survival.

I was so tired and cold, but I could not stop. From above, my master could see what I was doing. He was amazed. He was scared, shocked, and still trying to figure out what was going on.

"Go, Stanley! Go!" urged my master in a yelping voice summoned from fear and concern.

"Go, Stanley! Go!" were the best words my award-winning writing master could come up with as I struggled desperately to save this wounded girl. If I could speak, I would have made fun of him for that.

After her head and arms were secured within the confines of the rope, I grabbed it with my teeth at the start of the loop my master had created. I crushed my jaws upon the rope and pulled it as tight as I could into her armpits and around her neck. I looked up to signal my master to start pulling, but there was no need for that.

"I got it now, Stanley! I got it now, my boy!" yelled my master as he summoned every ounce of strength and adrenaline that he had in his storytelling body to lift this broken, wounded body from the depths of the ravine.

I am quite familiar with the sounds of my master. His snoring can sound like a wet, rusty saw trying to slice through frozen wood. I have heard his low guttural groans when he is frustrated, trying to find the perfect words to finish an important story. Rarely, I have heard him yelp a high-pitched sound, usually reserved for a finger burned at the fire or a toe stubbed while sleepwalking.

Now, as my master ushered all his strength and soul to pull this girl up toward safety, the guttural grunting noises he was making astonished me. The sounds coming from his body didn't seem like something that would emanate from an accomplished author, but there was a rhythm to the sound. He grunted, he growled, and he pulled! He grunted, he growled, and he pulled. Grunt, growl, and pull. My master worked with a furious rhythm that sent his mind into a depth of focus that can make a man do extraordinary things. His personality disappeared temporarily as his body worked to pull this girl out of the ravine.

Finally, the broken body was raised onto the trail leading toward our cabin. My master slumped to the ground, briefly looking at the wounded girl we were trying to save. I felt a bit guilty, because I had sunk my teeth into the girl's coat, and so my master had pulled me up from the bottom of the ravine as well. I know I would have never made it back up on my own strength. I always knew my master was smart, kind, and understanding. At this moment, Thomas Strong was about to show me an insurmountable toughness and desire that would never fade from my memory.

Our cabin was about five hundred yards up the trail. There was a simple but usable sled just outside the door. My master could have trekked quickly up to get the sled, but his instincts were now working stronger than mine. This wounded girl was barely alive, and I was exhausted and freezing to death. He realized it might take too long to make a trip back and forth from the cabin.

Thomas Strong summoned all his strength, reached down, and hoisted this wounded girl upon his shoulder. I was so proud of him, and I certainly realized it was worth my life to save this girl. I was frozen and exhausted, and I accepted the fact that there was no chance I was getting back to that cabin. As he took a step forward, I said good-bye to my life. But my master's step forward was only him planting his foot firmly in the snow so he could reach down and grab me. He was going to carry a broken girl and a frozen dog to safety.

"We'll be warm soon, Stanley, we'll be warm soon," was what my master said over and over again as he carried an unexpected, wounded guest and his faithful friend to another day of the warmth of life.

Chapter Twelve

A New Mission

The great writer Thomas Strong had traveled into this desolate environment and established our residence in this cabin in an attempt to reawaken his creative literary skills. In this regard, he had made the right decision. The travelers passing through our cabin were all interesting and compelling subjects. The stories these visitors brought flowed through my master like the first sip of water through a man escaping the heat of the desert.

Now, as my master gently laid this wounded, broken, and frozen body on a bearskin rug in front of the fire, this great storyteller worked swiftly and decisively to make certain that this scary story would finish with a happy ending.

"Not too close to the fire, Stanley, not too close!" my mastered yelled as I tried to warm myself.

He knew that if I toasted my frozen paws too quickly near the crackling heat of the fire, the chances for permanent frostbite damage would increase. As I struggled to pull back farther from the fire, I watched as my master dipped two rags into a bucket of lukewarm water.

"Oh, dear God. Oh, God," whispered my master as he ever so carefully wrapped the girl's icy fingers with the rags wet with warm water.

He then inspected the girl's injuries more closely and moaned some hopeless sighs of fear. I was confused as he picked up a large copper container that was used to remove ashes from the fireplace. He went outside and quickly heaped snow into the container, then brought it back inside, and placed it close to the fire.

My master then grabbed a glass and a bottle of whiskey and collected his thoughts for a moment. As he sipped the whiskey, I saw a mixture of calmness and determination developing in his eyes.

Amazingly, in the midst of this attempt to save this girl's life, my master was still concerned about my welfare. The container that he had quickly filled with snow had now melted into a shallow bath of warm water. He picked me up, placed me in the container, and soon I sensed the feeling coming back into my paws. I hate being in water, but I appreciated the warmth of this bath as much as the love I felt for my master.

Thomas Strong was certain that I would survive my battle with the elements, almost like he always knew the outcome of every story he had ever written. My injuries were minor compared to those of the twisted and tattered girl sprawled on the floor in front of our fireplace. Thomas Strong had wisely paused and taken a few minutes to determine the best course of action. He took a long drag of whiskey from his glass and then forged ahead into a tactical life-saving mission.

The victim had a number of gashes and cuts that needed attention. There was a particularly threatening wound on her neck, dangerously close to her jugular vein. If it had not been for the cold and snow, she might have bled to death already.

There were two injuries that made her body appear freakishly distorted. Her right arm was grotesquely bent backward at the elbow, and her fingers twitched nervously. Her right leg was limply hanging off her body, and her right foot was two inches farther below her left foot and awkwardly pointing toward the left leg.

My master evaluated all the injuries, and his quick assessment and immediate course of action most certainly gave this girl the best chance for survival. She was in shock and needed to be kept warm. As her body warmed in front of the fire, her flesh wounds would bleed faster. The author, now turned doctor, went outside and scooped up a ball of snow. He ripped off the sleeve of an old shirt and gently nestled the snow upon the girl's neck wound, and then he wrapped the old flannel sleeve around her neck. He was first tending to a neck wound that might be fatal, but he was also in a race to fix this girl's broken body before she came out of shock.

This girl was tough. She was strong. She had been bent, but she had not been broken! Her strong bones were intact, but she had a hyperextended elbow and a dislocated hip joint. Both injuries needed to be attended to before she came out of shock, or certainly, the pain would torture her.

When my master first started to reposition this girl's dislocated elbow, I heard a disgusting crunching sound that made me duck my head deep into the pool of the warm water in the copper container. After I raised my head back out of the water, I heard a gentle popping sound and a sigh of relief from my master. The girl's elbow had been placed back into position.

Thomas Strong was struggling to fend off the quite natural feeling of being overwhelmed. I was amazed at his decisiveness, but I was worried he was running out of energy and adrenaline. I leaped out of the warmth of the water in the copper tub and rushed toward him. He needed me, I needed him, and this poor broken girl needed both of us to help her.

My beloved master looked at me, and his visual instructions were clear, much more than any spoken orders from any language. He maneuvered himself to the left side of the girl and wrapped his arms around her left thigh as firmly yet as gently as possible. He then pressed his chest down upon her body to hold her securely in place. As his weight steadied her, he looked me in the eyes, and I knew I had to rise to the occasion. I sunk my teeth and firmly clenched my jaw around the tip of the girl's boot.

"Good boy, Stanley!"

I looked at my master and sensed his approval, and I struggled not to be overcome with the stress of the situation. I did what I needed to do. I yanked the tip of her boot as hard as I could, and I twisted her leg back into its normal position.

"Good job, Stanley!" my master yelped.

The pain of the girl's leg twisting back into position had started to rustle her from shock and out of unconsciousness. I went up to her face and gave her a kiss on the cheek as I watched my master place her knee between his chest and her hip, and then he quickly shoved the weight of his body forward. There was a thumping sound, something like a big round rock falling into a pool of murky mud. The girl's eyes opened briefly, just long enough to scare the hell out of me and my master, and we all three passed out from exhaustion.

When I opened my eyes, with the light of day emerging, I saw the full effects of the damage that had been inflicted on this girl. But as I turned and saw Thomas Strong in a deep slumber, I realized he had spent most of the night tending to the girl's many gaping flesh wounds. I don't ever recall him using a needle and thread before this emergency, but he had done a masterful job stitching the girl's deep and crooked neck wound. The great writer had performed heroically throughout the night, but our injured guest was still in a life-and-death struggle, and we did not yet know the outcome of this story.

I nestled up against her injured body as she warmed near the fire. Even if she were awake, I wouldn't want to hear the story of what happened to her. I was afraid to know. I got to know our new guest the way dogs get to know new friends. I licked her nose, and I sniffed her from head to toe. I gathered a strong scent of innocence and sweetness, but I also picked up the dastardly scent of the Pearson brothers. I nibbled a little bit on her ear to make her feel welcome and safe. Immediately, I liked her so much!

For two days and two nights, I curled up next to this girl's body and hoped she would recover. I barely slept. Every few hours, my master gently put tiny bits of snow in her mouth to try to keep her hydrated. He did the same for me. While he tended to both of us, I noticed a difference between the looks my master gave our injured guest and me, his best friend. He was quite familiar with all my expressions and behavior. He sensed I would be fine, and I could see that in his eyes. He looked differently at the girl, with trepidation and nervousness.

She was somewhere between unconsciousness and exhaustion. I was more confident than my master that she would recover. As I lay at her side, I sensed that her breathing was becoming more regular and stronger. As her recovery seemed imminent to me, I relaxed and finally slept for a little while. Well, it might have been a long while!

I was awakened by the stroke of a hand, caressing and softly petting my head. My master usually wakes me more ruggedly, with a hard smack and rigorous rubbing. But this time, there was a sweet voice unlike my master's whispering in my ear.

"Thank you, Stanley!" the lovely voice repeated over and over again. "Oh, Stanley! You saved my life!" she said softly as she kissed my head.

As the sound of her voice warmed my heart, she struggled to lean over and hug me, and I noticed the incredible stitching job that my master had done on her gouged neck. I was so proud of how he had carefully attended to all her many wounds. It was remarkable what Thomas Strong had done to help save this girl's life.

It was nice to hear my name spoken by her sweet voice, but I wondered how she knew it. I noticed that my master was in different clothes, and our injured guest was in much better condition than the last time I saw her. I realized that I had been slumbering for quite some time. It was a good, long, restful sleep, made better by awakening with two happy faces smiling at me. My master and the sweet voice of the recovering girl both chuckled at the bewildered expression on my face.

"Hey, Stanley, my name is Mikita! Promise not to ever call me Mickey, and I promise never to call you Stan!"

"My boy is named after Lord Stanley," my master blurted as he attended to his two patients.

"He hates being called Stan."

My master looked at me, and I nodded to him that I was okay. For now, the mission of the writer was not about words of ink being transitioned to paper. The talented author had used the same careful attention he normally used selecting words for his stories to give his full attention to Mikita. He patted me on the head and began to inspect the healing wounds of our new friend.

He first inspected her neck wound, and he seemed proud at the satisfactory work he had performed. As he continued to examine his fine medical work, a sense of contentment came over me. I thanked my lucky stars for three things: my master, Mikita, and the next log on the fire.

CHAPTER THIRTEEN

Cozy and Content

About a week had passed after Mikita had arrived. I was feeling fine. I had fully recovered from all my injuries sustained during the rescue effort of Mikita, and I already loved her! She was my new best friend. Mikita was quickly recovering from her injuries as well. My master had made a soft, comfortable resting place for her near the fireplace that previously had been my favorite napping area.

Each day, I nestled up next to Mikita and snuggled as close and tight to her as I could. She was resting and recuperating in a place that I once had regarded as my own slumber area, but I was happy to share my place near the hearth with her.

Thomas Strong looked different. For the last couple of days, he had a concerned look of determination on his face, but now, there was also happiness in his eyes. He continually nursed Mikita's broken body, and there was genuine purpose, care, and love. As the caretaker tended to Mikita and she continued to recover, I began to notice something. My master's heart, which had been broken by the tragic loss of his family, was now healing and being filled with feelings and concern for the welfare of Mikita.

I was so happy! Mikita was on the mend, and my master seemed alive again! Everything was great! There was one night the wordsmith authored a perfect fire, and above the flames, he cooked a rabbit stew. The warmth of the fire and the flickering orange glow it created, combined with the compelling aroma of the stew, overwhelmed my senses.

I didn't even hear the dogs approaching or the crunching footsteps in the snow coming toward the cabin. We were all startled as the cabin door swung open. Thankfully, it was our good friend Jan Ericsson entering the warmth of our dwelling. His arrival added to the special nature of the evening, but it also made me realize that I needed to be more aware. I had let my guard down, and I knew that I should have heard the approach of Jan Ericsson and his sled team. I vowed never to be unaware of the arrival of any travelers ever again.

Jan Ericsson was completely shocked to see the wounded Mikita resting by the fire, and my master was just as surprised by our friend's entrance. Usually, Jan Ericsson had a quiet greeting for us, as he slowly removed his outer garments and boots, but on this occasion, he was shocked into an excited dialogue.

"Holy hell, Tom! What the hell happened here?" was the astonished initial inquiry from Jan Ericsson.

"Sit down and warm up, my good friend," welcomed my master.

"How did she get here? Is she okay?"

"We have a wonderful fire tonight and a tasty rabbit stew," continued the host in an attempt to settle our friend.

"Tom, what happened here?"

"Jan, this is Mikita, and, Mikita, this is Jan Ericsson. Jan is our connection to civilization in Dawson City."

"Hey, Mikita, nice to meet you. Are you in pain? Are you all right?" inquired Jan Ericsson nervously.

"Calm down, Jan! I will tell you what happened to Mikita and how she ended up here, but you must promise it will be the only story that does not go south to Dawson City with you."

"Tom, is everything okay? I hope you are not in any trouble."

"Mr. Ericsson," interjected Mikita, "trouble brought me here, but the good nature and courage of your friends are the only reasons that I am alive," were the first words that Jan Ericsson heard from Mikita, and that seemed to calm him a bit.

"I think we are safe for now, Jan. We might be a little scared when certain people start making their way back down the trails," said Thomas Strong.

"Oh, Tom, I am sorry. I will do whatever I can to help."

"Just sit down and relax, Jan. Have some rabbit stew and I will tell you what happened."

The author began to explain what had taken place after we had found Mikita and how we had all three struggled but had managed to all get back safely to the cabin. As the story unfolded for Jan Ericsson, I nodded approval to the facts, and Jan smiled at me as if I were speaking as well.

There was a pause after Jan Ericsson had been regaled with the tale of our heroic rescue of Mikita. Our trusted guide had a sad smile that quickly turned into a look of determined consternation, and then his questions came quickly.

"Mikita, who did this to you? Do you know their names? Where did you meet them? Can you describe them to me? Do they think that you are dead?"

Mikita calmly provided answers to any questions for which she could construct a memory, and my master seemed composed as he listened to the horrible details. I was getting unsettled and upset listening to Mikita, because this was the first time I had heard how Mikita had arrived here. I realized at that moment that my master must have heard this before. Perhaps, during my long recovery sleep, Thomas Strong had urged Mikita to purge the horrid story. I looked at Jan Ericsson, and he looked right back at me, and he instantly realized that I had not heard these sickly details before.

The Pearson brothers met Mikita in Dawson City. She had been toiling at anything she could to earn a penny since she had been orphaned five years earlier. Her parents were both killed in a collapse of an unproductive gold mine not too far from where we were residing now. She didn't really have a permanent home, but her parents were well liked, and many families took turns providing Mikita with a place to stay. The tragic death of her parents somehow instilled a determination and work ethic in her not known by most young girls.

Mikita swept every floor, washed every window and dish, and cleaned every glass in all the homes, stores, restaurants, and saloons in Dawson City. What made her most valuable to eateries and bars was she was skilled with a knife, able to gut fish, and butcher wild game quickly and with efficiency. Mikita was also very good at tending to dogs, which, sadly, was how she ended up in the dangerous company of the Pearson brothers.

On a Friday afternoon, Mikita was recruited by Mother McCreary for a busy night of multiple duties in the kitchen of her saloon. Friday nights were always busy at Mother McCreary's Saloon and even busier during the season of rushing north for gold. There were enormous pails of fresh fish that needed to be cleaned and gutted, and later there would be dishes that needed scrubbing and glasses that needed cleaned.

Mikita had worked at a hard and steady pace all afternoon and evening. She deftly prepared the fish fast enough for the cook to keep up with the orders of the hungry patrons. She was now settling into the more mundane chore of scrubbing and cleaning the knives, forks, spoons, plates, and glasses that returned to the kitchen. The warm water and the gentle sound of the soapy rag rubbing the plates clean always relaxed Mikita, probably because she knew that the end of a hard night of work was approaching. She was cleaning everything that entered the kitchen faster than it was coming in, so she knew her night of hard labor would be ending soon.

Mikita's mind had relaxed and become complacent in the duty of her chores, but her hands diligently continued to clean. She was a bit surprised as Mother McCreary herself approached her from behind and grabbed her soapy forearm. Mikita had not heard her boss enter the kitchen and was briefly startled.

"It's just me, Mikita," said Mother McCreary. "I didn't mean to sneak up on you. I want you to stop cleaning for a while," the owner of the establishment, bearing her name, continued. "There are two men here on their way north. They are eating, drinking, and enjoying the comforts of a saloon for the last time in a long while. They asked for something special for their dogs. Will you take care of them?"

"Certainly, I know what to do," said Mikita.

Mikita opened the kitchen door and retrieved a large pail of fish heads that she collected earlier that day. She wouldn't dare walk through Mother McCreary's dining area with a bunch of stinking fish heads, so she exited through the back door of the kitchen and walked around outside the building. She headed toward the area a few hundred yards away where sled teams were normally secured.

Mikita was surprised to see the sled dogs all still harnessed and sitting upright, seemingly waiting for the command to pull forward. Even with the sound of Mikita's footsteps and the alluring scent of fish, the dogs remained stationary. Mikita placed a fish head in front of every dog. When the lead dog finally broke down and started to devour the savory morsel, the other dogs followed the lead. The dogs all snapped their jaws and dismantled the fish heads without ever moving from the start and go position. Mikita was happy to see the dogs eating but wondered why they were so alert and had not settled down.

Unbeknownst to her, while Mikita had been walking around the back of Mother McCreary's, quietly hauling fish to the sled dogs, the Pearson brothers were transforming a festive, happy establishment into a shocked and unsettled crime scene.

There were many people in this popular establishment at all times of day. Mother McCreary's often entertained travelers with plans to travel north, carrying not so securely in their pockets and satchels whatever money and valuable items that might be worth trading for important goods along the journey.

Dirk and Bob Pearson had planned to rob this type of patron and were less than thrilled with the limited bounty that did not quite fill their bags. It was late in the season, and everyone that had any sort of plan to head north had departed days earlier. As the two nimble-minded criminals vacated the premises and raced toward their sled team, it was quite apparent that the dogs harnessed to the sled were more intelligent than their owners.

As the Pearson brothers approached the sled team, an explanation for the dogs' behavior entered Mikita's mind. These dogs were well trained, and they were on alert, waiting for the cue to quickly leap into the action of a prompt departure. Just as Mikita began to realize that these dogs were set up for a quick getaway, she was simultaneously thumped on the head with a frozen log, rendering her unconscious.

The Pearson brothers were just simply half-assed stupid idiots. They had no plan or even one shrivel of organized thought in both of their brains combined. While their idea to rob the burgeoning pockets of the patrons at Mother McCreary's made some criminal sense, it was a limited success at best. They had no clue how to carry out their crime after the initial robbery.

The two lackluster outlaws never considered that all the people they had just robbed would certainly be able to recognize them in a court of law as witnesses, and maybe even more importantly, the two mopey morons would never be able to enter Dawson City again without fear of revenge from any one of the citizens of this growing community.

These two idiotic imbeciles had just left dozens of witnesses at Mother McCreary's. As the pair of nincompoops approached their stunningly well-behaved sled dogs, the Pearson brothers saw Mikita and, for some reason, began to worry about leaving a witness behind at the scene of their crime. In the cold and windy darkness, Mikita never heard the footsteps. Dirk Pearson picked up a log and moved quickly toward Mikita.

After he struck Mikita in the head, her body made a gentle crunch as she hit the snow. Dirk and Bob Pearson looked at each other, searching for one rational thought between two boneheaded buffoons. They could have just pushed Mikita out of their way and headed north with their well-trained dogs. They could have just left Mikita unconscious in the snow outside Mother McCreary's, and someone would have eventually found her and took her to safety. For some reason, these dubious dolts of delinquent behavior decided to load Mikita on their sled.

Maybe the Pearson brothers thought they were removing a witness from the scene of their crime, but Mikita hadn't even seen what had happened inside Mother McCreary's. The dopey duo dragged the extra weight of Mikita's body all the way north toward our cabin.

Maybe they thought that Mikita would be a productive prisoner for their journey. Maybe they thought she would be something to help keep them warm by the fire on the frozen trails. I am sure that many stupid ideas bounced around inside the skulls of the bewildered brains of the Pearson brothers as they approached our cabin. I guess in some strange way, I am thankful that these two corked-head criminal cronies decided to dump Mikita's body so close to our cabin.

The brothers probably panicked as they saw our dwelling, and then their desire to warm themselves overcame their underdeveloped plan about dealing with the unconscious young woman on their sled. The brothers saw a spot near the trail that they thought would be a good place to make a body disappear, and they just dumped her body, thinking she would freeze and soon be covered with snow, never to be found.

I thank God that the proximity of where Mikita was dumped allowed an opportunity for my stellar senses to become alerted. Mikita was so horribly injured as her body tumbled into the ravine. I am thankful that I did not sense the arrival of the Pearson brothers until after her body had finished twisting and turning downward through the rocks and trees, hurling toward the icy destination where I had found her.

It is strange to think of it this way, since Mikita was so badly wounded, but I was grateful for the stupidity of the Pearson brothers. If they had been smarter and just tossed her body off the sled in the middle of nowhere, she would have frozen to death before I ever had the chance to meet her.

Obviously, Mikita's memories of her involuntary trip north with the Pearson brothers ended after she had been thumped on her head, so my master filled in Jan Ericsson with more details of the brief visit by the Pearson brothers, and then he described what needed to be done to put Mikita's broken body back together.

I don't think Mikita enjoyed hearing these details, and she became removed and quiet. As the tale of her arrival concluded, Thomas Strong settled into a friendly conversation with Jan Ericsson. After a week of tending to and worrying about Mikita, I sensed my master beginning to relax as he spoke with Jan Ericsson. The two men drank and chatted, as many logs on the fire burned down to charred coals. I sensed Mikita needed a certain type of warmth not provided by flames in our fireplace, so I snuggled next to her and made sure she knew that I loved her.

CHAPTER FOURTEEN

———————·❋·———————

An Important Decision

The next morning, the writer and Jan Ericsson were doing their best to make as little noise as possible as they prepared for an early-morning hunt. The only light in the room was provided by the smoldering and almost-expired coals of the previous night's roaring fire. My master gently placed two large pieces of wood on top of the orange embers as I pretended to present the image of contented slumber. Mikita was still deep and far away in her dreams. Her face had a pristine look of contentment and solitude. I wanted to do everything I could to prevent her from being awakened from such a sweet moment of tranquility.

As the two men quietly tiptoed toward the door to exit the cabin, I noticed my master's hung-over, swollen, and barely awakened eyes glancing back at me. At that moment, I recognized his expression of approval. He smiled at me and closed the door of the cabin quietly, knowing that I would look after Mikita until he returned. I waited a few minutes until after the hunters had left and then quickly nestled myself as tight as I could next to the body of Mikita.

I fell into a cozy, comfortable, sleepy daze. In a vivid dream, I was brought back in time to the happiness of Thomas Strong's California estate. As I dreamed, I was running around in the glorious green grass of the fields, basking in the golden warmth of the California sunshine.

———

Still dreaming, I heard ordinary sounds and sniffed familiar scents and heard a voice calling me, which made me hop and skip toward the door where I knew I would welcome and greet my beloved master. As I raced through the halls of the house, I was surprised to see Mikita, instead of my master, kneeling down to welcome me at the door with a big, beefy bone. Before I even had an opportunity to chomp on the tasty morsel, I began smelling specific aromas that reminded me of quiet times spent between my master and me. There were the dark, rich scent of roasted coffee and the sweet smell of sizzling bacon crisping up in a pan.

I woke up salivating but was surprised to be all by myself in front of the fire. I was at first concerned but quickly thrilled to see Mikita slowly moving about the cabin, making breakfast. She saw me rustling around and looked right toward me, and then she smiled a lovely smile, just for me. I darted toward Mikita, but I made sure I didn't bump into her too hard. I realized she was still fragile, but I was eager to show my excitement about her recovery. I sat at Mikita's feet, and she slowly bent down to pet the top of my head. As she stroked my head with one hand, she placed a piece of bacon in front of my mouth with the other. All I could think about was how much I loved Mikita!

"Oh, Stanley, I love you," gushed Mikita as she continued to feed me thick chunks of juicy bacon.

We had a delightful time eating breakfast, and then Mikita let me out of the cabin so I could do my business. It usually doesn't take too long for me to relieve myself, especially considering the cold temperature and slushy conditions. Mikita giggled as I slipped around, trying to find a good place to go, and then she cheered me on as I raced back toward the door.

Mikita and I had a wonderful day together. She found a dusty old book, and she read to me as we snuggled under a blanket on the bearskin rug before the fire. The story she read was about a man lost in the wilderness for such a long time that he was presumed dead by his loved ones. The man survived because he wanted so desperately to see his family again. It ended up being a joyous tale, as the man finally made it home to his family. I related to this story, because Mikita was bringing a similar type of joy to my master and me.

As she was close to finishing reading the story, I could sense the sound of her voice thinning to a quiet whisper. I knew she was still weak and now probably tired, and the comforting sound of her voice had me a bit sleepy as well. I heard the gentle sound of the book cover closing, just before both our eyes closed, as we slipped into an afternoon nap.

After a short time, I was awakened by the familiar sounds of the voices of my master and Jan Ericsson as they approached the cabin. Mikita was also awakened as I rose and headed toward the door to greet them. The two men entered the cabin with just two small rabbits to show for their hunting efforts during the day. They were probably disappointed about their less than productive day as hunters, but they seemed more involved with a conversation that continued without interruption as they entered the cabin.

"There is not much time, Tom. The trails are already getting soft, and it is getting warmer this year earlier than normal. I need to head back soon," was the first thing I heard from Jan Ericsson.

"I know, Jan, I am aware of the temperature."

"Tom, you really need to think about this."

"Jan, all I have been doing is thinking about this situation!"

"Tonight is the last night I will spend here for three or four months, Tom, until after the mud and warm seasons."

"So it will be pretty isolated up here for a while."

"I know, Tom, and that is my point. You need to decide what cargo I am bringing south."

I have pretty good instincts when it comes to arguments between humans. I knew what my master and Jan Ericsson were quibbling about, but I wasn't sure if Mikita was following the conversation.

"Jan, I am not sure what to do. I don't think she is ready to travel."

"Tom, I think you need to—"

"Gentlemen," interrupted Mikita. "Please do not squabble on my behalf," continued Mikita. "I am feeling much better and stronger every day, but Mr. Strong is right. I don't feel ready for a lengthy sledding journey south."

"But will you be okay here, Mikita?" asked Jan Ericsson.

"Mr. Ericsson, I appreciate your concern, but I would not even be alive and talking to you if not for Mr. Strong and my best friend,

Stanley. I promise you that I will be more than okay. I am looking forward to spending time with my new family."

I was so enthused to hear Mikita say I was her best friend and overjoyed to listen to her say we were a family. I glanced at my master and noticed a tear rolling down his wind-burned cheek. I leaped toward Mikita as my master gave her a gentle hug, and all three of us were together as a family for the first time. As we enjoyed this precious moment of unity, Jan Ericsson threw a couple of big logs on the fire and exhaled a sigh of relief.

We soon settled in for an enjoyable evening. Mikita moved slowly about the cabin to help cook our dinner. It was the first time my master had seen her moving around on her feet, and I thought she was trying too hard to prove she was healthy and mended. When my master, Jan Ericsson, and Mikita finished cooking, I was happy to see my new best friend sit down and relax. Then we all enjoyed a nice meal before a crackling fire.

After eating, Thomas Strong and Jan Ericsson sat in two rocking chairs that they had moved closer to the fireplace, and they sipped whiskey and smoked cigars. I listened as Jan Ericsson described what the next three or four months would be like in our remote area.

As Jan Ericsson and Thomas Strong conversed by the fire, I heard something that was so similar to the sound of the scratching of quill on paper that my master made while he was at work. I looked up to see Mikita sitting at the author's writing desk, with her hand moving quickly. She seemed to be scribbling a story with a wooden pencil. Mikita was looking up at my master and Jan Ericsson and then back down again at the paper. I sat at her feet and waited patiently for her to finish her story, in hopes we would snuggle together as she read it to me.

When Mikita finally put down her pencil, my ears perked up, hoping to hear her lovely voice begin narrating a story. Instead, she revealed to me something more majestic and magical. On the paper was an image of Thomas Strong and Jan Ericsson sitting in front of the fire, chatting and sipping whiskey. I looked at the paper, then at my master and Jan Ericsson, then at the paper, and then again at the two men. I was dumbfounded, and I sat motionless and amazed. Mikita then showed her magical effort to the two subjects of her creativity.

"My goodness!" yelped my master as his glass dropped and broke on the cabin floor.

"Uuhhh . . ." was all that Jan Ericsson could manage.

"Mikita, this is amazing! Where did you learn to draw like this?" asked the dumbfounded writer.

"I don't know. I guess I got it from my mother. Growing up, I used to draw pictures of animals, trees, and people because it seemed to stop time for a while."

The room suddenly became quiet. That was very unusual, because my master was never at a loss for words, and Jan Ericsson always had a mouthful of syllables for the offering. Now, the only sound in the cabin was the crackle of wood in the fireplace and a little poof fart by me.

I gazed at the writer and the trail guide, and they were both scratching their heads. The two men looked at each other then looked at the picture that Mikita had drawn. They were overwhelmed, amazed, and impressed at the talent the drawing displayed. Mikita's artwork had seized a simple moment in time that completely captured the essence of two friends.

"Thank you, Mikita. You made an old writer and his friend look better than they should," was the best an overwhelmed author could muster.

Slumber was quickly coming upon us all. It had been a long day, and we had all eaten heartily and had earned a good night of sleep. The men had whiskey that eased them into a healthy slumber, and Mikita slowly placed herself down on the rug closest to the fireplace. I waited for Mikita to settle, and then I nestled next to her as softly as an excited dog could manage.

In the morning, Jan Ericsson enjoyed a nice breakfast before he began his journey back to Dawson City. He mentioned to my master that he had been happy to deliver his stories back to civilization, but in three or four months, the sledders would be returning from the Yukon and would be heading south, so they could deliver their own stories. He also said he might surprise us with a midseason visit on a horse sled if the weather was right. He looked at Mikita and then told my master that drawings with Mikita's artistic skill would make the tales of the north even more compelling.

"My good friend, Jan, the stories of the travelers coming home and Mikita's artwork will most certainly be delivered to the world," exalted my master.

"I think that sounds great, Thomas!"

"For safety's sake, Jan, don't tell anyone in Dawson City about Mikita. The Pearson brothers might have friends."

"I understand, Thomas. God bless, and good luck," offered Jan Ericsson as he exited and headed south toward Dawson City.

"We'll be fine!" yelled my master.

Mikita just waved good-bye and then sat down at the writing desk again. I sat closely below her, and I nodded in the direction of the desk where she had drawn that magical picture the night before.

"Draw me now!" is what I would have said if I could speak.

CHAPTER FIFTEEN

Family

Jan Ericsson's departure beckoned a sense of isolation to my master, Mikita, and me. Our trusted friend and advisor to all things of the north had thoroughly explained to us the nature of travel to the Yukon. The gold rushers needed the snow and ice of the arctic cold so their dogs could pull their sleds north toward potential riches. After making the arduous journey north, the travelers would find a place near a stream and set up a camp. Some set up tents, and other more industrious sojourners built rudimentary structures pounded together from the wood of nearby trees.

As the weather warmed, the ice and snow would melt, and the gold panners would begin working the site of the stream they had selected in hopes of finding instant wealth. The days became longer and the temperature warmed, but everyone that had journeyed north knew that the glowing sunshine and warming climate were not long-lasting in Alaska. Most of the gold rushers would have about three or four months to find their fortunes. Soon, the very long days of the northland summer would once again begin to become shorter, and the temperatures would plummet steadily toward the more customary chilly climate. There would be an early frost not like those in the southern states. There would be quick arrival of heavy snowfall, and streams would once again begin to freeze over, signaling the warning to start heading south. Timing is everything in Yukon travel.

It is best to head north as close to the warming weather as possible so as not to spend too much time in the frozen tundra, waiting for a chance to mine for gold. This strategy also increased the chances to encounter the danger of cracking ice and heavy snow. Likewise, the best strategy heading south was to exit the desolation of the northland just as the blustering cold started to harden the trails back into slippery, icy thoroughfares most suitable for dog sleds.

We understood that nobody would be moving north or south or passing by as the weather warmed. Jan Ericsson also had described a period of two weeks or so when everything near the cabin would start to melt. He called it the mud season, and he had warned us of the danger of this period. The quick melting of ice and snow often created unpredictable mudslides, a rapid rise in water levels in streams and rivers, falling trees, and treacherous footing. Jan Ericsson emphasized this danger before he left, because the temperatures this particular year were rising more rapidly than normal, which could be potential for more severe conditions.

Thomas Strong and I quite obviously listened and gave the utmost consideration to everything that Jan Ericsson offered in knowledge and experience. I know our trusted friend was worried about us as we nestled in for our first Alaskan summer. If not for Mikita, I might have been concerned about the lengthy separation from humanity. My master and I would have been fine by ourselves, living on our own and embracing the struggle of man versus nature, but Mikita's presence changed the dynamic of our existence. I couldn't imagine any situation that spending time with Mikita would not be productive, fun, and positive. I felt confident we would all be fine.

I looked at my master and I sensed contentment in his soul, and I knew the emotion he was feeling, because I felt the same way. There was a promontory moment when we both looked at Mikita, and she didn't even notice as we affectionately gazed at her. She was recovering so nicely, and that made us so happy.

The mud season seemed like it would be a period of isolation, and if it was spent in this cabin with just my master and me, the two of us might have felt a little lonely, but with Mikita here, we didn't think it would be such a bad thing. She was healing and getting healthier every day, and there was an opportunity for something special to occur. It was a unique situation that provided a chance for my master to reach into the heavens and grab back the love and zest for life that had been expelled from his heart after he had lost his beloved wife and daughter.

I had wished for this since the day Mikita came into our lives. I was hoping that Mikita, once beaten and broken and near death, could somehow manage to be the glue that made us a family, and maybe, she could heal Thomas Strong's broken heart.

Mikita was making a swift and continuous recovery that defied the laws of medicine. She had only been recovering for a bit over three weeks, yet she was moving about the cabin with only minor discomfort. Her once contorted ankle and dislocated hip did not prevent her from moving about when she felt the need to accomplish a chore.

I felt she was trying too hard to be a productive resident in the cabin. As each day passed, she participated in the cleaning, cooking, and tending to the fire alongside my master more and more, in such a manner that was above and beyond the call of duty for someone inflicted with such debilitating injuries.

I noticed an occasional wince as she labored around, and there were also frequent short breaths that were simply quick gasps for air as her battered body did its best to deal with her injuries. My master noticed exactly what I was witnessing with Mikita, and I was so thrilled that he put an end to Mikita's overexuberant caretaking efforts.

"Mikita, please sit down and listen to an old writer that needs to provide you with a message, not from a pen and ink on paper, but from my heart through the sound of my voice."

"Yes, Mr. Strong," responded Mikita as she slowly sat down without ever taking her eyes off my master.

"Mikita, I am thrilled and overjoyed at how quickly you have been recovering."

"I am feeling better every day, Mr. Strong."

"The day that Jan Ericsson left here, I most certainly became responsible for your well-being."

"Mr. Strong, I hope I haven't upset—"

"I am responsible for you, Mikita! My boy, Stanley, will keep you company and entertain you, and I will do my best to enhance your speedy recovery. I will be doing the cooking and stoking of our fire! You will relax, heal, and draw pictures."

"I don't want to be a burden, Mr. Strong."

The famous writer that had become a widower slowly positioned himself in front of the fire next to Mikita. There was a look of pale hopelessness but also consternation in his eyes as he placed his arm around her. He drew Mikita's body close with such tenderness and affection that my heart skipped a beat, and I actually held my breath while trying to take in this emotional moment.

"Mikita, you are by no means a burden." Thomas Strong's voice cracked as he tried to conceal his emotions. I jumped up and down in front of Mikita in an effort to display my agreement with my master. "The manner in which you arrived here was frightening and despicable, but nevertheless, you are not a burden, but a blessing for me and for my boy, Stanley," continued a man consumed by emotion, as I pawed and scratched Mikita's feet.

"Mr. Strong, you and Stanley are the only reason I am alive today. You both saved me and gave me a second chance at life."

"Mikita, you don't know me well enough to realize this, but you are giving this old wordsmith a second chance at life as well, and please stop calling me Mr. Strong. I want you to call me Thomas."

"Okay, Mr. Thomas," replied Mikita.

"Just Thomas would be fine, Mikita." My master chuckled.

I think I sensed it first, because dogs have superior instincts. Mikita, my master, and I were on the verge of something that might be special, perhaps like the bond that only loving family members can share.

My master cooked a nice rabbit stew dinner, and we all settled on the couch in front of some lackluster flames that needed a bit of attention. As my master got up to grab a few logs to replenish the fire, Mikita also rose and grabbed an old book. She began to read from it out loud before my master was done tending to the fire. The sound of Mikita's voice drew me close to her feet and even closer to slumber. As Thomas Strong finished adjusting the logs, he heard Mikita reading the story.

The tale being beautifully orated by Mikita was about a woman whose husband had been reported missing during the Civil War. The woman somehow felt in her heart that her husband was still alive and would someday come back to her. My master listened as Mikita's voice brought this tale to life, and it reminded him about how he futilely hoped and prayed his family would return to him. I watched closely as he listened attentively. In the story Mikita was reading, the widow's prayers seemed hopeless, but as my master's eyelids started to get heavy and his head tilted toward dreamland, he seemed hopeful and content.

I woke up the next morning to the sound of Mikita giggling. My master was still snoring away, and Mikita was holding her latest drawing close to his ruffled, snoozing head in an effort to compare its accuracy. She had awakened before us and seized the opportunity to capture an image of Thomas Strong at a rare moment of vulnerability.

Mikita carefully propped her drawing on his writing desk. She started a pot of coffee, and then she led me outside to let me take care of my morning business. Mikita smiled and wistfully chuckled as she watched me search for the best place to relieve myself. Just as I finished, Mikita and I heard a bellowing sound from within the cabin. It was my master bursting into laughter as his half-closed, early-morning eyes were suddenly cracked wide-open by the comical image of his face that Mikita had scratched from pencil to paper.

As Mikita and I entered the cabin, my master was still snorting quick bursts of laughter while his eyes beamed at Mikita with adoring approval. He hugged Mikita, and I leaped and ran circles around them. It was such a special bonding moment and just another wonderful moment on our journey toward becoming a family.

CHAPTER SIXTEEN

---•❊•---

The Landscape

The time spent alone in the cabin provided such cherished memories for my master, Mikita, and me. During the day, we all did the chores required to keep us warm and secure. Firewood was brought inside, the floors were swept, and dinner was prepared. We always had a blessing before our evening meal, and we were thankful as we finished as well.

Each night we spent enjoying the closeness that was so quickly blossoming among us. We were all three alone in the wilderness, but we all had skills that kept us smiling, laughing, and entertained.

Thomas Strong was obviously a prolific storyteller. I felt so cozy as I nestled into Mikita's lap, and then we listened carefully as the award-winning writer weaved a wondrous story for our ears only. Each night his voice became more vibrant, and his tales became more jovial and enthusiastic.

Mikita anxiously absorbed my master's stories, and I enjoyed them just as much. I was thrilled to listen to all the details of the glorious tales, but when my master would complete his story, Mikita would begin to read from one of the old books in the cabin, and I relished those moments just as much.

Mikita's voice brought life to the stories of dusty old pages. She didn't read in a whisper, nor was it too loud in an attempt to command the room. Her voice mesmerized the old author and me like a woodwind instrument gliding through the notes of Tchaikovsky.

When Mikita read to us with such perfect pace and rhythm, we were like very young children listening to a bedtime story. Each night ended with us cradled to sleep by the sounds of Mikita's voice, the crackling of logs in the fire, and the whipping wind outside our cabin that sounded so cold but only made it feel warmer inside.

One of my skills was the ability to fill in the dull moments of our days with any type of behavior that might encourage smiles, chuckles, or laughter from my master and Mikita. I flopped around on my back, leaped over furniture, and chased down anything that seemed to be moving and alive on the cabin floor.

My best skill was the ability to start a new day. I usually rousted my master and Mikita, probably a bit earlier than they wanted to rise. I was very good at waking them, because my cold nose and gentle tongue kisses effectively woke them, while also being cute enough to prevent any agitation. This skill was of great benefit to me as well, since I usually needed to make some yellow snow as the new day arrived.

One morning, after I had rustled Mikita from her evening of sleep and I had finished greeting the new day with my call to nature, we returned to the sanctity of the cabin to the sweet aroma of bacon sizzling in a pan above the fire. Thomas Strong was in a good mood, and he was making a stellar breakfast. Mikita moved swiftly about the cabin to help him prepare our meal. My master had been reluctant to let Mikita help in this manner, but now he was grinning and had a sense of satisfaction on his face. I read his expressions almost as well as Mikita had read the stories from the old books. He knew that Mikita was healed and healthy. Her recovery was amazingly quick and was in perfect timing with the end of the mud season.

"Hey, guys, let's have a nice breakfast, and then maybe we can get out of this cabin for a while today."

"That sounds like fun," replied Mikita as I jumped up and down with approval.

"We won't go too far, just a little walk around the grounds. Are you sure you are up for it, Mikita?"

"Yes, Mr. Thomas, I am fine. Are we going to bring Stanley?"

I jumped and raced all over the cabin.

"Just Thomas," said my master, "and let's tease him for a while to make him wonder if he is going with us, but you know Stanley is coming."

Soon, we ventured out of the cabin on a perfect day to explore and familiarize ourselves with the area near our cabin. The temperature was slightly above freezing, and the ground felt firm beneath our feet. It occurred to me that it was strange to have spent so much time in our cabin and yet have not really known much about the area surrounding us.

As we exited the cabin, my master awkwardly tried to steer Mikita north in an effort to prevent her from looking south, toward the location on the trail where we had found her. Mikita understood and appreciated the gesture, but as my master stumbled and slipped, I realized Mikita was going to be the leader of this recreational expedition.

We all looked south down the trail that had brought all of us here. It was strange to see this path as it glowed with magnificent golden sunshine. It was a narrow trail that had brought such a wide spectrum of visitors and emotions. As we began our first day outside the cabin, I think we all silently agreed that we were fortunate this path had brought us together.

As we moved away from the cabin and started to head north, we saw the wide, flat opening to the east where all the sled teams had been secured and used as a resting place. Again, just like the trail, it looked quite different in the beautiful, warming glow of sunshine.

The three of us started walking and headed north on the trail that so many travelers had embarked upon, and after just a few hundred feet, I began to see things that had been so close but I never really noticed. I peered at my master, and I knew he felt the same way.

As we continued slowly strolling north, we noticed just off the trail to the east, two enormous pine trees towering toward the sky. The mighty pines were standing about fifty feet apart. My master and Mikita tried to hook their arms around one of them, but they would have needed at least four more arms for that to be accomplished.

As they attempted to hug the tree, it dawned upon me how uncommon it was for two such strong members of the same species sharing such proximity to survive but also to successfully flourish. I tilted my head toward the sky and examined the two trees. As they reached farther toward the sun and sky, they became increasingly entwined and tangled together. I wondered if they were fighting for territory or reaching out to each other for companionship.

As I daydreamed about the relationship of the two gigantic pine trees, my master and Mikita began carving their initials into one of the trees. Thomas Strong worked the letter *T* into the bark and was working on the *S* of his last name as Mikita had already crafted a large *M* into the tree and had almost finished the *SS* of my initials. I thought the ceremonial carving was almost completed, but my master was not quite finished, and he carved one last letter into the tree.

It was by far the most significant letter etched into the bark. Just to the right of the artistic *M* Mikita had carved, he slowly dug another *S* into the tree. I looked up at the letters that appeared on the tree. Now, the second letter of all our initials included the letter *S*. As I was trying to figure out what that meant, I watched Mikita hug my master, and as they embraced, I noticed a tear slowly trickling down her face. I was slow to realize what the *S* had meant, but soon I realized what the letters carved into the bark had made most official. The letter *S* was now a common link for all of us, which stood for our last name, Strong. We were a family. We were a strong family for sure!

After that revelation at the pine trees, we looked toward the west, and the curiosity became evident in the eyes of the father figure of this trio. There was a steady slope grading down toward the sounds of a bustling stream. We carefully tracked down the grade and then peered upon the retired gold mine. It had been the original reason for the construction of our current dwelling.

There was a big hole carved into the side of a steep, rocky hill, which was poorly protected by a broken-down, rotted fence. Protruding from the entrance to the mine was a wooden slide that led down to a sparkling stream that had many shallow pools and bustling water that appeared perfect for gold panning.

It seemed like an ideal location for mining the golden treasure, and it made me sad that so much effort had been put into this mine with little results. Then again, I was happy that this place was now the home of my Master, Mikita, and me, and I was so thankful for that.

CHAPTER SEVENTEEN

---◆❈◆---

The Big Rumble

As the weather warmed, we spent more time outside the cabin. The soft, muddy ground had hardened quickly, but I noticed that there was still so much snow in the hills above our cabin. Even though it was warming, when we ventured outside, my paws quickly got cold and my master's old bones stiffened, well before Mikita needed to head back to the cabin for warmth.

We watched Mikita set snare lines to trap rabbits, and the next day, she entered the cabin with a bounty for rabbit stew. We observed as she smashed a rock into the slushy ice at the side of the stream, creating a bubbling hole of frozen water. Soon she had a bucket full of fish that we filleted, sizzled in a pan above a steady fire, and then devoured with pure satisfaction.

I had so often heard my master's friends calling me a spoiled little runt. I never really understood why they would say that, because for my entire life, he had been taking care of me the best way he knew. I loved him for it, and I always expressed my appreciation for his efforts.

Now, as I watched Mikita cater to each and every need of her new family, I realized the selfless nature it takes to care for loved ones. I learned and realized that those sacrifices are not so difficult, especially if your efforts are made for loved ones that appreciate and care for you.

Then, one day, as I watched Mikita tending to our needs, it dawned on me that we were all loved ones. We three would all make sacrifices for the one another's happiness. Mikita loved my master and me as much as we loved her. I was so happy when I realized this. I bubbled with joy. If I had a tail, I would have wagged it. I looked right into the once-lifeless eyes of Thomas Strong. He sensed my newly found joy, and I also was keenly aware that my master's heart was whole again.

With that growing warmth in our hearts, many simple things brought smiles and laughter to all three of us. When the weather was nice, we went fishing or set traps for rabbits and patrolled the area around the cabin in order to become familiar with our surroundings. If the weather became inclement, we would tend to do chores and clean the cabin.

Regardless of what each day brought to us, every evening was the same. We would eat a family meal, with me at the feet of my master. I always enjoyed it when he gave me a little bit of leftovers at the end of his dinner. After the table was cleared, we always ended up relaxing on the bearskin rug together. My master and Mikita would take turns picking a book to read. I would sit between them as they took turns reading paragraphs from wonderful stories.

The sound of the voice of such a wonderful man like Thomas Strong always put me at ease, relaxing me in a way that is difficult to describe. Perhaps his voice affected me like a mother singing a lullaby to her child, but it wasn't quite as sweet as that. It was more like the continuous sound of a locomotive engine, slowly and rhythmically ushering you to sleep, while you lay in a cozy berth on an evening train.

When Mikita read aloud from the books, her voice was similarly comforting as the narrative voice of my master. Her voice was not a dainty, feminine whisper, nor did it contain the sturdy and tough sound that would be representative of her arduous existence. Her voice had a calming, even flow. It was a voice that could compel you to listen in a quiet room, yet was also powerful enough to draw attention. Mikita had a voice that could calm and command. Simply, she had the voice of a leader.

One particular night, after a filling and satisfying meal, we settled down to read a story. The fire that evening was a boisterous one and provided toasty warmth to our sanctuary. I drifted off into a tranquil slumber and was soon followed into this peaceful state of nocturnal bliss by my master and Mikita. Soon, I was awakened by a rumbling, which seemed to be of an intestinal nature. My more acute hearing and sense of smell made me the only one in the room to wake. I looked at my master and at Mikita, and judging from the less than familiar scent of the gas and the crooked smile of contentment on Mikita's face, I realized that she had broken wind in her sleep. I closed my eyes and went back to sleep, knowing that girls pass gas just as well as men and dogs.

At dawn of that same night, I woke with a sense of fear and distress from a more imposing rumbling noise. I rose quickly and rustled my master and Mikita. I scurried about the cabin and felt a nervous tension I had never experienced before. My master and Mikita looked at me with concern, trying to figure out what was wrong, but then the floor of the cabin started to shake. There was a brief pause of complete silence, which was immediately followed by thunderous, violent cracking sounds and scary, floor-rattling movements in the cabin. We all scurried about the cabin, trying to figure out what to do, but the shaking event ended almost as quickly as it started.

Thomas Strong and I had lived in California and had experienced a few earthquakes, but from the way he was acting, this seemed unique and unfamiliar to him. He checked on Mikita and me and then went toward the cabin door. When he opened it, his jaw dropped in astonishment.

"Oh my God!" was all the writer could manage.

Mikita and I quickly followed him to the open door and were equally stunned at the level of natural destruction around us and how close it came to consuming us. The warmer-than-usual temperatures of the season had caused an icy sled beneath the heavy, wet snow on the hills above us, and a massive avalanche had crashed into our quiet existence.

The monumental weight of the heavy, wet snow sliding down the slope of the hillside had ripped up trees and grabbed big rocks in a powerful, formidable example of gravity. The rumbling snow, broken trees, and tumbling rocks had filled the ravine that my master and I had found Mikita. The trail heading to and from the cabin was also inundated with snow, large rocks, and debris. The area that sled dogs had been accustomed to nestling and making comfortable snow caves had been completely obliterated. I looked at Mikita, and she looked at me with the same expression of amazement as we both looked at the two big pine trees that had been so special to us. The massive trees had actually prevented the landslide of snow and debris from bringing harm to our cabin.

"Look down there!" yelled my master.

My master was pointing down to what used to be the gold mine and the flowing stream. Now, both the useless mine, and the frozen stream were just an enormous pile of snow. In our minds, all of us absorbed the immense destruction and then headed back to the sanctuary of our cabin, which, thankfully, had been spared by Mother Nature and those two big pine trees.

As we neared the cabin, we all noticed a subtle hint of natural grace. There was a tiny bit of sunlight refracting from the rising foggy mist of the fallen, turbulent snow. It was oddly beautiful. We entered the safety of the cabin, and after we had all collected ourselves, I noticed that we all three were shaking. My master and Mikita were cold, but the quivering of their bodies was more due to the shock of what had happened surrounding us. While I was utterly impressed and awestruck with this disaster, my shaking was more due to me walking around in that big pile of slushy snow. I moved quickly toward glowing fireplace in an effort to warm myself. I also hoped that the image of me toasting myself might calm down my master and Mikita.

I woke a while later with Mikita nestled next to me in a restful sleep and my master just a few feet away. He was snoring prolifically on the rocking chair nearest the fire. It might seem odd to have such a peaceful moment in what would be considered by most people to be a perilous time. There certainly was an enormous degree of carnage outside our cabin, but the heat of the fire and the warmth of our hearts within the cabin prevented any disturbance to our tranquility.

CHAPTER EIGHTEEN

---⦿---

Shoveling Strategy

The morning after the avalanche of snow, I woke from a deep and peaceful sleep to the sound of my master's voice. His tone sounded a bit different than normal. It sounded stern and determined but also uncertain. That was a bit strange to hear, because as a writer, Thomas Strong was always sure of every word he spoke or penned on paper.

He was talking to Mikita about what to do with the mountainous piles of snow surrounding us. We really didn't need to move too far from the cabin, and there was access to our woodpile through the side door of our dwelling. His concern was that the large amount of displaced snow might melt too quickly in what was so soon after the mud season. If the snow melted rapidly so soon after the mud season, the ground surrounding our cabin might become circumvented, and the foundation of our dwelling might shift so much that it would be unsafe to live in.

He decided the best way to protect the integrity of the cabin was to move as much snow downhill as possible, south of the cabin. His reasoning being that as it melted, it would flow away from our safe haven. For three days, my master and Mikita tirelessly moved, pushed, and shoveled snow and debris below harm's way. His strategy was his strength, because on the fourth day after the avalanche, the sun rose with brightness and power, and the temperature warmed quickly.

The first few days of rising temperatures were a delight for a warm-weather dog like me, but it was still really unsafe for me to explore. There were such interesting and unfamiliar sounds around me, like a symphony orchestra playing newly invented instruments.

The rapidly melting snow provided a soft whispering, sound that reminded me a bit of autumn leaves blowing around in the wind. There was also the more rugged noise of ice cracking and snapping as it shifted. The most consistent sound was the shallow grinding, whisking sound of heavy snow sliding all around us. All these noises were new to me, and each by itself might have made me nervous, but together, they joined in rhythm to create a performance that I enjoyed.

For the next few days, there were prevailing clear skies that provided the bright sun an opportunity to melt away all the remaining excess snow. The increasing temperatures and sunshine rapidly ushered in the joy of spring. After a week or so of again being surrounded by deep, squishy mud, the sun and spring breezes solidified the earth around our cabin. It seemed like the first time since my master and I had arrived, it was more pleasurable to be outside the cabin. The walls of the cabin had protected us and provided security throughout the harsh elements of winter.

After spending so much time contained in a small dwelling, we were all happy to spend time setting snare traps for rabbits and searching for moose hoof prints. There was a wealth of canned food supplies, and my master felt confident that would sustain us through the spring, well before Jan Ericsson would visit us with more sustenance.

Certainly, the fresh meat of wild animals would be a welcome treat, and Mikita continued to show us her vast trapping and hunting skills. Mikita was very skilled at setting traps, and we had prolific success in capturing rabbits.

One afternoon, we all slipped into a midday nap after overstuffing our bellies with rabbit stew. My master and I woke simultaneously to a repeated high-pitched whistling sound followed with a hearty thump. We both headed toward the door of the cabin, and we peered out to see Mikita shooting arrows into one of the big pine trees that had protected us from the snow slide. She was focused on aiming the arrows toward a target she had made on the tree and had not noticed us watching her archery performance. The arrows in the tree were all bunched tightly together due to her consistent skilled performance. After Mikita launched her last arrow, she realized we were watching her, and she smiled, beaming with pride. She was happy because she sensed that we enjoyed her display, but more importantly, she knew her innate skills of hunting had not been eroded by her injuries.

"Rabbit stew is fine," she said, "but venison is a heartier meal, and hunting moose is more fun than trapping rabbits."

"From the looks of things, that is not good news for the moose around here," was my master's reply as he chuckled and scratched his head in amazement.

The next day, Mikita prodded us into a morning wake-up that was much earlier than usual. She wanted us to go out with her in search of moose, and she explained to us that the brief period when the dark of night begins to turn into the dawn of daylight is the best time to track moose. She enlightened us that the most sensitive survival mechanisms of a moose are not working at full capacity in the early-morning hours.

We followed Mikita out of the cabin, and as we walked into the wilderness, we tried to walk as quietly as she did. While we worked our way between trees and brush, I picked up a powerful scent and heard the distant sound of footsteps. We were not yet too far from our cabin. The aroma I was picking up had the strong scent of a big animal, and the stepping sound was quick but heavy. Instincts told me this was a moose moving about nearby, and I quietly tugged at Mikita's leg and pointed my head toward the location of the moose.

"Good boy," whispered Mikita ever so softy.

She quickly positioned herself behind a tree, and I nestled behind her, close at her feet. Mikita slowly waved her hand to attract the attention of my master, and then he followed her hand signals and hid himself behind a tree. As we all quietly waited, I noticed the scent of the moose getting stronger and the sound of the footsteps getting louder. Suddenly, Mikita looked down at me with a gaze of approval. She leaned against the tree as she deftly loaded an arrow into her bow. Mikita took a deep breath, and all was briefly quiet. Mikita then whirled quickly from behind the tree and released an arrow toward the unsuspecting moose.

The arrow whizzed through the air and thumped directly into the neck of the moose. We watched in amazement as the mortally wounded animal raced quickly and erratically in the direction of our cabin. We hurriedly followed its bloody path and found the dying animal had tumbled down the slope near our cabin and landed halfway up the ravine near the old gold mine.

"Stanley. You are a good hunter!" yelled Mikita.

I felt so good that I had helped with this great success, and my master was laughing a triumphant laugh as he tossed me about. Mikita began roping the moose in preparation for dragging it toward the cabin. My master and I watched Mikita in amazement as she continued to exhibit her wilderness skills, but then I was distracted by something sparkling in the stream below. It was a sensational and noticeable glimmer in the water. I was immediately attracted to the beautiful shine, and I rushed down to the stream and began pawing at the glistening objects with curiosity.

My master heard my paws tapping into the water and made his way toward me to figure out why a warm-weather dog would be thumping around in a frigid stream. He bent over to pull me out of the cold water. As he began to pick me up, his grip loosened, and I fell back into the stream. Thomas Strong was overwhelmed and excited as he recognized what I had seen.

"Oh my Lord...Oh . . . oh my God," were the words that sent us into frozen disbelief and ushered in a changed existence for all three of us.

CHAPTER NINETEEN

---✤---

Unexpected Wealth

The shiny sparkles in the stream that had drawn my attention were large nuggets of pure, natural gold. As we all began to survey the area, there were so many chunks of shiny yellow metal with the same characteristics, nestled aloft in the bed of the stream, begging for our attention.

American magazine had purchased this property for Thomas Strong so he could tell the stories of people in pursuit of the very element that now glistened underneath us. I thought of all the people that had sought shelter in our cabin on long journeys, subjecting themselves to the treacherous elements of northland travel, searching for what now sparkled right at our feet.

"How could this be?" asked Mikita as she wondered out loud.

"I really don't know," was all that the prolific writer could offer for an explanation.

"Well, I suggest we start picking up this gold before it sinks into the river bed or gets washed downstream," was Mikita's logical statement that snapped us all back from our haze of amazement.

My master stood with his feet in the freezing water of the stream, scratching his chin. He appeared to be in some sort of shock or just simple disbelief.

Meanwhile, Mikita picked me up and took me back to the warmth of the cabin. She had noticed that I was shaking. I thought it was from the excitement of seeing all the gold, but Mikita knew I

---

was cold and needed the warmth of the cabin. She placed me by the slow-burning coals of a heavy fire and kissed my head.

"Stay here, Stanley, I will be back soon."

I trusted Mikita and watched her move about the cabin for a minute or two before I started to meander into slumber. I noticed Mikita exiting the cabin with two large leather satchels in her hands, and then my eyelids began to close for a nice nap. As I drifted off, I heard the sound of my master outside the cabin laughing and sounding more joyful than I had heard him sound in a long time.

My lovely nap was ended by three simultaneous sounds. The first was the thud of wood entering the fireplace and the crackling and popping that follows. The second was a gentle tumbling sound that probably seemed louder because of its actual proximity to my snout. The third was the boisterous laughter of my two best friends as I was completely awakened to the sight of Mikita rolling a huge gold nugget in front of me.

"We are rich, Stanley!" cheered Mikita.

"Stanleeeeeey!" Thomas Strong yelped at me with a joy that I hadn't heard in so long.

I sprung up with enthusiasm and excitement and leaped at my happy master. He reached out to hug me, and gold nuggets fell all over the floor. I briefly felt bad because I thought I had made a mess, but then Mikita opened her arms to welcome me as well, and a similar result occurred as she hugged me. There were nuggets of gold all over the floor of the cabin.

The shiny pebbles were atop Thomas Strong's writing desk and also in a pile glowing beautifully before the fire. Mikita held both of her hands in front of me, and the sparkle of gold shining from her palms and the happiness in her face warmed my heart almost as much as the first day Mikita started feeling better after her injuries.

It is not very often that an incredible writer like Thomas Strong is at a loss for words, but I watched as his facial expressions went from joy, disbelief, amazement, bewilderment, and back to joyfulness.

Mikita sat down on the floor and seemed suddenly overwhelmed. She began to quiver, and sobbing followed. I rushed to her and licked her face to try to usher a smile. I wasn't sure why she was so suddenly acting sad, and as my master noticed the sudden change in her emotions, his joyfulness instantly faltered.

"I shouldn't be here. I don't deserve this," was what Mikita managed to utter in a scratchy voice.

"Oh my goodness, Mikita, if anyone deserves this, it is you," was my master's immediate response.

"You and Stanley saved me. I love you both so much, but this makes me feel afraid for having too much happiness."

Mr. Thomas Strong had never given an order to anyone in his entire life. He never even gave me orders. It was funny to listen to his voice trying to have the sound of authority.

"That's nonsense, Mikita. You deserve to be happy. Everyone deserves to be happy. If you think you are too happy, get up and throw a couple of logs on the fire, clean up all the gold nuggets off the floor, and then make dinner for me, you, and Stanley."

There was a brief, quiet pause in the cabin, and we all were looking back and forth at one another. The expressions on all our faces were kind of like when everyone in a room is wondering who passed the gas. Mikita stood up and picked me up. She kissed my head and placed me in my favorite place by the fire. I watched as she hugged my master and then wiped a tear from his cheek. She knew what the yelling of his orders had meant, and she responded perfectly.

"Dinner will be ready soon, but both of you will clean up the gold nuggets spread all around this cabin floor, and somebody needs to drag that moose closer to the cabin so I can butcher it," Mikita ordered with a chuckle and a smile.

As we ate dinner, my two favorite people still had looks of shock and amazement controlling their faces. They were definitely both happy, but the quiet of the room made it easy to hear the sound of their brains wondering what needed to be done. Soon, the voice of Thomas Strong ended the silence.

"I traveled here in search of stories," he began. "I didn't come up here in search of gold, and I didn't come up north looking for a new family. Now I have found both, or both have found me, and it is the best story of all to tell."

Mikita stood up and took a couple of deep breaths. I noticed she felt comfortable but was also being thoughtful. Usually, I have a good instinct for what people are going to say and do, but I really wasn't sure what Mikita was thinking.

"Well, Thomas and Stanley, if this is going to be the best story of all to tell, we need to get as much gold out of that stream and mine as possible."

My new best friend and the now-established guardian of Mikita heaved bellowing laughs, and they began to calm and chuckle with happiness. Mikita raised her arms in celebration and did a little jump and skip toward her new father figure, hugging him with love that had previously been reserved only for me.

I was not jealous of this expression of emotion between two people that needed that kind of connection. I was thrilled, however, when both of them looked at me, smiled welcoming smiles, and allowed me to leap into their arms.

What soon followed was a strategy discussion about how to extract as much gold as possible from the stream and mine before the weather started to turn into the coldness of winter. The return of frigid north air would freeze the wealthy stream and also signal the return of the travelers heading south back toward civilization.

Mikita had the most experience working and garnishing the products of nature the northland provided, so it was natural that her voice was most prevalent in the conversation.

Mikita did most of the talking, and the writer did most of the listening. I watched the way Mikita gestured with her hands and the way her head confidently moved from side to side as she spoke. I remember the sound of her voice as she explained to my master what was the best way to harvest our recently found fortune. It was the sound of confidence that her tone portrayed. I wasn't quite sure what the expression on the face of the brilliant writer Thomas Strong was, as Mikita devised our strategy. He seemed perplexed, confused, and amazed all at the same time. I was just happy to enjoy the show.

Mikita explained to us that the snow avalanche had crushed the interior structure of the mine and forcefully thrust the hollow walls out into the stream. A mountain of icy snow still rested in front of what used to be the opening of the mine, and there was also that bounty of large gold chunks bouncing about among the rocks of the stream's bottom.

Mikita had a three-pronged strategy, and each facet had all our particular skills considered. Mikita would work up from downstream, scooping up as many hefty nuggets of golden treasure as she could handle. The famous writer Thomas Strong was now bonfire chairman. His job was to construct an enormous fire, each day, in front of the icy snow pile at the opening of the mine. Mikita anticipated that as the snow melted it would reveal bigger chunks of gold that had not been completely expelled from the mine. As my master collected enormous chunks of gold each day, it was obvious Mikita's prediction was correct.

I had the best job of all three of us. It wasn't the hardest or more difficult job, but there were responsibilities that required my smarts and intelligence. I was in charge of bringing the afternoon bounty back to the safety of the cabin. It was fun and certainly the warmest and coziest of all the tasks at hand. I snuggled up near the fire inside the cabin, keeping warm and toasty. I was completely comfortable, but I did have a leather strap loosely wrapped around my neck. The strap maintained a brown leather satchel that was light in weight and empty, and it was no bother at all, as I enjoyed my fireside slumbers. I snoozed, napped, rested, and waited for one simple signal that snapped me to attention.

"Stanleeeeeeeeeeey!" my master and Mikita yelled simultaneously to spring me into action. I bolted toward the door of the cabin and whisked my way through a custom-formed passageway covered by a hanging piece of thin leather at the bottom of the door. Mikita had that made just for me. I rushed down the slippery slopes of the banks of the stream toward my two favorite people, who had both suddenly become prolific gold miners.

Thomas Strong and Mikita always enjoyed my hurried arrivals down toward the mine. They yelped my name, Stanley, jumped up and down, and received me with laughter every time. They loaded up the leather satchel attached to me, and then I headed back up to the cabin.

"Go! Stanley! Go!" Mikita always yelled as I bolted up toward the cabin.

I was so proud of this job. I was not a cold-weather dog, but I could scurry up the slope to the cabin ten times as fast as Thomas Strong and Mikita, with half the effort.

When I returned to the cabin with a satchel full of gold, I had another important responsibility. Underneath Thomas Strong's writing table, Mikita had loosened a floorboard and created a hiding spot for our newfound fortune. I knew the spot, and I knew what to do to make the latest deposit.

I lay down on my side and then pulled the loose leather strap from around my neck, which released the satchel filled with gold from my body. I then carefully placed my paw on the exact spot in the floor that Mikita had instructed me to do so. I pushed down, and as my paw disappeared into the floor, the other end of the board lifted up, revealing our secure hiding place. I then slid the gold-filled satchel into the opening in the floor. Pushing the floorboard back into the proper position was the easiest of my tasks, and it completed my duties.

I was proud after completing my task, and I went back to resting by the fire, waiting for the evening delivery of gold from my master and Mikita. What I never realized was that I was the only one delivering gold to the cabin. Mikita used my fleet feet and smarts to get the afternoon bounty quickly to the cabin. I could bolt up to the cabin in just a minute or so, while it usually took Mikita and Thomas Strong a lengthy ten minutes, and maybe more depending on the weather, to get from the mining area back to the cabin.

Soon, gold rushers would be returning from the north. Some might have struck it rich, but many others would be tired, hungry, and desperate. Mikita knew that it was essential to gather the gold and transport it up into the cabin as quickly as possible. This would give less opportunity for desperate and hopeless travelers to notice a chance for a quick score.

Whatever gold my master and Mikita collected in the afternoon, they left down by the mine. If travelers came across my gold-mining friends returning to the cabin at the end of the day, they wouldn't be carrying anything that attracted attention. They never told me this, but I figured it out for myself after a few days. It became obvious as I noticed I was the only one lifting up the secret floorboard.

CHAPTER TWENTY

---✦---

How Did He Get Here?

It had been a few weeks of continuous accumulation of gold from a mine that once was assumed barren. It was stunning how this abandoned mine had become such a prolific source of this most precious metal. The air was warm and the ground dry, and we only needed a small fire to cook our dinner and keep the cabin warm as we slept. The summer season in the northland is very short, and for a warm-weather dog like me, that made each day more special.

One evening I was frolicking in front of the cabin, playfully jumping up and down as Mikita and my master chuckled and laughed at my attention-grabbing performance. A starry, silver darkness began to settle upon our cabin, which encouraged us to settle back into our dwelling for dinner and a restful evening. As I bounced around and headed toward the door, I glanced up at the sky and noticed just how many stars were already beginning to sparkle. I thanked them all, because they were all my lucky stars, and I was so grateful for the wonderful life I was now living.

The next morning, I heard the creaking of the cabin door opening, but I hadn't heard the sound of Thomas Strong or Mikita rising from slumber. I jumped quickly to attention and then immediately relaxed as I saw the friendly face of Jan Ericsson smiling at me.

"Hey there, Stanley. There's no sneaking up on you," whispered Jan Ericsson.

As I was greeting our surprise guest, I wondered how he had traveled here. My familiar friend noticed the perplexed look on my face and opened the door of the cabin. His mode of transportation was a horse pulling a wagon on wheels. I was amazed at the beauty of the mighty, hardworking horse, but I was also embarrassed that I didn't hear the heavy footsteps of the horse or the wagon wheels rolling toward our cabin.

"How do you think we brought all the heavy stuff up here, Stanley?" Jan Ericsson chuckled.

I excitedly led him back into the cabin, and inside, both of our friends were slowly awakening. I rushed toward Mikita and tried to hasten her rising to greet a beautiful day and our special friend. I was in such a hurry to show Jan Ericsson how wonderfully Mikita had recovered. She slowly stood and stumbled a bit as she went to greet Jan Ericsson. I noticed concern on the face of our friend, as her initial movements appeared slow and awkward, but she was hardly awake. Soon I saw a happy expression upon our visitor's face as Mikita moved quickly about the cabin to make coffee. Much slower to rise than Mikita was his friend Thomas Strong, who also stumbled while waking.

The writer rose, and then he moved toward the veteran guide that had become a trusted friend. The two men met in the middle of the cabin with a sturdy hug that shook the remaining Alaskan air out of Jan Ericsson's coat. Thomas Strong seemed less surprised than I was about our friend's arrival. Jan Ericsson had promised him a summer visit if the weather was right and the trails were dry and solid. We were all happy to see Jan Ericsson and even happier as the supplies he brought us were carried into the cabin. There were big sacks of flour, coffee, beans, and sugar, along with jars of honey, fruits, and vegetables.

Jan Ericsson seemed so happy to be with us again and thrilled with the remarkable recovery of Mikita as she moved swiftly about the cabin.

"I am stunned, Mikita, by your recovery," gawked Jan Ericsson. "You should slow down."

"I need to move quickly and keep busy, Mr. Ericsson," replied Mikita. "If I don't, I feel I am wasting time."

Mikita began serving coffee and started to organize the new supplies. Thomas Strong and Jan Ericsson slowed her down and helped move the new sustenance to the appropriate places. Then everyone was more delighted as they worked together to cook a glorious breakfast.

As we ate our breakfast, I started to grow impatient and began scratching on the floorboard below Thomas Strong's writing table. My eyes were darting to and fro, quickly looking into the eyes of my three friends in the cabin. Mikita and my master were looking at each other with uncertainty.

There was no doubt that Thomas Strong and Mikita trusted Jan Ericsson, and my instincts told me that they were more afraid for his well-being if he became aware of the wealth that was now secretly harbored in our cabin. I understood their trepidation, but that didn't stop me from pulling Jan Ericsson by his pant leg and opening up the floorboard.

"Oh my goodness!" exclaimed Jan Ericsson. "Oh my! Unbelievable! Oh my! Oh wow!"

"Calm down, Jan. You just said *oh* four times in about three seconds." Thomas Strong laughed.

"What happened?"

"The warm weather created a slippery base under the snow, and it was an avalanche that crunched down quick and hard," began Mikita. "The two big pine trees slowed and stopped the onslaught of snow toward the cabin, but as best as I can explain, the sudden pounding down on the mine crushed the hollow tunnels and expelled the shiny bounty that probably would have taken years to dig out of the rocks."

"Well, happy days!" blasted Jan Ericsson. "You came up here to write stories about people risking life and limb in pursuit of the riches of gold, and the gold leaps right into your lap."

Everyone was laughing. Everyone was yelling. Everyone was hugging. I was so excited, and I felt such an incredible sense of joy. I leaped higher than I ever had before, and I found a new way to express myself as I raced around the cabin. It was not a bark and not a howl. It was a screeching yelp that I had never made before, and my new audible behavior made the loud sound of joyous laughter in the room increase even more.

After a few minutes of raucous celebration, everyone began to settle down. I looked at the faces of Thomas Strong, Mikita, and Jan Ericsson as they sat down with a funny glow upon their faces. I guess Jan Ericsson's arrival and knowledge of our good fortune made everything seem more real for my cabinmates. Soon, Jan Ericsson brought up something that my master and Mikita had not yet even considered.

"How much do you think all that gold is worth, Thomas?"

"Not really sure. I don't have any clue how much it weighs, and I certainly don't know the current price of gold. I guess the only thing I am sure of is there is plenty more gold down there." My master chuckled.

"There is so much more gold down by the mine," added a smiling Mikita.

"Well, let's just see how you have done so far," said Jan Ericsson as he headed toward the bunk farthest away from the fireplace. Out from under the bunk, he pulled a scale that had been left behind by frustrated miners. They probably didn't get to use it very much.

It was a balancing scale that looked like the artwork you might see in a painting on a courtroom wall. My master had written many stories about legal issues, so I knew what the scales of justice looked like. For this particular scale, there were weights of specific measures that you placed on one side, and then you placed gold on the other side until the scale was balanced.

The biggest problem with this particular scale was that the largest measuring weight was one pound. We had already accumulated much more gold than a one-pound measure, and so we had to do a lot of balancing acts to figure out how much gold was in the cabin. After twenty-eight turns that evening with the single-pound weight on the scale, we realized how much gold we had so quickly accumulated.

"My, oh my, Thomas!" bellowed Jan Ericsson. "That's twenty-eight pounds of gold, and sixteen ounces per each one of those shiny pounds. When I left Dawson City, the price of gold was nineteen dollars an ounce."

"Mikita, you do the math," crackled my master.

Mikita started scribbling away on a piece of writing paper with a pencil. Thomas Strong paused and rubbed his chin. Jan Ericsson scratched his head in curious anticipation. I joined in by tilting my head from side to side.

"There are sixteen ounces in a pound. Right now, we have twenty-eight pounds, and gold is worth nineteen dollars an ounce. When you multiply sixteen, times twenty-eight, times nineteen . . ."

"How much, Mikita?" yelped a childlike Thomas Strong.

"Our total is eight thousand five hundred and twelve dollars!" screeched a jubilant Mikita.

"Unbelievable!" yelled Thomas Strong.

"You guys are rich!" exulted Jan Ericsson.

"Aaaaaooooooh," I yelped again in an attempt to add to the excitement of the atmosphere.

"This is barely scratching the surface of what is down near that mine," offered Mikita.

"There sure is plenty more where that came from," agreed the writer turned gold miner.

"Jan, why don't you stick around for a while and help us mine as much gold as possible?" asked Thomas Strong. "Then we can all share the wealth."

"I am ready to help . . . and ready to earn a few shekels." Jan Ericsson laughed.

Mikita had a big smile on her face as she readied herself for another day of mining the golden ore. It seemed obvious to me that Mikita was truly the leader of our now-prolific gold mining operation. She prepared to exit the cabin for another day of work, and without saying one word, Thomas Strong and Jan Ericsson followed her lead and got set to head down to increase our wealth.

The first day with Jan Ericsson helping our gold-gathering process proved bountiful. The friendly and knowledgeable guide was tougher and more rugged than his personality let on. When it came to mining, he really was worth his weight in gold.

Also, when it was my time to do my gold-carrying duties, it was easier to hear three voices yelling my name. Jan Ericsson was astonished, and he laughed at how quickly I made it down to the mine to do my job. As I made my way back to the cabin, I noticed the weights of the satchel were becoming heavier than they had ever been. The extra weight didn't bother me, because as I rushed up the slope toward the cabin, I heard the encouraging cheers of my friends.

"Go, Stanleeeeeeey!"

"Atta boy, Stanley!"

"Wow!" yelled Jan Ericsson. "He is something else!"

At the end of each day, there was obviously happiness and joy being shared among great friends and good family.

One evening, there were a few quiet moments as my master and Jan Ericsson huddled in front of the fire for a private discussion. They were exchanging short sentences, and they were both nodding agreement with each other's statements. When they were done, the writer in the room sat before Mikita and me and provided an important message.

"We need to finish our mining in a couple of weeks and then try our best to hide any evidence of our great fortune. My trusted friend, Jan Ericsson, has warned me that before it even snows here, the weather further north will have already started to chill. There will be many desperate people returning from the north and heading toward us.

"Also, it will probably be the most unsuccessful and hopeless travelers that will be arriving here first," continued Jan Ericsson. "Desperate people do desperate things, and if they knew there was a pile of gold inside this cabin, this sanctuary could become a very dangerous place."

"I understand," agreed Mikita. "I am familiar with the evil nature that can sometimes spill out of people."

"This has been so much fun, and I don't want anything to happen that would taint it," said a thoughtful Thomas Strong.

My master was being smart, and certainly, a man who already would be considered wealthy had no need to be greedy. We settled into a restful evening with only one other discussion about mining. It was concluded that I would make two runs up to the cabin each day instead of just one. With the extra hands of Jan Ericsson, there was more gold to be hauled up the hill. I was happy to be given the extra responsibility. I would do whatever it took to make everyone in the cabin happy.

As I glanced around the dwelling as the evening came to a close, I observed the three smiling faces surrounding me and realized at that moment I didn't need to do anything to make them happy. I was so content, and I felt myself drifting off to sleep. I was consumed by a cozy bliss, and then I was even happier when Mikita snuggled with me and gave me a silent look of adoration just before we fell asleep together by the fire.

CHAPTER TWENTY-ONE

―・❀・―

A Gold-Mining Team

For the next week, every condition of our circumstances seemed to be working toward the benefit of our prolific mining effort. The skies were clear, and the bright rays of the sun seemed to point out each of the sparkling nuggets of gold that were nestled within the pebbles of the stream. As the warm temperatures and powerful sunshine poured down upon the mine, the heavy layers of snow surrounding the area swiftly began to melt and dissipate into the stream. Each day, more area along the banks of the stream appeared from what was once covered by an enormous blanket of snow, revealing more gold nuggets for me to carry up to the cabin.

Having Jan Ericsson working with us was worth more than just an extra body and two more hands. He was a strong man with a wealth of experience working outdoors. He was gathering as much gold as Thomas Strong and Mikita all by himself, and soon we needed to create another hiding place under the floorboards. Jan Ericsson's efficiency around the mine was always the first topic of conversation in the cabin after a long day. My master and Mikita always had something to say about his productive performance.

"Mr. Gold, that was another day of heavy lifting," Mikita would joke.

"Hey, Jan, you are making me look bad in front of Mikita and Stanley." Thomas Strong laughed.

―

With Jan Ericsson's help, the gold was piling up underneath the floorboards at an unbelievable rate. Everyone was happy with our continued success and the rapid growth of our wealth. Each night the cabin was filled with laughter and stories about how the new fortune would be spent.

Having Jan Ericsson in our cabin had another great benefit to me. Naturally, the two grown men would spend the evenings tending to the fire, sipping wine or whiskey, smoking cigars, and telling stories about the adventures they had experienced. Each night, when the two friends ventured into their own world of legendary tales and tobacco smoke, it left more time for Mikita and me to spend with each other.

Mikita would nestle next to me on a blanket near the fire. She would have a little snack for me, and she would stroke my head gently until we were both comfortably settled. She always had a book in hand, and she would read out loud to me. Sometimes I didn't even try to understand the words, but I could see the fire making sparkles in her angelic eyes as she read from the pages, and the sound of her voice always warmed my heart and soul.

At night I fell to sleep so comfortably attached to Mikita, with our bodies mingled so closely together and our hearts even closer. As I slept, I dreamed of images and scenes that gave me heavenly warmth. As I snored away, I dreamed of sepia sunrises climbing over pine trees, magnificent sunsets settling into the Pacific Ocean, and full moons shining silver light onto beautifully still lakes.

In the morning, I woke from my dreams the same way every day. While I was still half asleep, I would reach for Mikita with my paw. As I began to realize she was not lying next to me, my senses swiftly became more alert by the sound of her feet moving about the cabin.

Mikita was always the first to rise in our dwelling. I always woke soon after her, and before I even had all four paws on the floor, she would lean over and scratch my head. I would open my jaws to release some sort of early morning yelp of joy, only to be hushed by Mikita.

"Sssshhhhh, Stanley," Mikita would whisper.

She would start the morning coffee and begin cooking breakfast. When the aromas of coffee and bacon wafted through the cabin and stirred the slower, older men out of slumber, Mikita would order them to clean up the mess they had made the previous evening. She had grown up working for next to nothing at all kinds of jobs, taking care of people she didn't even know. Mikita was a hard worker with a soft heart, but there was no taking advantage of her.

After a week of prolific mining, we actually needed to make a third hiding place under the floor. As the bounty of gold under the boards continued to grow, my master and Jan Ericsson avoided weighing the shiny harvest for fear of jinxing our overwhelming good fortune.

There was an evening when the two men finally agreed that they should weigh how much of the precious metal we had accumulated. That same night, I felt a chill in my bones, and when Mikita let me out to take care of my business, it was a cold and crispy air, and there was a feathery dust of snow beginning to fall. When I reentered the cabin with snow melting on my head, everyone knew some important decisions needed to be made.

Thomas Strong and Jan Ericsson began to weigh the gold that had not previously been measured. It took a long time to weigh everything that had been hiding under the floorboards of Thomas Strong's writing desk. Mikita and I sat closely together and watched the two men work slowly and carefully. As they balanced the scales, they also discussed what needed to be done to ensure our well-being and the safe transport of our riches to the banks of Dawson City.

"The snow is coming down, Tom, so I need to get my horse and wagon heading south as soon as possible."

"We'll be glad to get rid of you," joked my master.

"If it is snowing here already, winter has certainly arrived up north," warned Jan Ericsson.

"Let's finish weighing our nuggets, my good friend, Jan, so you know how much you are worth as you travel south."

"There sure will be a smile on my face as I pull into Dawson City."

Mikita and I had fallen asleep long before the process of weighing the gold was completed. I think we both thought that the monetary value of the gold was not as important as the precious new family that had been forged.

"Eighty-eight pounds!" screeched my master in a high-pitched yelp that woke Mikita and me.

"Oh wow, Thomas! Oh my goodness, Thomas!" barked Jan Ericsson.

"Mikita, do the math."

Mikita was still not fully awake, but she gathered herself, grabbed a pencil, and started to do the arithmetic. The same pencil that she had used to create her wonderful drawings now scratched the paper as she multiplied numbers that were as equally impressive as her artwork. When Mikita was done tallying up our total, she slowly placed the pencil down and paused. She was waiting for someone to ask what the results of her arithmetic were.

"Is gold still nineteen dollars an ounce?" asked Mikita with a smile.

"Well?" simultaneously asked Jan Ericsson and Thomas Strong.

"Twenty-six thousand seven hundred fifty-two dollars!" yelped a thrilled Mikita.

Everyone was beaming with happiness with the staggering total of our surprising mining efforts. Suddenly, for some reason, I felt an instinctual sadness, because I knew that Jan Ericsson would be leaving soon.

During the night, Thomas Strong and Jan Ericsson discussed many things. All the discussion was about the personal safety of all of us and the best way to transport our golden treasure back to Dawson City.

Jan Ericsson needed to head south with his horse and wagon. He needed to bring a story or two for publication in *American* magazine. The stories that he would be carrying would not be the amazing story of Mikita's horrible arrival and amazing recovery. There could also not be the tale of our surprising gold mining exploits. If people read about Mikita, a couple of bad men might come back looking for her, and if people read about all the gold stashed in our cabin, a whole helluva lot of people might come looking for an easy score.

The writer Thomas Strong gave two stories to deliver for publication. There was a dramatic tale about how an avalanche almost wiped out the cabin, which was mostly true. The other captivating yarn described the feeling of loneliness, isolation, and boredom of being in a cabin in the middle of nowhere, hoping for something to happen. In this fabricated story, my master did mention how the company of his dog and best friend, Stanley, was so important to him.

I understood the story was mostly fiction, but I knew in my heart the only true words within that story were about me.

Thomas Strong and Jan Ericsson had agreed that the only things of value that our guide and trusted friend should transport south to Dawson City while traveling by himself were the stories written with black ink on white paper written by my master, combined with the drawings he himself had created for publication in *American* magazine. Again, fear for safety was an issue. The fewer people that knew Mikita was here was better for her safety.

So many people were aware of the role Jan Ericsson played in getting Thomas Strong's stories to the public. Stories scratched out on paper were only worth something to Thomas Strong and *American* magazine.

If Jan Ericsson encountered any troublesome characters on his solo journey back to Dawson City, they would see the tales of the northland and probably greet him with pats on the back and send him on his merry way. On the other hand, if they found gold in his possession, they could threaten him with violence and ask where he had managed to obtain such good fortune. This could bring great harm to a man traveling alone and could lead to a dangerous encounter in our cabin, which we all certainly wanted to avoid.

My master, Thomas Strong, and our good friend Jan Ericsson had decided that the gold should stay nestled safely under the floorboards until the end of season of returning gold rushers. As planned, we would welcome the tired sojourners with smiles, a warm fire, a hot meal, and open ears that listened to all the details of their adventurous stories.

My master had planned to write the tales of the returning adventurers, but now there would be the added bonus of Mikita etching drawings of these returning survivors. *American* magazine would be getting more than it ever would have been expected. Of course, the artwork would have been composed by "anonymous artistic travelers."

The words and drawings would be carried personally to Dawson City by the characters that were described in the pages and captured in the drawings. We would ask all our returning visitors and storytellers to promise not to mention Mikita upon their return to Dawson

City. We knew they all would understand after hearing how she had arrived here.

These adventurers would be exhausted and weary, and the ability to transport a record of their own perilous journey would probably be worth more than any gold that they might have discovered. I had instincts that made me worry about how many of these stories would turn out, and I think the writer Thomas Strong felt the same way. We wondered how the final chapter of most of these tales would conclude.

At this point in the season, there would be many people traveling on the trails between our cabin and Dawson City. There would be tired travelers returning from the north, and there would also be so many of the typical Alaskan hunters looking for elk and moose. So it was planned that when the season of traveling south was near completion, Jan Ericsson would return, and we would all depart safely with the heavy weight of fortune, gliding easily down the trails toward Dawson City.

In the morning that Jan Ericsson left the cabin and headed south toward Dawson City, Thomas Strong, Mikita, and I all began looking at one another in a strange way. It was as if we were trying to figure out the rules to a game that none of us had ever played. We were waiting for untold stories to arrive and hoping that there would be more joy than sadness and more safety than danger.

After Jan Ericsson's horse and wagon clippety-clopped down the trail toward Dawson City, the cabin was relatively quiet. The fire crackled, and sometimes the wind howled, but the loudest noise came from beneath the floor. We all heard it loud and clear even though it was a quiet, silent call. We took turns peeking at the floorboards, and we all heard the messages sent from our friend beneath the wood. Without words ever spoken, we were all thinking about the same things. The gold was asking us if we would be safe, if we would be in danger, and if we were ready, willing, and able to protect the family we had become.

The night after Jan Ericsson left, Mikita made a delicious venison stew, and after we finished eating, we all huddled closely near the fire. This was usually the time when Mikita would entertain us by reading from a book. On this night, my master read a passage from an old *American* magazine. It was a sad offering from a talented man that was saying good-bye to the many readers that enjoyed his stories. In the article, he explained his deepest thoughts, and he felt his hand and mind would not cooperate enough anymore to author any interesting work.

Thomas Strong had written these words before he decided to take this adventure north. It was obvious he had penned these words at a time in his life of the utmost despair, when he was consumed with feelings of desolation.

As he finished reading his own words, a tear rolled down his cheek. Mikita noticed his emotions first and lifted her hand to wipe away the tear, but I was quicker and licked it away with my tongue.

"I love you both," said my master in a voice that sounded scratchy with emotion.

Thomas Strong hugged Mikita and me with a strong sturdiness, and yet still it was a gentle grasp.

"I love you. You are my family," was the last thing we all heard as we all welcomed a deep sleep.

CHAPTER TWENTY-TWO

---·◦·---

Adventurers Start to Return

A few days passed after Jan Ericsson had departed, and each day it got a little colder, the wind howled a little louder, and snow began to fall with a steady consistency that quickly changed the landscape surrounding our cabin. It was amazing how suddenly old man winter thrust himself upon us.

Our mining season was officially over. The plummeting temperatures and continuous snowfall clogged the stream with slushy ice and made the paths heading down to the mine too treacherous.

One clear but frigid night, Mikita let me outside to do my business, and I noticed her staring into the sky in a ponderous way. She usually offered encouragement and laughter to help me achieve my relief goals, but on this night, she was focused on something else.

When we returned to the cabin, Mikita sat down at Thomas Strong's writing table, grabbed a pencil and piece of paper, and began scratching away with incredible determination. For thirty minutes or so, Mikita was focused and unable to distract. She had a detached look on her face, almost as if something had taken control of her. As she finished what she had been drawing and laid her pencil down, I noticed her expression return to normal, and then I watched as her face exuded satisfaction.

I was happy to see Mikita looking so pleased with her efforts, and I went to her to see what she had drawn. When she showed me the picture that she had etched, my happiness turned into wonder.

Mikita had magnificently drawn the image she had absorbed outside the cabin such a short time ago.

She had interpreted the landscape, the snow-burdened trees, and the silvery shimmer of the moon as it tried to force its way through the clouds. Somehow, with just a chalky black pencil, she managed to capture the sense of white snowflakes floating through the air. I swear, if you looked at that picture long enough, you could almost see the wind blowing.

Thomas Strong was famous for being able to use the written word to tell stories that painted pictures, but when he first glanced at Mikita's most recent drawing, he was rendered speechless. He stared for quite some time at this remarkable piece of art, and Mikita stared at him, happy to see that she had done something that could impress a man like Thomas Strong. I stared at both the writer and the artist, and I was so proud that my two best friends were both blessed with such dynamic talent.

"Mikita, this is the beautiful scene of where we are now, and it is a place we will never forget, a place we will forever be together."

"I feel so lucky to be here with you and Stanley. I don't know what came over me. In my mind, the drawing just seemed to come together with purpose," was the modest response of the artist.

"It is remarkable, Mikita," responded my master. "Maybe your drawing is like the three of us, something great that came together with a purpose."

After a relaxed pause of comfortable satisfaction, my master added wood to the fire and began cooking some fish that Jan Ericsson had brought us. Mikita went to find a story for our usual evening reading session. The chef, Mikita, and the hungry dog would soon be eating a scrumptious dinner, followed by a storytelling session in front of the fire.

Soon we were all eating some tasty flame-broiled fish, which tasted even better with the side dish of contentment. As we finished eating our delightful dinner, we settled near the fireplace for a cozy family evening. Suddenly, I went from a lazy happiness to red alert as my instincts snapped to attention.

"What is it, Stanley?" asked Mikita as my head twisted and my restlessness became obvious.

"Stanley, my boy . . . what?" asked my master as I lurched my head toward the door.

Quite quickly it became obvious to my master and Mikita why I was on high alert. Sounds that we had not heard in a while were beginning to get louder. There was the synchronous sound of paws pounding into the snow, a man yelling encouragement, and that silky smooth sound of the rails of a dogsled sliding through the snow.

Thomas Strong, the storyteller, began to realize this would be the first story he would hear about a return from the adventures of the northland. He went to the door with Mikita, and as the door opened, we saw three men bringing a team of twelve dogs to rest. These men cared about their dogs, with one traveler in particular being so skilled and making certain that the team was safely secured in just a few minutes.

I remembered how I felt the first time I met a sled team. I was in awe of their strength and power and how they seemed to combine all their energy as a team, and I felt that again as the dogs settled into the snow, and the men headed toward the comfort and warmth of our cabin.

The three men entered the cabin, and they began to remove their coats and shake the wintery cold from their bodies. I felt relaxed and comfortable with men I did not yet recognize, but I became so excited when I heard a familiar voice.

"Hey, Stanleeeeeey!" chirped my friend Payuk as I pawed at the floor and then rushed to greet him.

Payuk was the experienced guide that was the first to deliver travelers to our cabin, and true to his word, he delivered both men back south to safety. As I continued to welcome Payuk, my master reacquainted himself with the Fahrun twins, Wolfgang and Dietmar. Mikita was unfamiliar with this group of weary adventurers, but she was quick to provide warm coffee and join in with the greeting of our tired travelers.

Thomas Strong was thrilled. I could sense his excitement. These men would be the first to provide him with an ending to a story. He had listened to all the stories about the hopes and dreams of the adventurers heading north, but most of those yarns seemed similar. The documentation of what happened in the Yukon would certainly be more dynamic and interesting to the storyteller and to his readers.

After our guests had warmed and settled, the writer sat down at his table, grabbed his quill pen, opened his inkwell, and shuffled a few pieces of paper with an enormous sense of anticipation. Wolfgang and Dietmar, the Fahrun twins, alternated sentences, telling the story of their adventure.

"We traveled north from sunrise to sunset, and then we would set a camp," started Wolfgang.

"One day, we rose as usual for another full day of travel, but our sledding ended earlier than expected because we came across a lake, which seemed perfect for ice fishing to catch for our dinner," continued Dietmar.

"We ate a nice fish dinner, and after a good night of sleep, we were charged and ready to surge farther."

"After a few days of successful travel, we came across a place that seemed would be ideal for mining."

"We settled by an area that overlooked a large bend in a frozen stream," continued Wolfgang.

"We began chopping down trees and built a simple small log cabin," said Dietmar as he used his hands to help describe the motion of chopping down trees.

"It only took a couple of days to build our rudimentary dwelling, but we had to wait a week or so for the frozen stream to thaw and allow us to mine," offered Wolfgang.

As Payuk listened to the Fahrun twins tell their story, he patted me on the head and stroked my belly. I noticed a crooked smile of satisfaction on his face. The Fahrun brothers continued to relay their experiences to their host and prolific writer, but it started to become clear that their story was not an astonishing tale of dangerous adventure.

Payuk beamed with pride as the Fahruns' travels continued to bore my master. His job as a guide was to limit the danger of northland travel and make it safer for his less experienced clients, and therefore, it was less dramatic. A good writer like Thomas Strong realized the central figure of this first story of a successful return should focus on the professional guide that had proved his capacity for dominating the unpredictable northland and how he delivered the Fahrun twins back south unharmed.

"Payuk," said Thomas Strong, "your skills as a guide have made my first tale about the return of adventurers from the north quite a bit boring."

"Sorry, Mr. Strong . . . just doing my job," responded Payuk.

"Payuk, you shouldn't be sorry. You should be proud. When you carry my story with you to Dawson City, it will be more about your unique skills and instincts. Those talents made the Fahruns' journey as uneventful as possible, and for that, you are the hero of this expedition."

Wolfgang and Dietmar nodded in agreement with the award-winning storyteller. Soon, Payuk sat close to my master's writing table, and he tried to explain some of his innate skills that were imperative to frigid north traveling. He spoke in explicit detail about how to know when the sled team is tired and when it can be pushed just a little bit farther. He described the ideal place to set up a camp and the surest way to guarantee that the ice on a frozen lake will not collapse beneath you.

Soon the conversation between Payuk and Thomas Strong was fading into the background for the rest of us in the cabin. The snap, crackle, and popping of the fire were more prominent on the earlobes of the Fahrun twins, Mikita, and me.

Mikita and I snuggled and listened to Payuk educate Thomas Strong. The weary Fahrun twins were soon snoring in rhythm, and Mikita and I followed them into slumber as the writer and subject continued along. As I drifted off to dreamland, I had a strange thought that there had never been any mention of gold in the conversations with the Fahruns or Payuk.

We were all sleeping comfortably, until Dietmar Fahrun tripped over me as he headed toward the door to answer an early-morning call to nature. The thud of the clumsy Fahrun as he hit the floor and the yelp that was forced out of me woke everyone else in the cabin much earlier than would have been preferred.

Payuk rose and exited the cabin to tend to the dogs. In a few minutes, we were all awake, eating breakfast, and enjoying the company of good friends. Soon, a thunderous noise filled the cabin. It sounded like a lumberjack's saw slicing through a huge tree. We all looked to find Dietmar, the man responsible for waking us up much too early, snoring like a slug and sleeping on the floor in front of the fire.

One thing I noticed, and became more obvious as we all spent a restful day in the cabin, was that Payuk and Mikita were making eye contact as if they were familiar with each other, and the quick glances became more frequent as the day progressed. They were just curious glances between two people that perhaps recognized each other. It seemed that Payuk knew Mikita, but out of respect to his host, he kept his uncertain thoughts to himself.

The day quickly evolved into an evening meal, complete with wood, wine, whiskey, wind, and wild tales. The Fahrun brothers would be leaving with Payuk in the morning. They would be carrying with them what might seem like a boring story about twin brothers traveling up and back from the Yukon. Perhaps the story was not a thrilling struggle of life and death, but instead, a genuine story about the dedication and instinctual skills of Payuk, the best guide in the northland.

The next morning, Payuk rose first, so quietly that he only jostled me as he went outside to tend to the dogs. By the time Payuk reentered the cabin, Mikita had brewed a fresh pot of coffee and the Fahrun brothers were nearly finished dressing themselves for the final leg of their journey back to civilization.

"Hey! My good man, Payuk, let's say we get the heck out of here before we get too comfortable," squawked Wolfgang Fahrun.

"Are we ready to take to the trail?" asked Dietmar.

"The dogs are rested and can't wait to work," responded Payuk.

The twin brothers were bouncing with anticipation like anyone would when a long journey nears completion. They thanked and hugged Thomas Strong and Mikita, patted my head, and bolted through the door. Payuk took a bit more time to exit. He thanked my master for his generosity, and then he whispered something in his ear that prompted a look of bewilderment from the writer's usually stoic face.

Payuk put his arms around Mikita, and then his arms gently enveloped her body. As Payuk's embrace with Mikita was complete, he turned toward me to say good-bye. He had a tear streaming down his face, and I sensed emotion in a man that previously had seemed as solid and sturdy as a stone.

"Take good care of Mikita, my good friend, Stanley," were Payuk's last words before exiting the cabin.

Payuk had said the same thing to my master, which had caused the amazed look on his face. Mikita would later explain that she and Payuk knew each other from working in Dawson City. The night that Mikita and Payuk were glancing at each other and communicating with their eyes, she finally managed to tell Payuk what the Pearson brothers had done and where they had left her to die.

Payuk was extremely upset because he had witnessed the abusive nature of the Pearson brothers many times in Dawson City. Many times they had taken advantage of the good nature of the kind people of a quickly blossoming community.

The tear I saw gliding down Payuk's wind-burned face was a combination of sadness for Mikita's pain and gratefulness for a friendly French Bulldog and a lonely author that helped save her from an icy grave.

Payuk was already my friend. I liked him the minute I met him, and now I was missing him already and wishing to see him soon. It would probably be a while before I saw my good friend again, when again he would playfully tap my head and scrub my belly.

I think Mikita sensed my feelings for Payuk. At the end of the day, Mikita warmed my heart and made me miss Payuk a little less. She had been working on a drawing all day. It pictured Payuk down on one knee in front of the fire, patting my head and rubbing my belly. I was overcome with happiness. I so badly wished I could speak so I could thank God for friends like Mikita and Payuk. Then I looked at Thomas Strong, the best dad a dog could have, and I knew he sensed what I was feeling.

Mikita also knew how much I appreciated her artwork. That night as I slept, I dreamed of a glorious heaven, and when I was awakened by a loud cracking pop in the fire, I looked around and realized my dreams had not transported me anywhere. A warmth and contentment overcame me as I realized I was in heaven on earth.

CHAPTER TWENTY-THREE

---·◦·---

Just Two Return

For a couple of days, Thomas Strong, Mikita, and I rested in the glow of our fire, and we basked in a warm sense of contentment, knowing that the Fahrun twins and Payuk were safely headed home. Our dwelling was very tranquil and quiet, but there was a constant sense of silent happiness that was obvious to us all.

My wordsmith master and Mikita were beginning to relate to each other without having to utter a word. They smiled, tilted their heads, nodded, and gestured to each other in a manner that was very similar to my method of communication. For me, this was such an amazing development, because I could understand each syllable of body movement and subtle signal of their silent dialogue, just as any reader would be able to understand the words of Thomas Strong's writing. The nonverbal language developing between us formed an even more compelling attachment within our family.

It was a silent, crystal clear evening when I heard another sled team approaching our cabin. As usual, I noticed the impending arrival first, and I alerted Mikita by tilting my head toward the door. She headed toward the fire to begin heating water for coffee, and the resident writer and host observed these signals and rose to greet our visitors.

My master waited until he heard the sound of footsteps crunching closer toward our cabin. When he opened the door, it was just two travelers that entered, both wrapped in layers of clothing that made it difficult to recognize them at first. The two visitors began to unwrap and remove the garments that had kept them warm. Soon, as each layer of frosty winter gear was removed, the exhausted bodies of two warm-hearted women were unveiled. There was a relaxed sense of relief upon their faces because they were in a warm, safe place and closer to home, but the sadness in their eyes told the story of their loss before they even uttered a single word.

Maureen Winston and Mandy Bagley had arrived here before heading north with their husbands Jack and Ted. The brave women had returned to our sanctuary with only the last names of their husbands. Somehow, the hearty appetite of the unforgiving northland devoured the bodies of Maureen's husband, Jack, and Mandy's husband, Ted.

"Jack won't be joining us," was the sad statement of Maureen.

"And neither will Ted," whimpered Mandy.

The two women had been traveling with focus and determination. They wanted to get back to civilization as soon as possible, and the constant work of sledding helped keep their minds from thinking about what they had left behind. As these two powerful women removed each layer of frosty cover, their bodies began to weaken, and the emotions that had been pent up inside overcame them.

Thomas Strong was so sympathetic, and he and Mikita helped the two sturdy but exhausted women to a warm place in front of the fire. The women sipped coffee, settled, and eventually calmed down a bit.

I felt so bad for them. They seemed to be embarrassed by the tears they were shedding. We were all curious to hear what had happened to their husbands. Jack and Ted were both friendly and lovable men, but when the sorrowful ladies felt strong enough to talk, the topic was surprising.

"Ladies," started Thomas Strong. "I know you have met my boy, Stanley, but you have not yet been introduced to Mikita."

"I know you, sweetie!" said Maureen Winston as she grasped Mikita's hand.

"Yes," continued Mandy Bagley, "you are that delightful girl that waited on us at Mother McCreary's in Dawson City."

Mikita seemed to struggle to recognize the two women. I noticed Mikita had a sudden moment of clarity, and then she was fumbling in her mind to find an appropriate response. She had now recalled the two women, but only because their husbands were more memorable. Jack Winston and Ted Bagley were exuberant and boisterous, and they overshadowed their wives when Mikita had served them. I watched as Mikita's face turned pensive as she tried to select each word of her response with care and consideration.

"I remember you both, and I remember your husbands, Jack and Ted," was the beginning of Mikita's carefully crafted response. "They seemed like happy men that loved life and loved their wives, and I am so sorry for your loss."

I tilted my head toward Thomas Strong and observed his reaction. He was astonished that Mikita would remember the names of two men she had met only briefly. Maureen and Mandy rose and hugged Mikita. They were also surprised by how she managed to recall the names of their spouses, and perhaps Mikita's memory of their departed husbands helped them to realize that Jack and Ted would never be forgotten.

"How did you end up here, honey?" asked Maureen.

"I see scars that probably brought you here," proffered Mandy. "Yet somehow, I think maybe this place has helped heal your wounds!"

The two heartbroken women seemed more interested in talking with Mikita about her story than telling the writer in the cabin what had happened to their spouses. Likewise, the great author in the room was in no hurry to pry and ask the questions of Maureen and Mandy that would only prompt painful answers.

Maureen and Mandy sat closely with Mikita, and they listened to the horrid tale of how she arrived here. My master moved away from the conversation, simply because he did not wish to remember those painful details one more time.

As Mikita revealed her horror story to the two recently widowed women, I noticed them touching her hip and then her ankle as Mikita described her injuries. Then all the eyes in the room turned toward me, and Maureen Winston scooped me up off the floor and gave me a powerful squeeze after Mikita described how I had somehow managed to find her in that icy ravine. Soon, Mandy Bagley was hugging Thomas Strong, as Mikita was telling the two women how grateful she was to be alive, living with her new family.

When Mikita had finished her story, I noticed a peaceful look appear on her face. Thomas Strong had told her the way she had been rescued, but otherwise, she would have never recalled any of the details of how she was now alive and well, residing in this cabin.

The telling of her tale to the two women had been some sort of cathartic experience. She looked at Maureen and Mandy and thought it might also help them talk about their tragic story. She grabbed their hands with care and without any words, only a look of genuine sincerity in her eyes. She gently assuaged the women to describe the painful details of the tragic demise of their husbands, Jack and Ted.

The great writer in the room did not even ask a question; he only had to pick up his quill pen and start scratching notes. He glanced at Mikita with an expression of approval, like a teacher that has watched a student figure out a difficult problem. Then he looked at me with a queer look of bewilderment as Maureen and Mandy opened up to Mikita and described the harsh memories of their still very recent wounds.

"When we started our journey," began Maureen, "our husbands Jack and Ted were on a joyride, and Mandy and I did our best to take care of them."

"We enjoyed their happiness," added Mandy, "and took care of many things that often went unnoticed by our husbands."

"Mr. Strong, do you remember when we arrived here on our way north?" asked Maureen.

"Yes, I remember."

"And you wrote a story about us?" asked Mandy.

"Yes, I did."

"Looking into your eyes now," continued Maureen, "I am recalling how you observed us upon our arrival, when we first met you and your boy, Stanley."

"I remember, Maureen." Thomas Strong nodded.

"I don't have much doubt about what you wrote about us," continued Maureen.

"Right now, you look more sad than surprised," observed Mandy, "so it seems obvious you didn't have much faith in the return of our husbands."

When the Winstons and Bagleys initially arrived on their journey north, I was the one that had bad instincts about the fate of Jake and

Ted, and my master had sensed that from me. When the two couples left our cabin, we were both concerned. My master repeatedly told me that he hoped the two couples would avoid danger.

"I had hope for all of you," consoled Thomas Strong, "but you were the first to arrive without a guide, and I was worried about all four of you."

Thomas Strong, the writer, and Mikita, the survivor, embraced Maureen and Mandy, and they all joined together as a tight group in front of the fire. I found a toasty spot at their feet, and I listened as the widows opened up their hearts and recalled how the powerful promise of an exciting adventure ended up having such a sad conclusion. My instincts had been correct about Jack Winston and Ted Bagley, but there is no satisfaction in being correct when the result is such a tearful outcome.

Maureen and Mandy slowly offered their story to the sympathetic ears inside the fire-drenched cabin. Their journey north began with four days of swift and trouble-free travel into the Yukon Territory. Then the Winstons and Bagleys came across a spot that seemed ideal for mining. There was a wide curve in a stream that seemed ready to defrost and some flat ground flourishing with sturdy pine trees. The couples were happy to be done traveling, and they enthusiastically chopped down trees and built a cozy log dwelling with remarkable efficiency. They had listened and learned from experienced travelers of the northland, and everything appeared promising, secure, and safe.

They chopped down tall, narrow trees that could be cut into pieces and made ready to be lifted into place. The tree branches filled with the vibrant green of pine needles were sliced away from the long logs, and the smaller subsidiary branches were also removed and placed in a big pile.

The long tree logs were stacked upon one another, and then the men secured them into a square cabin structure using traditional dovetail notches. In not too much time, a nice ten-foot-square room had been established, and it reached just about a foot or so over their heads. Jack and Ted cut two stools from a big log and used them to stand up high enough so as to place the large pine branches across the top of the structure. They would use those same stools to sit in front of the fires they soon would build every evening. They layered the branches horizontally and then vertically to create a three-foot layer of protective cover.

The pine branch roofing system was rudimentary but most successful technique for Yukon travelers. The smoke of a fire within the cabin could escape through the roof, and the heat from the coals rising up from inside prevented any snow from collecting above. Sometimes, there might be an accumulation of snow that would melt through the branches. A simple canvas tent was then set up inside the dwelling, and that whisked the melting snow away from the center of the living space.

While the men were providing a roof over the heads of their wives, the women went about providing the warmth of their habitat. The industrious women ventured to the frozen stream and retrieved brick-size rocks to construct a safe fire pit in the center of their new residence. Maureen and Mandy then went to work on the small branches that were left over from the construction of the dwelling. They worked their fingers into bloody blisters as they stripped the pile of small twigs into fine mulch that turned into a comfy and soft floor. The men had left a small entryway in the side of the cabin facing the stream down below, and the women completed the finishing touches on the dwelling by hammering two blankets that covered the hole but also allowed easy entrance and exit.

This home was certainly temporary, but the first night spent inside provided memories that would last forever. Maureen and Mandy tended to the sled team, and they sensed the dogs were relaxed. It seemed as if the dogs knew that their hard work was completed and had earned them a well-deserved respite.

When the women returned to the dwelling, Jack and Ted had already stoked the first fire within the cozy walls, and the aroma of pine needles and burning wood smelled like the warmth of a family Christmas. The smoke of the fire rose up toward the pine branch ceiling, escaping into the crystal Yukon night, leaving only warmth and a sepia-toned flickering light that added a healthy glow to the cold and weather-beaten faces of the four travelers. They now had some sense of home and security in this faraway place.

In unison, Jack, Maureen, Ted, and Mandy all took a collective deep breath, followed by a sigh of relief. All their faces appeared more relaxed as they settled into the safety and security of the best shelter they had shared in a while. It had been a number of long days of hard travel, but the coziness of their new residence reminded them of the night they spent in our cabin. They only had some scraps of jerky left to eat, but they did manage to protect and preserve two fine bottles of wine for this exact moment.

The bottles opened, and as they savored the wine, they talked about their journey and expressed joy and happiness that they were able to share this adventure together. Soon, Jack and Maureen Winston were huddled together in a combined dream of contentment, and Ted and Mandy Bagley similarly fell deeply into a duet of dreams.

Just before sunrise, Jack and Ted were awake and headed out to the stream to fish for breakfast, lunch, and dinner. They had topnotch flies knotted on sturdy line attached to short bamboo poles. After a short while, it was obvious that the fish seemed disinterested in their flies, but they did notice that the curve of the stream had created a slush pool that slowed the fish down to almost a standstill. Quickly, the bamboo poles became spears, and within a short time, Jack and Ted returned to their wives with a bounty of fish, just as the morning coffee was being served.

"Maureen and Mandy," interrupted Thomas Strong, and he interjected, "It seems like everything was going so well."

"What went wrong?" asked Mikita.

"The time we spent up there was surprisingly peaceful and happy," responded Maureen.

"We were so happy and just coming home. We were coming home . . . coming home," continued Mandy before she broke down in tears.

CHAPTER TWENTY-FOUR

Happiness

The two heartbroken women resumed the dialogue of what had happened while they were in the vast desolation of the Yukon. As the skilled writer Thomas Strong and the warmhearted Mikita listened intently, they both smiled and nodded, as the story that had started out going so well began to turn into a tragedy. I sensed anxiousness in the cabin as we all waited to find out what had gone horribly wrong during our friends' journey.

"Jack and Ted started out panning for gold with great determination," started Maureen.

"Our goal was to find enough gold to start our own small hotel," continued Mandy. "We had wealthy parents that would have provided the money for us . . ."

"But we wanted adventure and independence," completed Maureen.

The women described with great detail how the men in their lives began to lose interest in the labor of panning for gold. Each day, the time that Jack and Ted spent working the stream grew shorter and shorter. They weren't having much success, and the lack of rewards became frustrating. Finally, the rest breaks taken by the men at the side of the stream turned into entire days of uninspired laziness.

While the two unsuccessful miners had given up on the fantasy of the quick riches of the gold rush, this journey ultimately provided them with something far more valuable than any currency.

"One beautiful day, Jack and Ted returned to the cabin, and they both seemed different," offered Maureen.

"They came to us with a burlap sack of freshly speared fish, and they both gave us a handful of wildflowers," Mandy said with a slight chuckle.

"We had an amazing evening of tranquility," continued Maureen.

"And many more after that." Mandy giggled.

After the captivating dreams for golden grandeur came to an end, Jack and Ted began to relax, and they became more aware of the natural beauty of their picturesque surroundings. This newly found awareness for Mother Nature's artwork began to manifest itself into a greater appreciation for the women that had sacrificed so much to make this incredible journey with them.

For one month, the two couples were happier than they had ever been before. Each day, the men would fish for the two couples' dinners, and they also hooked enough small fish to provide meals for the resting sled team.

If there were fresh animal tracks near their dwelling, Jack and Ted would follow the trail with bow and arrow to secure a larger feast. The men had a rifle and handgun as well, but they had limited ammunition and usually preferred to save the gunfire for protection against desperate and hungry animals or maybe desperate travelers.

While the men were fishing and hunting, Maureen and Mandy ventured out into the sprawling hills that reached so far into the clear blue sky, which made their tiny dwelling appear even smaller as they gazed back down upon it. The women gathered wild berries and fresh herbs that added additional flavor to their evening meals. They picked aromatic flowers that vastly improved the atmosphere and scent in their tiny cabin. Maureen and Mandy also took the time to examine the bark of various trees and always returned with something that made a warm cup of delightful tea at the conclusion of the day.

Some evenings, the two happy couples would sit outside their small shelter, savoring the interesting flavor of the tree bark tea. They didn't speak much during these times, as they all absorbed the massive beauty of the enormous star-filled sky. The natural, artistic masterpiece that enveloped them made them appreciate their own existence more than they ever had before.

Jack Winston and Ted Bagley began their journey with their wives toward the Yukon in pursuit of a shiny yellow metal. The harsh travel through the northland did not provide any significant wealth from gold that they had sought, but the men were rewarded with something more precious. The two men had a greater appreciation and deeper love for their wives, and the women they loved felt wealthier than they had ever imagined possible.

The glorious romantic time seemed like a honeymoon for the two couples, but the brief warm season would quickly be coming to a close. The winds would soon begin to howl warnings of another impending frigid winter. The length of days would hurriedly diminish, and the temperatures would plummet just as quickly. When the snow began to fall, it would only be a matter of days before the trails heading south would be suitable for sledding. Fortunately, their rested team of dogs was anxious to begin working again.

Jack and Ted woke one morning by the sound of water dripping into the fire, sizzling and sending a puff of steam toward the pine branch roof. As they exited for their usual morning fishing session, they encountered a foot of snow on the ground. They looked up to see a slushy mess of icy snow that burdened the integrity of their dwelling's pine branch roof.

The men didn't feel comfortable letting Maureen and Mandy sleep under a shelter that did not seem secure. Jack and Ted woke their wives and urged that it was now time to head home. The men went to fish for the last time, while the women secured their belongings and harnessed the dogs for travel.

The return trip would probably take five or six days of rigorous sledding to make it back to Dawson City. The two couples had twelve healthy dogs and mostly downhill trails. They hoped to shorten their return by setting camp every other night, and the alternate nights, the ambitious trekkers would sled straight through the night.

Jack, Maureen, Ted, and Mandy started out early the next day, waving good-bye to a place they would always remember as home. After a long day of productive sledding, they made a camp under an enormous pine tree that had already had the lower limbs removed by previous sledders, who were also kind enough to leave a ring of stones in a perfect place to start a fire. When the safety of the warmth of fire had been established, the men took pots and gathered the purest snow they could find to melt into water. The women tended to the dogs. They fed them fish and secured them on the other side of the pine tree in a location that was neither too close nor too far from the fire.

Finally, after a long day that made the friendly foursome weary to the bone, they settled under the massive pine tree. An enormous salmon was soon sizzling in a pan above the fire, and the pair of husbands and wives managed tired smiles as they pulled the flesh of the fish from the bones and fed each other with consideration and care. The two couples were satisfied with what they had accomplished that day, and their eyes began to close as the flames of the fire quickly diminished.

Jack was the only one roused by the rustling behind him, near where the dogs were resting. When he raised his head to try to figure out what was going on, his heart immediately pounded into high gear as he saw the menacing silver eyes of a pack of wolves staring right at him. The flickering flames of the fire were reflecting in their desperate eyes, which gave them an intimidating, devilish glare.

Soon the evil eyes became less visible and appeared to be withdrawing from the fire, but then Jack heard the sounds of his defenseless sled team whimpering in panic. He kicked Ted to wake him, grabbed a flaming log from the fire, and rushed to defend his loyal and hardworking dogs. A half dozen wolves were salivating and snarling, ready to pounce upon the vulnerable and chained-down dogs. Jack circled the pine tree as quickly as he could, driven by a furious adrenaline rush that he had never experienced before. The biggest wolf, the leader of the pack, was closest to the two lead dogs of his team.

Jack was not a violent man, but he lunged at the biggest and baddest wolf and slammed the burning log that was clenched in his right hand smack between the ears of the snarling threat. It crushed the animal's skull and made a sound like a sledgehammer pounding upon granite. Jack then waved the still burning log at the other now-awestricken wolves. He looked fiercely at them as he lowered the flaming log and lit their dead leader on fire. Ted appeared just as the shocked wolves began to disperse, and he fired a couple of shots from his revolver that didn't find any target.

"What the hell was that?" yelled Ted.

"Trouble!" weakly responded Jack as his adrenaline rush was swiftly expiring.

"Well, Jack, you sure sent them a message," hacked Ted as he watched the leader of the wolf pack burn into ashes.

"I think they'll be back," said Jack discouragedly as he kicked the burning corpse of the dead wolf in the head and went to wake the women. There was a new sense of urgency for an even more rapid and efficient journey south.

For two days and two nights, they relentlessly forged on in pursuit of a safe return to civilization. The couples alternated the responsibilities of the journey with efficiency and intelligence. While Jack and Maureen rode the rails of the sled and guided the dogs, Ted and Mandy would rest on top of the sled. After a while, the couples would switch positions.

When they stopped to change roles, they did it quickly, with the similar instinctual awareness of any animal that is being pursued by predators. Maureen and Mandy were concerned about how hard the dogs were working, but each time they stopped moving, the dogs expressed no desire to rest. At each brief pause in the journey, the sled team seemed more restless and anxious to return to the duty of pulling the sled. The men, the women, and the dogs were all worried about the same thing.

The wolf pack that had interrupted their happiness and compelled them on this hurried drive home was following them.

Chapter Twenty-Five

Happiness Turns Horrible

After two straight days of continuous sledding, everyone needed a rest. Jack and Ted decided it would be better to set a camp in an open area so they could see any potential danger as it approached them. Daylight was beginning to give way to darkness as the group established camp. As always, the women tended to the dogs. Meanwhile, Jack and Ted hurried toward a dense group of trees at the end of the clearing. They ripped and pulled at every dead branch they saw and dragged it all back toward the camp. After breaking the branches into fire-worthy kindling, they started a fire and then headed back to procure some more fuel for the bonfire they were trying to create.

Jack and Ted knew that wolves didn't like to approach fire, so they built a towering blaze that rose high into the starlit sky. The two couples huddled together to plot their strategy for safety, and the surging flames cast four endless shadows behind them across the snowy ground.

As the fire was being assembled, Maureen and Mandy had taken inventory of everything that could be used for defense. There were four shells left for the rifle and six rounds loaded into the revolver. They had four bamboo poles that had been used to spear fish, and they had a number of knives that had been used mostly for filleting meat and fish.

The dogs were restless and agitated. The flat ground upon which the camp was established was difficult for them to settle. The open area was warmed by the sun during the day and then chilled by the dark of night, so the snow was icy and stiff, which made it troublesome for the dogs to bury themselves deep into a snow cave and get comfortable. Maureen and Mandy comforted the sled team and tried their best to pull them closer to the safety of the fire, but the training and instincts of these incredible animals kept them from coming too close to the warmth of burning wood.

While the women were dealing with the dogs, Jack and Ted took burning limbs from the huge fire they had constructed and built several smaller fires in a semicircle around the dogs in an effort to protect them. The two weary and worried couples gathered in the safety of the fires they had created and devised a schedule for the long night ahead.

"Listen to me," barked Jack. "This is what we need to do!"

Ted, Maureen, and Mandy were all listening and willing to follow Jack's instructions.

"Ted, you will stay with Maureen and Mandy on this side of the fire, and keep your ass awake with the rifle in your hand!"

"Got it, Jack."

"I'm taking the revolver and going to set on the other side of the fire to protect the dogs."

"Do you want to take shifts for dog watch?" asked Ted.

"Ted, listen to me, and listen to me good," urged Jack. "If our wives don't make it, I don't want to go home, and if the dogs don't make it, none of us are going home. Do your job, and I will do mine! Protect our wives, Ted."

Maureen caught the eye of Jack as the foursome moved closer together toward a supportive group huddle. In a brief second, she conveyed pride in the way her husband had grasped control of this threatening situation. Jack gave his wife a subtle nod of thanks, which he also hoped would calm her before the dangerous threats of the impending long night.

Jack headed around the bonfire to protect the dogs with a loaded revolver in his hand and a mission to accomplish. Ted, Maureen, and Mandy gathered close together, keeping watchful eyes for wolves behind the flames, all hopeful and determined to survive the night.

The night seemed to be progressing safely. The men were alert, and as Jack added smaller wood to the surrounding fires, Ted tossed a few pieces of heavier lumber on the central bonfire. Everything seemed optimistic, but soon an inevitable weariness overcame everyone in the camp.

Wolves can sense the exhaustion and weariness of the prey they are pursuing. The pack follows along, waiting for the best opportunity to strike.

The wolves waited patiently as all four pairs of human eyes struggled to stay open, and then they watched all eight eyelids flutter up and down before finally closing.

Jack had just briefly slipped into an involuntary state of sleep when the high-pitched yelping of his dogs being attacked snapped him to attention. He leaped up quickly and rushed toward his dogs. He was immediately alert, and his actions were decisive. A pair of wolves had attacked the two lead dogs of his team, and as he ran closer to try to defend the dogs, he realized they were mortally wounded.

The final moments of Jack's life were filled with fury and rage, which is sad, because he was a jovial sort of person, and he hadn't spend much time in his existence being angry. He cocked his revolver and fired two shots, each of which ended the lives of the two evil wolves that had killed his lead dogs. Jack then moved closer toward his sled team, and the dogs were looking at him and howling, as a raging wolf blindsided Jack and sank his dastardly fangs into his neck. As the man and the wolf both simultaneously slammed into the icy ground, Jack managed to fire a round into the chest of his killer. In a tangled mess of good and evil, they both crumpled together in a pile of death.

It all was happening so quickly, and when Ted came racing around the fire, he scrambled toward his friend and hurled the dead wolf away. He immediately realized Jack was gone and looked up into the sky in despair. While Ted was asking God how and why this could happen, another wolf slammed upon him and crushed his throat with evil efficiency. The last sound Ted heard was his wife, Mandy, firing his rifle, shattering the skull of the wolf that had ushered his demise, and the final image his mortal brain absorbed was his wife, Mandy, dropping to her knees to bid him a tearful farewell.

In just a brief moment, these vicious animals systematically ended the lives of Jack and Ted and destroyed the lives of Maureen and Mandy. Amazingly, the two women quickly calculated what needed to be done for survival. Maureen picked up Jack's revolver, which had three rounds left. Mandy already had the rifle, and three shells remained. The four most aggressive wolves had attacked and now were dead. In the distance, Maureen and Mandy saw two sets of silver-star eyes watching their movements.

The fearless women approached the two remaining wolves with steady determination. The eyes of the wolves remained steady and focused on the women as they drew closer. Since these wolves had not attacked, they were probably followers in their pack, and now they were about to follow their leaders into the great beyond.

Mandy aimed the rifle between the eyes of the wolf on the left, and Maureen set her sights on the wolf to the right. They blasted simultaneously. Mandy's rifle destroyed the wolf to the left, but Maureen's pistol only wounded the wolf on the right. The women moved toward the injured animal and found it struggling for breath and certainly bound for death. Maureen pulled a knife from her belt and slammed it into the throat of the wolf.

"I hope you howl all the way to hell!" yelled Maureen.

"Tooooo HELLLLLLLL!" howled the two women as they headed back toward camp to ready their dogs for travel and to try to find a way to salvage what they had left of their lives.

The story of these two heroic and determined women was jaw-dropping. There was a long, dramatic silence at the end of this horrible tale. Only the crackling of the burning wood in the fireplace interrupted the utter silence in the cabin. After Maureen and Mandy finished their tale, there was an overwhelming sense of remorse in the cabin. The storyteller, Thomas Strong, felt troubled about sending this horrid tale to be printed for profit, and the women felt guilt like so many other survivors of tragedy. The recently widowed ladies had one last part of their tale to tell, and sweet Mikita gently lifted their final burden with a simple query.

"How did you say your final good-byes?" asked Mikita.

Maureen and Mandy described how they rested the men they loved on top of a woodpile on a frozen lake. They lit a fire below them and watched as the fire melted the ice beneath them. Soon, the fire was rising into a glorious blaze, and the bodies of Jack and Ted peacefully slipped into the water, leaving only a brief plume of steam rising toward the sky.

Mikita had been listening intently to the women as they spoke, but I noticed the writer in the room was not just penning a story. He was quietly lifting up one of the secret floorboards, and when he realized I was aware of what he was doing, he tried to buy some time.

"Mikita, please draw a picture of Maureen and Mandy by the fire, and perhaps Stanley should be a part of the drawing as well."

"That's a great idea," agreed Mikita, and I obliged by leaping into the arms of the grieving women.

As Mikita scratched and etched away to form a captivating image of Maureen and Mandy and me, the storyteller was quickly composing this most recent tale. I again noticed him messing around under his desk, and he tried his best to make it look like he was just tying the laces of his boot. Mikita's artwork and the writer's story were completed almost at the same time. The women admired Mikita's drawing and were so pleased with the way Thomas Strong had recorded and written their story.

The award-winning author hugged Maureen and Mandy, and it was obvious he felt a strong connection to the recently widowed women. I lived through the desolate period of time after Thomas Strong had lost his family, and I sensed he related to the two women in that regard. I also realized that my master had an admiration for the strength and determination of these relentless ladies.

"Ladies, with all you have been through, I can't compel you to listen to me, but I can only ask for your ears," started the host of the cabin.

"Thomas, you have been so gracious. Please speak your mind," replied Maureen.

"You seem upset, please, Thomas, talk to us," continued Mandy.

The great wordsmith had been working hard and fast in his literary brain to choose the perfect words he was about to utter, but he appeared uncomfortable, because he was uncertain if they would be well received.

"Maureen and Mandy," started Thomas Strong, "when you leave here tomorrow morning, you will take Mikita's drawing and my words with you to Dawson City."

"Yes, Thomas," the women agreed.

"And now you must promise to me that your tale will end the way it ends on the pages I have written."

"Thomas?" queried Maureen.

"Your story will have a different ending that will not be written with ink on paper, and it will only exist in the hearts and memories of both of you, Mikita, myself, and my boy, Stanley."

"What ending? What story?" asked Mandy.

The fortunate gold miner approached Maureen and Mandy with a leather satchel that seemed to be of significant weight. He guided them toward the fireplace, and they all sat down together. Thomas Strong reached out to grasp their hands. When my master opened the satchel and revealed its contents to the women, they appeared dumbfounded.

"I want you to take this gold home with you and start that hotel you dreamed about opening with Jack and Ted." The host of the cabin quickly raised his hand to thwart any potential negative response from Maureen and Mandy. "I came up here with my boy, Stanley, for the stories, and I ended up with a new daughter and a pile of gold. We had so much fun gathering up the gold each day, but we really didn't earn it. You earned it. Your husbands paid for it, and I refuse to let you depart without some of our good fortune. Don't worry, we have plenty more stashed away around here," finished my master, and everyone chuckled.

"Thomas, I don't know what to say," said Maureen.

"I'm speechless," added Mandy.

"Perfect," laughed Thomas Strong. "Not knowing what to say and being speechless are exactly what I want from you when you get back to Dawson City."

What followed was such a peaceful evening, and soon Maureen and Mandy faded quickly to sleep in front of the fire, both with smiles on their weather-beaten faces that crinkled as they snored. The author poured a drink and looked content as he scribbled some notes at his desk. I looked toward Mikita and watched her as she observed Thomas Strong. Earlier that night, he had called Mikita his new daughter, and her face expressed happiness without even a smile. I knew how she was feeling, and I leaped into her arms just as the tears of joy began to stream down her face.

The next morning, the two toughest women we all had ever met headed to Dawson City to finish their long journey. The gold my master had given them was hidden deep within the gear of their sled, and we were all confident they would make the last leg of their adventure without much difficulty.

Soon after their successful return to Dawson City, they boarded a steamship and headed to San Francisco. Maureen and Mandy bought a hotel and quickly renovated the establishment into a classy place for the many interesting people traveling to the hilly city by the bay in Northern California. The hotel was an immediate success, in large part due to all the publicity garnished from their story in *American* magazine.

The women named the hotel Strong Manor, and the restaurant just off the lobby was called Jack and Ted's. Maureen and Mandy started a tradition of leaving two small chocolates, one for each pillow, on the beds of new arrivals. The owners of the hotel took the time to etch the *M* of their initial on each chocolate. It was the kind of personal touch that made their hotel so successful.

CHAPTER TWENTY-SIX

---·❋·---

Maruk Drags Francis Back

After Maureen and Mandy left and headed home, the writer, the now newly established daughter of the family, and I spent the day relaxing and enjoying the casual pleasure of having nothing much to do. My master seemed happier than he had been in a long time. Mikita was so cheerful. I ate up all the joy in the room, and I became the happiest dog in the world.

As usual, Mikita couldn't help herself and soon was busy organizing, arranging, and cleaning our dwelling. She noticed that the scale we had used to weigh the gold was noticeable from under its hiding place beneath the bunk. After she pushed it back out of view, Mikita removed a very unique object from below that same bunk. I had no idea what she had discovered, but it seemed to make her happy, and the sweet sound of her laughter soon filled the cabin. Mikita's chuckling quickly ceased and was replaced by a high-pitched musical melody. I listened in amazement as I had never heard anything like this before.

"My goodness, Mikita!" howled my amazed master. "Where did you find that? When did you learn to play like that?"

"It was under the bunk next to the scale, and I learned how to play the mandolin when I was just a little girl."

It is rare when a talented writer is rendered speechless, but Thomas Strong was once again amazed and surprised as another special talent of Mikita was unveiled.

I jumped up and down in front of Mikita because I wanted her to continue to create those pleasant sounds. Her fingers moved quickly across the strings of the small musical instrument, creating a high-pitched composition of sound that was so pleasant to my ears. As Mikita stroked and strummed, she established a brisk rhythm, and as I sat before her, I noticed she kept the pace of her music by tapping her foot up and down upon the floor. The sound of the music and the movement of her foot mesmerized me. Soon, my head was bobbing up and down in time with the music.

I loved and admired Mikita, and I wanted to be a part of anything that made her happy. I was watching Mikita's foot keeping time, and I was focused on the up and down tapping motion of her toes. I didn't even realize what I was doing, but my master and Mikita were suddenly laughing and staring at me while they both chuckled with delight. I looked down at my right paw and noticed it was tapping upon the cabin floor in perfect sync with Mikita's foot.

There was laughter in the cabin, and as Mikita played a quicker rhythm, my paw kept pace and tapped the floor faster. Mikita's music seemed to get louder as the volume of the laughter in the room increased. We were all enjoying our own little world, so much so that nobody even noticed my friend Maruk had entered the cabin. He didn't want to startle us, and he stood quietly by the door until I noticed him. As I rushed to greet the skilled guide, the music and laughter were instantly replaced by conversation.

"Hello, Mr. Strong," started Maruk.

"Welcome back, Maruk," greeted the host of the cabin.

"I am happy to be here again with you, but I need your help right away."

"What is wrong, Maruk?" asked my master. "Is it Francis?"

"Yes, he is outside. It is my duty to bring him home. Please help."

Thomas Strong bolted out the door with Maruk and quickly returned with the nearly frozen body of Francis Krausse. Just like his brother, he had fallen through the unsafe ice of a deep lake and would have been dead already if not for the efforts of Maruk.

The clothing of Francis Krausse was frozen stiff, and he didn't seem to have much life left in his body. The great writer and the skilled guide moved him close to the fire. They were about to slice off his frozen clothing in a hurried attempt to warm him when Mikita interrupted them and took control.

"Stop!" Mikita yelled. "Slow! Slow! Slow! You have to warm his body gradually."

I know my master knew about the strategy of warming frozen bodies gradually, because he had saved my paws with that concept the night we found Mikita. That night, I just had some frozen paws, but Francis Krausse appeared to be frozen through, and I guess my master's panic got the best of him for a moment.

"Maruk, this is Mikita," said Thomas Strong. "I think maybe we should listen to her."

"I think so," responded Maruk. "Where did she come from? I didn't even notice her until she started barking orders."

Mikita had been working quickly as soon as Maruk and my master went out to get Francis Krausse. She quickly poured water into three pots and hung them over the fire. By the time Francis Krausse was lying before the fire, she already had rags soaked with warm water.

"Pull him a little farther away from the fire, and place these warm rags over his legs," instructed Mikita. "And be gentle!"

I watched Mikita work quickly with decisiveness and determination. She wrapped Francis Krausse's hands with rags soaked with lukewarm water and then carefully poured the same tepid water on the frozen coat covering his chest.

Mikita knew what she was doing. A dumbfounded writer, an amazed northland guide, and a proud dog watched as a young woman that had once been so close to a frozen death was now desperately trying to thaw an icy body clinging to life.

The strategy of patience Mikita was executing was actually just common sense but usually hard to follow by someone tending to a loved one that is freezing to death. My master had used some of these techniques while helping to revive Mikita. She was about to explain that a body frozen from exposure shouldn't be subjected too quickly to heat, and then she glanced at my master and me and realized that explanation wasn't necessary.

Slowly, the warm water melted the frozen clothing of Francis Krausse. Then Thomas Strong and Maruk cut the clothing off his thawing body and wrapped him in a blanket, about ten feet from the fire. Every once in a while, they slid the slowly warming body of Francis Krausse closer to the fire.

I was actually very helpful with the slow and careful movement of Francis Krausse toward the warmth of the fire. My body has always served as a temperature gauge of fireplaces. If the wood is stoking, I am positioned farther from the fire. As the wood and coals start to cool, I naturally move closer. As I gradually progressed toward the glowing hearth, so did the warming body of Francis Krausse.

Mikita, my master, Maruk, and I were all exhausted. As the chances for survival of Francis Krausse increased, our adrenaline was diluted and the inevitable need for sleep overcame us. I woke before everyone else, responding to the first noises of the new day. There was a guttural groan and a deep breath followed by a dry cough. I turned my head to see Francis Krausse rising to his feet before the fire that had warmed his bones and, thankfully, brought him back to life.

As he straightened and stretched his body, the blanket that had been wrapped around him fell to the floor. I let out a quick yelp, and Francis Krausse quickly turned around. He was naked and obviously healthy, because he was sporting some morning wood. This type of wood wasn't for use in the fireplace, but it definitely proved he would survive!

"For Christ's sake, Francis, will you cover yourself!" yelled the disturbed host.

"Mr. Krausse, it was treacherous and difficult to get you back here, but seeing that is going to cost you more!" Maruk laughed.

All the men laughed heartily, and I howled in amusement. Mikita was awakened by the ruckus, fortunate to have missed the full-body display of Francis Krausse. As always, Mikita rose quickly and hurriedly tended to the needs of everyone in the cabin. She took a pot from above the fire and headed for the door of the cabin. She let me outside, and as I did my business, she filled the pot with snow that soon would be melted into water. Mikita started a pot of coffee and then made oatmeal with sugar and a jar of peaches added for delightful flavor. We all ate quietly, but soon it was decided by all that Francis Krausse and Maruk should stay here another day, just to ensure the complete recovery of our now thawed-out friend.

For a while that day, there was an interesting dynamic in the room. Francis Krausse didn't remember very much about how he had arrived to the safety of our cabin. Maruk had all the details of the eventful journey home, but his modesty made it difficult for him to elaborate about his heroics. Also, Maruk was more curious and interested in hearing the details of Mikita's arrival.

Little by little, a comfortable dialogue was established. Maruk described what he had done to pull his boss from the broken ice and frigid water, and Thomas Strong painfully offered the horrid details of how we had found Mikita.

I looked around the room and absorbed the emotions on the faces of all the storytellers. I saw expressions of fear, joy, amazement, and relief. I realized that I was in a room full of survivors, and I was thrilled to be in their company.

Thomas Strong, the great writer, had survived a bottomless depression caused by the loss of his beloved wife and daughter. Mikita had survived despicable abuse and broken bones. Francis Krausse had amazingly survived his frigid frozenness, and Maruk had once again survived another perilous journey to and from the northland.

The storytelling and tales flowed more fluently as the day progressed. As the writer was scribbling down notes, Mikita was scratching a beautiful drawing of Francis Krausse and Maruk.

Hours of nonstop yammering immediately halted when Mikita showed her artwork to everyone. Once again, she had captured the essence of our visitors.

"I am amazed!" yelped Francis Krausse.

"Wow," Maruk mumbled softly.

He was a rugged young man with many skills, but he was humbled by the image presented to him, and Maruk's brain failed to offer any words toward his tongue.

As Francis Krausse and Maruk continued to gaze with amazement at Mikita's drawing, the great author and storyteller sat at his desk and began to compose this latest tale. The quill in his hand moved swiftly from the inkwell and glided over the paper so smoothly that it certainly promised a great story.

As Thomas Strong wrote, Mikita picked up the mandolin and entertained everyone with upbeat melodies. My paw started tapping again, and soon Maruk was tapping an empty pot with a wooden spoon, and Francis Krausse was whistling louder than Mikita's mandolin.

It really was a special day. We were all so pleased with the recovery of Francis Krausse and simply overjoyed in the relaxed company of good people. As the afternoon turned into evening, I realized something about these visitors and their story. In all the fireside chatting and the telling of tall tales, there was never any mention of gold.

Their stories were about adventure, battling with the elements of Mother Nature, and their will to return home. I knew the value of gold was the great reward of the difficult journey, but I was now beginning to think that the effort and struggle of the journey might be more important.

I watched as Thomas Strong handed the story he had written to Francis Krausse. I looked at my master and tilted my head back and forth. He looked back at me with understanding, and I was certain he knew what I was thinking. Truly, the stories are worth more than the gold.

The next morning, Francis Krausse and Maruk headed south toward Dawson City. Gold was never mentioned during their entire visit, and somehow that didn't seem important. They left with a greater appreciation of their lives, a well-written story, and a spectacular drawing, and I thought those things were more important than any shiny metal.

Chapter Twenty-Seven

Good Friends Return

The cabin was all our own for the next few days. There were no weary travelers to tend to or care for, and my master, Mikita, and I were content to amuse one another as best we could. I jumped up and down, rolled over, and did anything I could to make my two favorite people smile and laugh.

Mikita was a better entertainer. She played the mandolin and whistled tunes that filled our dark cabin with comfortable joy. One evening, the smiling author sat at his writing table and began scratching pen to paper. After a while, he sat next to Mikita and showed her what he had been writing. Mikita smiled, laughed, and then began experimenting with new sounds on the strings of her instrument.

In a short time, Mikita settled into a state of composure. She winked at me, and I rushed to sit at her feet. I glanced up to see her gazing at my master, in search of the approval that a daughter wishes and hopes for from a father.

Then, Mikita started to play a gentle melody, and she began singing a song about our lives together.

She played and sang so sweetly.

I arrived here broken, so painfully.
My wounds are now distant memories.
True happiness is having a family.

I have my dad and my friend Stanley.
Please, God, keep my loved ones safe with me.
Dear God, keep my loved ones safe with me.
We spend long, cold nights happily,
as long as the fire burns majestically.
I love my dad and my friend Stanley.
Please, God, keep my dear ones close to me.
Dear God, keep my dear ones close to me.

Mikita's performance was so captivating, but it ended quickly with the sounds of a dog sled approaching the cabin. I headed toward the door as I usually did to greet the new arrivals, and Mikita laid down the mandolin and opened the cabin door. We stood in front of the cabin and watched as the sled team approached, but they were not slowing down and didn't seem to be interested in stopping.

As the sled was quickly whipping by our cabin, I felt a sickening chill, and my stomach turned. There were two men on the sled, and I knew who they were. As they passed the cabin, both their heads turned to look back. I was hoping that they didn't have a good-enough look to recognize Mikita. The sled slammed by quickly, and I was hopeful everything would be fine. I turned to go back inside and looked to Mikita to open the door, but she was shaking, petrified, and in a state of shock. I scratched her leg and bit on her pants, and that gained her attention. She moved sluggishly and opened the door of the cabin, and as we both entered, Mikita fell to her knees on the floor.

"They saw me!" Mikita cried out. "They saw me! They saw me!"

Thomas Strong had been preparing for visitors. His fire building, water boiling, and coffee making was immediately interrupted, and he rushed to Mikita.

"Who saw you? What happened? Who?"

"It was them . . . it was those men that . . ."

"Calm down, Mikita. Everything will be all right."

The protective nature of the father figure in Thomas Strong gently ushered Mikita to a comfortable place in front of the fireplace. As he finished resting her body down and he felt that she was calming down, he moved toward his writing desk and sat down. His head sunk down low, and I could tell from the look on his face that his brain was busy thinking about what would be our best plan of attack to accomplish safety for all of us. He knew trouble was coming, and he wasn't sure if he could prevent the oncoming evil from hurting his family. The Pearson brothers had seen Mikita, and he knew they would be back.

Thomas Strong loaded the revolver that Jan Ericsson had given him for protection. He placed a chair close to the door and sat down, waiting for the trouble to arrive. I kept close to Mikita to provide comfort, but I kept my eyes and ears open. The night was long and stressful, but soon the blackness of night was turning into the welcome light of day. As the morning of the new day began, our anxious tension slowly drifted away.

We all were so tired, especially me. I had stood watch all night as my master occasionally slipped in and out of involuntary unconsciousness. My ears listened to the sounds outside, my eyes were on the door, and my heart kept me awake to protect all of us.

As the sun rose, I nestled close to the fire, and my eyes were struggling to stay open. I watched Mikita go into the butcher room, and I remembered her saying something about rabbit stew for dinner. My eyes slammed shut, and I dropped into a depth of stellar slumber. Suddenly, the door of the cabin smashed open, ending my deep sleep with a rush of adrenaline.

The first thing I saw as my eyes opened was the no-good, dirty pieces of shit Pearson brothers. Thomas Strong was napping on the floor, and Dirk Pearson quickly picked up his revolver.

"How are you, old man?" Dirk Pearson laughed.

"Where is the girl?" asked Bob Pearson.

"Yeah, where is that bitch?"

"She didn't die?"

"You must have saved her."

I was getting so aggravated, but I wasn't growling, and I was doing my best to keep quiet. I was so mad at myself for letting my instinctual guard down and allowing these assholes to threaten my family. Somehow, Thomas Strong was remaining calm, and the smartest man I knew actually began to act stupid with great success.

"Boys, boys, what girl? What are you talking about?"

"Don't mess with us, Thomas," barked Dirk Pearson.

"Where is she?" hacked Bob.

"Gentleman, relax, take a load off. Why all the anger? Have some coffee."

Dirk Pearson bent down and grabbed my master's neck and then slammed his head into the floor. I was so angry. I needed to do something, but I knew I only could do so much against such evil men, and I needed to choose my opportunity to assist as wisely as possible.

"Where the hell is she?" were the last words that filthy piece of garbage Dirk Pearson ever uttered.

"Right here, you bastard!" yelled Mikita as she suddenly appeared from the carving room.

Mikita had quietly loaded a crossbow and fired an arrow right through the neck of Dirk Pearson, and his head twisted to the side in a look of bewilderment. The arrow protruding from his neck made a sickening, crunching sound as it hit the floor, followed by the thud of his dumb head.

Just as Dirk Pearson's dead head hit the floor, I recognized my one and only opportunity to help, and I leaped with all my might at his equally despicable brother, Bob Pearson. I smashed hard into his shoulder, and he was surprised by my strength and fury. He lost his balanced, and his head slammed hard into the fireplace. He probably would have remained unconscious for some time, but his hair caught fire, and he rose screaming in pain.

The few seconds Bob Pearson spent swatting his hair to try to put out the flames that were scorching his scalp were just enough time for my master to gather his revolver from the floor. Bob Pearson tried to kick me and missed, and he awkwardly slammed to the floor. We all laughed at him.

"You little runt," were his last words as he started to reach for his pistol.

"Go join your brother in hell!" screamed Thomas Strong as he cocked his revolver and blasted a hole in Bob Pearson's face.

"Stanley! Stanley!" screeched Mikita as she rushed to pick me up.

Mikita hugged me, and then we both collapsed into the arms of our father. It was an amazing moment of unity. Within a room filled with bloodshed and two dead bodies, there were peace and tranquility among us. Together, we collected ourselves in a lumpy pile, only to be startled by the creak of the cabin door opening.

"What the hell happened here, Thomas?" yelled John "Bullman" Foreman.

"Holy shit, Writer Boy!" gasped Louis "Loser" Bostock.

Writer Boy had been reaching for his revolver, but the sound of his friends' voices was like music to his ears. He raised his hand to wave a welcome and snorted a shallow sound that resembled laughter.

"Thank God you guys made it back," said the Writer Boy.

Chapter Twenty-Eight

Clean Up

The demise of the Pearson brothers and the immediate arrival of Bullman and Loser were such strange moments that combined astonishment, relief, and joy. In just a few heartbeats, we had defended ourselves, avenged the horror Mikita had suffered, and suddenly were welcoming beloved friends. Kituk had been tending to the dogs outside, and as he entered the cabin, we all snapped back into reality.

"Oh man . . . these assholes!" Kituk barked. "Let's go right now, clean this garbage out of here before they stink the place!"

It was obvious Kituk had encountered the Pearson brothers before, and he had absolutely no respect for them. We watched him drag Dirk Pearson's body across the cabin floor, and then he slung him outside.

"Who snapped his neck with the arrow?" asked Kituk.

Thomas Strong pointed a finger toward Mikita. Bullman and Loser had jaws agape, and Kituk nodded approval toward Mikita as he dragged the body of Bob Pearson out of the dwelling and slammed him on top of his equally dead brother.

"Did you blow that hole in his face, Mr. Strong?"

"Well, ah, yeah!"

"Good for you!" yelped Kituk. "These bastards have been creating havoc up and down these trails for years."

"We didn't want to kill them."

"Mr. Strong, if you didn't kill them, they would have killed you. Now let's get rid of this trash and clean up in here."

Kituk took control of a messy situation with determined efficiency. Bullman and Loser had trusted their lives to him in the treacherous Yukon, so they listened to everything Kituk had to say, and they encouraged Writer Boy to do the same.

"Thomas, listen to Kituk," urged Bullman.

"I think I know what he is doing," said Loser.

Kituk was moving quickly, barking orders, and explaining his actions all at the same time. He dipped two rags into the warm water above the fire and then tossed them on the floor and then asked Mikita to clean up the blood. He ushered the men outside and told them to remove the clothing from the Pearson corpses. He told Thomas Strong to light the clothing on fire as Bullman and Loser helped him drag the dead bodies downhill.

Kituk stopped moving the bodies in the exact place that the Pearson brothers had discarded Mikita. Perhaps it just looked like an ideal place to dump a body, or maybe Kituk had been guided by his Native American instincts and he was bringing these two evil men back to a place of their utmost treachery.

"Okay, guys, go back to the cabin," ordered Kituk. "I will take care of this from here."

Along their journey, Bullman and Loser had learned to listen to Kituk. They turned and headed quickly up the trail back toward the cabin. They began to tire as they approached the dwelling. As they slowed and collected their breath, they heard a sickening chopping noise from the trail down below. Then there was a long silence. We all waited for Kituk to return, and soon Mikita opened the door to check on him. We both observed him on his knees, feeding the dogs.

"Ten fingers and ten dogs," was his matter-of-fact statement as he stood and entered the cabin.

When everyone was settled back in the cabin, Kituk explained why it was necessary to act quickly and dispose the bodies of the Pearson brothers. He spoke of the wonderful reputation of this cabin and described it as an oasis to so many. If travelers knew that garbage like the Pearson brothers had visited here and had become a threat, it would discourage anyone from stopping here and ruin the whole beauty of this sanctuary in the snow.

"Mr. Strong, people have read your stories, and this cabin is like a warm haven to so many people, and some may never even make the journey here. But this place is special, and criminals like the Pearson brothers can't be allowed to taint that image."

"So, Kituk," the famous author chirped as he waved his finger back and forth, "I guess there will be no mention of the Pearson brothers in your adventure story!"

"No, sir, no, sir," responded Kituk, "but I could use your professional expertise to iron out the details of your friends' adventures."

"Certainly, Kituk, I will be happy to help." Thomas Strong chuckled. "Let's see if we can make you the hero that saved these two fools from the cold jaws of the north."

Everyone was laughing as Thomas Strong put his arm around Kituk and led him toward his writing table. So much had happened in such a short time, and it was a welcome sight to see Mikita begin her usual evening routine. I loved the way she managed to tend to everyone without ever making her efforts noticeable. She was so smooth and had such grace.

Bullman and Loser settled down and finally could relax. Thomas Strong seemed enthused to have an interested and aspiring writer asking his advice. The learned author was bellowing something about paying attention to details. Then there was a brief silence in the room, and it was easy to hear Kituk as he asked the advising writer a question.

"Which one is Bullman, and which one is Loser?"

There was boisterous laughter in the room. Thomas Strong almost toppled from his chair. Mikita buckled over and dropped a stirring spoon. Bullman and Loser were cackling, and they pointed at each other as if to ask who was who. I was so excited and leaping around chaotically, bouncing off all my friends.

That night in the cabin, the usual things like dinner and the fire seemed typical, but it really was a most memorable night, because of the faces in the room that flickered in front of the fire. I watched everyone in the room with great intensity. As the night progressed, I became overwhelmed with the realization that I was surrounded by a group of extraordinary people. This unique collection of personalities somehow managed to lift every individual in the room to a level of contentment, and that can only be found within a true family.

At the writing table sat Thomas Strong, a prolific author, who was helping Kituk, a courageous guide of the Yukon, to develop his storytelling skills. Mikita was crouched on the floor, scratching her pencil into a piece of paper, capturing the mentoring moment between the established scribe and the potential wordsmith.

Bullman and Loser weren't really doing anything amazing, but I watched as they sipped whiskey, and I noticed their bodies slowly relaxing. The stress of their journey melted from their faces so softly, like an ice cube disappears into a glass of scotch.

After Mikita had finished her drawing of the two writers, I jumped between Bullman and Loser and struck a pose that was too cute for Mikita to ignore. It was a nice drawing, but it was even funnier, because during the time it took to create the sketch, the two men in the picture had passed out and were robustly snoring.

Mikita laid down her pencil about the same time Thomas Strong and Kituk had polished up the story of how Kituk had guided Bullman and Loser up through the Yukon and back. Mikita picked up the mandolin and stroked a few high-pitched chords between the dozing heads of the weary adventurers. Bullman dropped his half-filled glass to the floor, and Loser spilled what was left in his glass all over his friend, and they both groggily regained awareness.

Mikita began to fill the room with delicate and ethereal musical sounds. The snapping and crackling fire provided a perfect backdrop to her mandolin play, and the waving orange warmth of the fire created a magical atmosphere for Kituk as he read to us the story he had just composed with the help of my master.

Kituk's story had moments of danger, like when the first brutal storm slammed at them quickly and caught them off guard on the trail. It had some exciting parts, especially when he explained how they managed to bring down a moose. We all laughed when Kituk described how Bullman got his leg tangled in the dog harnesses and was dragged around like a rag doll for a hundred yards.

The story was very well written, and it captivated our attention. Strangely, the most enjoyable thing about the story was that there weren't too many perilous situations, and it actually seemed somewhat uneventful. The lack of any life-and-death struggles or impending disasters didn't lessen the importance of the story. The tale was more about the skill of Kituk, the author of the story and the guide of this particular adventure. The words rightfully described Kituk as a quiet hero. The fact that there were no major problems along the way was a credit to his experience and skill as a guide. Thomas Strong thought that was an accurate depiction of the events, and Bullman and Loser nodded in approval.

Similar to most of the stories told in our cozy cabin, the lengthy yarn woven by Kituk had no mention of any gold-mining histrionics. The most consistent theme within the tales of the returning adventurers was more about discovering what they valued most within their hearts and souls, much more so than the value of any precious metal.

"So you knuckleheads traveled all across God's creation and have nothing to show for it but Kituk's story and Mikita's drawings?" Writer Boy laughed.

"Oh, Writer Boy, you know we didn't come up here to try to get rich," cracked Bullman.

"We were too rich before we got up here," added Loser.

Bullman picked his coat off the floor and fumbled with a little satchel in one of the pockets. Loser smirked and Kituk chuckled as Bullman tossed a small bit of gold onto Thomas Strong's writing table.

"It's not much, but it's something," stated Bullman.

"It's embarrassing and probably not even enough to buy you one of those fancy new typewriter machines they are selling in San Francisco," cracked Loser.

"You guys shouldn't be ashamed," was Writer Boy's sarcastic retort.

"Mikita, would you get the scale so we can see just how much gold my good friends have procured from the depths of the great north."

"I would be happy to." Mikita giggled.

Mikita placed the scale on the writing table and showed Bullman and Loser how to use it properly. As the two men busied themselves balancing the weights and their satchel of gold, my master and Mikita began removing the floorboards that were hiding our hefty treasure. Before Bullman and Loser had finished measuring the meager amount of gold they had gathered, they almost knocked the scale off the table and onto the floor as two men that had always been difficult to impress stood stunned.

"Holy damn!"

"Good God!"

Bullman and Loser were wealthy men, and so was Thomas Strong. The amazing thing about the sparkling gold filling up the deep space below three floorboards was how it had accidently fallen into our lives.

"And all Mikita and I had to do was walk down the hill behind the cabin, and Stanley did all the heavy lifting. He was like a regular pack mule hauling that gold up the hill into the cabin," yapped Writer Boy as he picked me up and laughed at his friends.

CHAPTER TWENTY-NINE

---◦◦◦---

Exit Strategy

After two days of relaxation and jocularity, Kituk seemed to grow restless, and Bullman and Loser realized it was time to finish their journey and head south toward Dawson City. The men gathered around Thomas Strong's writing table and strategized about a safe return to civilization for all.

I noticed that Mikita appeared unsettled, perhaps because she was uncertain about her future. She was so happy to have the life with a new father and me and all our visitors. Her life in the cabin had provided her with a loving family and genuine purpose. I followed Mikita as she headed outside, and when the cabin door closed behind us, Mikita sat down and she began to cry.

"Oh, Stanley, I don't want to have to say good-bye to you."

Perhaps Mikita was afraid of losing the love of her new family because of what had happened to her in the past, but there was no way I was ever going to say good-bye to my wonderful friend, and I was sure her new father felt the same way. I scratched my paws in the snow and tilted my head back and forth in my best effort to look dumbfounded by her concerns. I leaped up to kiss her, and when she bent down to give me a playful pat on my head, I yanked on the collar of her coat and pulled her down into the snow. I bounced on top of Mikita and was so thrilled to hear the sound of her laughing. As we rustled around in the snow, our eyes connected, and at that moment, Mikita knew that forever and always, we would be together.

As Mikita and I were frolicking around outside, the men had decided on the best course of action for a safe return for everyone. Thomas Strong, the writer, had taken control of the situation almost as if he were authoring the ending to one of his dramatic stories. He was most concerned that Kituk got his friends home safely, and since Kituk had already managed to bring his two best friends to and from the Yukon, he trusted the knowledge and instincts of the reliable guide. The last leg of the journey was probably the easiest stretch of terrain for a guide like Kituk. He was so trustworthy that my master diverted from the plan he had arranged with Jan Ericsson, and he asked Kituk to bring the bounty of all the gold we had collected back to civilization, along with Bullman and Loser.

Kituk would head toward Dawson City, carrying a story that he had cowritten with Thomas Strong. He also had Mikita's two latest drawings to go with the story that would certainly be a page-turner in *American* magazine.

Writer Boy, Bullman, and Loser agreed that Thomas Strong's two best friends would head back to his estate in California and wait for our return. My master needed to have one conversation before he could relax, and I watched as he pulled Kituk aside to communicate an important message.

"Kituk," started Thomas Strong, "you are an amazing guide with instincts and bravery."

"Thank you, sir."

"I am not sure if traveling through the frozen tundra of the great north as a guide is the life you want, but if you go with my friends to my estate in California, I promise to do whatever I can to help you begin a writing career."

"Thank you, sir. I have learned so much about writing from you already, but this life is all I have ever known."

"You have storytelling talent, so you think about what you want to do as you head back to Dawson City."

"I will, sir, thank you."

My master explained to everyone that he felt the need to stay at the cabin for a few more days because he was waiting on one memorable adventurer that had yet to return. Charles Tarkenton had been the last to visit our cabin on his trek northward, and he was the only explorer that set out braving the challenges of the Yukon by himself.

"Charles Tarkenton was different from everyone else. He seemed determined and at the same time lost, kind of like me when I first got here. I need to wait a bit longer for him to return."

"We understand, Thomas," said Bullman.

"We will head to your estate in California and have it opened and ready for your arrival," encouraged Loser.

"Just don't burn it down, you knuckleheads." Writer Boy laughed.

My master moved toward Mikita and gave her a loving hug that only a father could give to a cherished daughter. He had sensed Mikita's anxiety about her future. Thomas Strong thought he had established himself as a father figure to Mikita, but he began to realize the people Mikita had trusted the most in her life always vanished and somehow let her down. He somehow knew her feelings. She was afraid that our impending departure from the cabin might change the course of our blooming family, which had brought us all such happiness, and the great writer had the perfect words to halt Mikita from any more unnecessary worrying.

"Gentlemen, when you arrive at my estate, please be sure to prepare a room for my daughter, Mikita."

Mikita had been so tough, durable, resilient, and strong, which made it even more emotional for all of us as she gasped for breath, sobbed, and slumped deep into the arms of the man that had adopted her as his own daughter.

"She'll need a drawing table and a music stand!"

"Certainly!" agreed Bullman.

"We're on it, Writer Boy," chipped in Loser.

There was a brief group hug in the center of the cabin, which might have seemed a bit too corny if you didn't know everyone in the room as well as I did. These were all exceptional people, with genuine love and respect for one another. Mikita was the first to move away from the huddle, and she immediately resumed her diligent caretaking duties.

The next morning, I woke a bit earlier than usual, and Kituk, Bullman, and Loser had not yet risen to prepare for the final leg of their journey. Thomas Strong was still sawing wood like a lumberjack in a timber-cutting contest, but Mikita was nowhere in sight. Soon the cabin door opened, and Mikita entered and quickly ushered me outside. I did my business in short time and headed back toward the cabin door, but then I noticed that Mikita had been busy composing a beautiful drawing of the abode that had provided us with so much happiness.

"Stanley, sit right there," ordered Mikita as she pointed at a spot near the door.

Of course I obeyed her request, and soon a detailed image of me squatting in front of the cabin was completed. Mikita had done a great job depicting me in the drawing. She had highlighted my best features and downplayed the few flaws in my appearance. It was the first time I was the main subject of one of her drawings, and I was so thrilled to see this image of me sketched on a piece of paper. I liked the way I looked in the drawing, but I was happier to see the relaxed expression on Mikita's face.

As Mikita and I headed back inside the cabin, the door opened, and Kituk rushed outside to ready the sled team for the trip to Dawson City. Inside the cabin, another reunion of the three great friends was coming to an end. There were hugs and handshakes and some vigorous slaps on the back.

"Get the hell out of here, my boys," barked Writer Boy.

"We couldn't get out of here fast enough, Writer Boy," said a sarcastic Bullman.

"Hey, Thomas," started Loser, in a more serious tone. "We will see you soon in California."

"Take care of this word scribbler, Mikita," was the final request of Bullman.

"I will, I will," assured Mikita.

"Take care of your family, Thomas," beckoned Loser.

"I will, I will," promised Writer Boy, "and just make sure you don't lose my gold on the way home."

Soon Kituk, Bullman, and Loser were gone, headed south on the trail to Dawson City. I could tell my master was having second thoughts about his decision to stay behind and wait for Charles Tarkenton. The sled team left behind by the Pearson brothers was rested and ready for travel, so we easily could have followed Kituk and headed home.

The next couple of days were much different from any other time my master, Mikita, and I had spent together in the cabin. We were happy and occupied our time in the same manner we had done before. The writer quilled words onto paper, and Mikita cooked, cleaned, played the mandolin, and worked on drawings. I just spent the majority of my time curled up near the fire, basking in the glow of flames and family.

It was obvious Thomas Strong wanted to go home. Mikita and I both sensed his restlessness. Our ride back to civilization was supposed to be provided by Jan Ericsson, the man that had brought us here. The great writer wanted to end the story, and there was a rested and eager sled team willing to pull his new family toward the comfort of his California home.

He had traveled such a long way to this desolate cabin in a desperate attempt to find something that might rekindle a spark in his soul. The widowed author never could have imagined the unpredictable story of his days spent inside this cozy cabin.

"Mikita, please start preparing yourself and Stanley for the trip home."

"It won't take long to get ready," responded Mikita.

"I am giving Charles Tarkenton one more day, and then we are getting the hell out of here."

That night, the three of us were a bit more quiet than usual. Obviously, there was a significant amount of introspection taking place. This night might be the last we would spend here. We all knew that this rustic dwelling was not the greatest place to live, but our lives had been made greater because of it. The great author did not write that evening, and Mikita didn't draw, play the mandolin, or read out loud from a book. We were occupied by our thoughts and memories, and soon we all drifted peacefully to sleep.

My senses and instincts snapped me to attention early the next morning. A sled team was approaching, and I was hoping to see Charles Tarkenton pulling up in front of our cabin. Thomas Strong had made the decision to stay and wait for him, and I knew his arrival would mean we could go back home to the lazy warmth of our California estate.

I rushed toward Mikita and nudged her while licking her face to wake her. As I roused her, I scratched the floor with my paw and jerked my head in the general direction of the cabin door. Mikita understood the signals I was sending and stood up quickly, and we both moved swiftly to greet the man we both felt would be our last arrival. As Mikita reached to open the door of the cabin, my instincts recognized that the approaching sled team was not heading south toward Dawson City but actually approaching from the south. Just as Mikita and I exited the cabin, we welcomed Jan Ericsson and his sled team as they pulled into view. He waved at us as he ushered the dogs to a halt.

I felt a pang of guilt because Mikita and I were initially disappointed that we weren't welcoming Charles Tarkenton. I was ready to go home, and I knew Mikita was curious and looking forward to the opportunities that a life in California could provide her.

As Jan Ericsson began to secure his dogs, Mikita rushed to help him. I watched them work together, and I realized how crucial Jan Ericsson had been in the evolution of our happiness. He guided us here and advised us about survival in the frozen north, and when he visited, he always brought a great sustenance of supplies. My brain stalled as I wondered about what our lives would have been like without all the efforts of this thoughtful and dedicated friend.

CHAPTER THIRTY

Charles Tarkenton Returns

There had never been any certainty regarding the length of our stay in this cabin, which had now become a source of vitality and had rejuvenated my master's spirit. Jan Ericsson was a smart and observant man. He enjoyed the connection he had with such a great writer as Thomas Strong. When he first brought us to this remote cabin, he really wasn't sure what would become of us. He had made many trips to bring supplies up to this remote dwelling, and so many times, he carried Thomas Strong's words back to civilization. A man of his experience would have a problem not noticing the unattended sled team burrowed into the snowdrifts outside our cabin.

"That's a nice sled team out there, Thomas," barked Jan Ericsson as he entered the cabin.

"Yes, it is, Jan!"

"I don't recall leaving any dogs up here, Thomas!"

"Well, the dogs just showed up one night looking for a place to rest. Mikita fed them, and they have been nesting here ever since."

"I've never seen anything like it," offered Mikita. "They pulled up with nobody guiding the sled and haven't moved since."

"I passed your friends on the way up here," responded Jan Ericsson. "They urged me to get you home safely. I think you made a good decision, Thomas. Kituk is a great guide, and the weather conditions are perfect for travel right now."

"Jan, I know we made plans to bring all the gold back together as we left here."

"You don't need to explain, Thomas."

"I feel I should explain, Jan."

"Thomas—"

"The gold under the floorboards started to feel like something out of an Edgar Allan Poe story. It just felt like danger, and Kituk seemed so sure of himself. I just wanted the gold gone!"

"I understand, Thomas . . ."

"When we get back to Dawson City, you will have a healthy bank account!"

"That will be nice!"

"And with Kituk and my friends trekking the gold home, we can now relax and enjoy ourselves, without any worries about lugging precious metal through dangerous territory."

"So I can relax, Thomas?"

"Just settle down, Jan. Mikita and Stanley are in charge of getting us ready to embark on our safe journey home. Just settle tonight, and we will be on our way tomorrow morning."

There was a silent understanding in the room that was louder than the avalanche that had shaken our cabin and opened up the gold mine below. Nobody in the room cared to discuss the details of the missing sledders. The Pearson brothers were easily forgotten. I watched Jan Ericsson as he quietly observed his friend Thomas Strong and Mikita.

I noticed a smile of contentment on the face of Jan Ericsson. The talented, lost soul that he had guided to this cabin one year ago was in better shape than when he had first left him here. The heartbroken man he brought to this magical cabin was now recovering from the loss of his loved ones and seemed to be healing from painful memories of a life that now seemed so distant and far away. He was even more amazed at how Mikita had already forgotten the pain of her broken bones, and her recovery seemed complete. Jan Ericsson only noticed smiles and giggles from Mikita, and now she only seemed hopeful for the future.

Thomas Strong stood up quickly and ended what seemed to be a long, thoughtful pause in the cabin. He poured two whiskeys and handed one to Jan Ericsson, and they clinked glasses in a toast.

"To great friends and second chances," was Thomas Strong's toast.

"Indeed, Thomas, indeed," replied Jan Ericsson.

Mikita whisked around the cabin with her usual care and consideration. She cooked, monitored the fire, and generally attended to everyone. After the last plate was cleaned and the last cup of coffee poured, Mikita worked hard to usher two tired old men into an artistic opportunity in front of the fire.

Thomas Strong looked rumpled and weary, and Jan Ericsson appeared beaten down by the wind and weather, but they sat next to each other, still exuding happiness. Mikita crafted another masterful drawing that captured everything that was most important about the relationship between these quality individuals. After a while, the two subjects of Mikita's drawing were struggling to keep their eyes open, and the fire was beginning to dwindle.

"Hey, guys, wake up," yapped Mikita as she turned her drawing toward Thomas Strong and Jan Ericsson.

"Wow! Oh my goodness!" exclaimed Jan Ericsson.

I was thoroughly enjoying the look on my master's face as he watched Jan Ericsson overcome by the amazement of Mikita's artwork. The collective joy in the room seemed a perfect way to conclude such a wonderful evening. The two men were laughing and hugging, and Mikita was smiling and beaming with happiness. As I was absorbing all the emotions flourishing inside the cabin, my right ear flickered, and then my instincts clicked into high gear. I headed toward the door, knowing a sled team was approaching, and Mikita was right behind me.

Mikita and I bounced out of the cabin with such enthusiasm, hoping to welcome Charles Tarkenton, and were looking forward to listen to the tale of his journey and experiences. The dogs slowed as we greeted the team, but the happiness that Mikita and I felt was short-lived as we noticed the one body on the sled was slumped over and lifeless. I knew it was Charles Tarkenton, and I had a sick feeling that he was in big trouble.

As Mikita and I reached the sled, I recognized a weather-beaten and weary face that somehow resembled Charles Tarkenton. It looked like he might be dead as Mikita pulled him off the sled and gently rested him on his back. I was panicking a bit, and I was upset about the condition of Charles Tarkenton. I did something I don't do very often. I howled as loud as I could.

"Aaaaaaaahwwwwooooooh!"

My howl was a surprising release from the stress of the situation, and it also alerted Thomas Strong and Jan Ericsson that there was a problem outside. They rushed through the cabin door, and as Jan Ericsson tended to the sled team, Mikita and my master carried Charles Tarkenton into the cabin. They carefully placed him near the fire, and the smartest man I know began pacing the floor, trying to figure out the best course of action to help the wounded traveler.

I remembered how my master had gathered his thoughts so quickly and with determination when he executed his plan to save Mikita. She was in shock and unconscious most of the time as we had worked to save her, but somehow she remembered and looked at her new father with trust, eager to listen, and help in any way possible.

"He's in shock!" yelled the author of authors. "Mikita, gently remove his gloves and boots."

"Yes, sir."

I was scurrying all over the floor, not sure what to do. I looked up at my master, and he was doing the same thing. He stopped bouncing around long enough to pour a big drink, and after gulping it down, he refocused on the task at hand.

Mikita had finished removing Charles Tarkenton's gloves and boots. Thomas Strong knelt down and grabbed the injured man's right hand and then pulled his middle finger up toward his palm, separating it from the other fingers. When he let go of the finger, it snapped back toward the other digits, which seemed to please my master. He repeated the same procedure on the left hand with the same result. Then, we all watched Thomas Strong induce the toes of Charles Tarkenton to wiggle up and down.

"Well, I don't think his back is broken, and his arms and legs don't seem to be displaced."

"What do you think is wrong?" asked Mikita.

"He is wheezing, and taking short breaths. We need to take off his coat and take a look under his clothing for wounds."

Thomas Strong was a writer by nature, but again he found himself making split-second crucial decisions in an effort to save a life. He knelt with Mikita alongside the unconscious visitor and began to unbutton his coat. When the first button popped open, Charles Tarkenton gasped for a breath, and his eyes opened with a strange expression that made it appear he was searching for reality.

"Calm down, Charles, you are safe in my cabin. I'm Thomas Strong. I've been waiting for you."

As Charles Tarkenton became more alert and aware of his surroundings, the depth of his breathing increased, but so did the volume of the wheezing noise escaping from his lungs. As his two caretakers tried to help him, Charles Tarkenton made a weak effort to prevent his coat from being opened.

This is sad to say, but I knew Charles Tarkenton was never going to leave this cabin. I went to him and licked his cheek, as Mikita and my master opened his coat, cut open his garments and shirt, and found a horrible mess on the right side of his torso. I tried as best I could, but I don't think I concealed my anguish, and I think Charles Tarkenton couldn't help but notice the other two concerned heads hovering over him, bowing in despair.

There were two ribs badly broken and pressing so hard against the skin that it was amazing the bones had not burst through the flesh. The entire right side of his body was a blackish purple, and on the edge of that cloudy bruise was a crimson-red border, which was rapidly growing in size.

So much had happened in just a couple of minutes. We had gone from a frantic effort to trying to save a friend to the solemn realization that there was nothing we could do to prevent the demise of Charles Tarkenton. There was a strange tranquility that overcame us, and there was a peacefulness in the air.

"Oh my!" blurted a surprised Jan Ericsson, interrupting the silence as he entered the cabin.

The well-traveled tour guide had seen many things, but he wasn't expecting to walk in to see a man's body looking like it was ready to explode. There was a brief moment of uneasiness that was lifted away by the man gripped with pain.

"It's okay, Thomas," whispered Charles Tarkenton as he gripped the storyteller's hand with surprising strength. "Before I leave, I want to tell you about my journey."

"I am listening, Charles," the great writer responded as he lowered his head closer to listen to the crippled voice of a mortally wounded man.

"Let's get the most important thing out first, Thomas." Charles Tarkenton somehow managed to muster a crooked smile. "Just in case I can't finish with all the details."

Thomas Strong wasn't sure whether to laugh or grab a pencil and paper, so he did both. Mikita put a pillow under Charles Tarkenton's head and a blanket over his fractured body, while Jan Ericsson pressed a glass full of whiskey against his lips for easy sipping. I licked his fingers and did my best to relax him by looking happy and cute.

"My journey was a success, Thomas. I had my moment with our creator," declared Charles Tarkenton, "and I had a few good chats with my father along the way."

"I am happy for you, Charles, that your journey was a success," were the comforting words of Thomas Strong as the author hurriedly tried to capture the profound final words of a weakened man who had the strength of his experiences keeping him alert and alive.

"Thomas, please don't think my words are deranged or erratic because of my wounds," begged Charles Tarkenton.

"Just relax, Charles, I'm with you."

"As I spent more time alone surrounded by such majestic landscape, all the sights and sounds started to join together in a collaborative voice."

"I'm listening, Charles."

"The constant rustle of the wilderness and steady whispering of the wind through the trees began to construct sentences in a language I was not familiar with, but strangely, I understood. The clouds in the sky altered the sparkle of the stars and also sifted the glow of the moon, just enough to create punctuation to the sentences."

Charles Tarkenton was having more and more difficulty breathing. Jan Ericsson helped him sip his final whiskey from a cup, while Mikita placed another blanket over his broken body. I just licked his fingers and tried to make him smile.

CHAPTER THIRTY-ONE

---※---

One Last Story Before We Go

Charles Tarkenton was struggling through enormous pain in a final effort to prove the invaluable worth of his journey. I noticed a strange distortion of time as the words started to rapidly rush from the mouth of Charles Tarkenton, but all the images of the scene moved distinctly slower.

"I was traveling by myself," began Charles Tarkenton, and I noticed every head in the room gradually leaned closer, as if in some sort of slower motion, as we all tried to listen.

"I was by myself, but strangely, the farther I got away from civilization, I felt less alone. I had a wonderful trip northward, with no problems or difficulties. It was really unexpected smooth traveling, and that allowed the opportunity to really absorb the unique landscape surrounding me.

"At the end of one long day, I was ready to pack it in and camp for the night, but the dogs pulled me farther. They didn't want to rest, and somehow I trusted their instincts and kept moving."

"That is amazing, Charles."

"I had fallen asleep on the sled when the dogs stopped abruptly, and I tumbled down and woke quite quickly. I fell right in front of a small alcove in the side of a steep embankment, a perfect place for a single sojourner to reside."

"Those dogs brought you where you needed to go," chirped Jan Ericsson.

"Amazing," mumbled Thomas Strong.

"I started to gather wood for a fire, and as I was returning to my new dwelling, I looked toward the sky and saw a moon so enormous and radiating with heavenly attraction. The picturesque scene captivated me, and I dropped some of the wood that I had collected. As I bent down on my knees to pick up the kindling, I looked below and saw a stream shimmering in the silver glow of the moon."

"It sounds like a beautiful place," offered Thomas Strong.

"Are you okay, Mr. Tarkenton?" asked Mikita.

"I'm fine, darling," whispered Charles Tarkenton into the ear of Mikita as the young woman provided care and comfort in what we all knew where his final moments.

"Charles, Charles, tell us . . . please tell us what you learned," beckoned Jan Ericsson.

"It's hard to explain, but the enormity and the magnificence of the scenery at first made me feel tiny and insignificant. As some time went by and I listened to the language of the sounds of the north, and I absorbed all the beautiful images surrounding me, I began to feel as if I were a part of everything, and I began to feel larger than my own existence."

"Charles, I am so glad you made it back here," whispered Thomas Strong as he squeezed the dying man's hand. "There was a time when I also felt small and meaningless, but I was brought back to life by the people I have met here. People like you, Charles."

Charles Tarkenton gripped Thomas Strong's hand with his last ounce of strength, and he nodded in agreement with what the storyteller had just said. He turned toward Mikita and smiled, and then his eyes peacefully closed.

There was a monumental silence in the cabin that seemed like an eternity, but it probably was only a minute or two. Everyone always seemed to know what to do, but in this unique situation, my master, Mikita, and Jan Ericsson were saddened and disoriented by the passing of such a wonderful man. I also was confused by the powerful emotions in the cabin, but I noticed Charles Tarkenton's hand had fallen to the floor. I grabbed the sleeve of his shirt with my teeth and pulled his arm up so that his hand rested over his heart.

"Good boy, Stanley," thanked my master.

"That's a sweet boy, Stanley," whispered Mikita."

"This is so sad!" bellowed Jan Ericsson.

Jan Ericsson was right. There was overwhelming sadness in the cabin, but we knew we had to bury Charles Tarkenton before we headed home. We needed to pay the utmost respect to the remains of such a compassionate and thoughtful man.

We made a fire on the northernmost point of the open flat ground where the dog teams resided. After the snow melted and the ground had softened underneath the fire, Thomas Strong and Jan Ericsson dug a grave. While the men were digging, Mikita and I were inside the cabin. Mikita was wrapping Charles Tarkenton's body in a favorite blanket of ours, one that we had spent many nights snuggling closely together in front of the fireplace.

I noticed Mikita was crying, and I went to comfort her. She had never met Charles Tarkenton before the night of his demise, but I sensed that his departure was a reminder of what had happened to her. I realized Mikita's tears were both of sadness for Charles Tarkenton and also for the happiness of the life she now had with her new family.

"I love you, Stanley," whispered a sobbing Mikita as she hugged me and squeezed me a bit too tightly.

We laid Charles Tarkenton to rest at the sunrise of the next day, in a ceremony full of all the respect and honor that he deserved. Jan Ericsson and Thomas Strong gently placed his body in the ground, and the two solemn men slowly began to cover his body with the earth they had just displaced.

Mikita began strumming softly on the mandolin that had so often provided joyful entertainment. The sounds she was creating from the strings were of biblical nature. She organized her rhythm and began to sing.

Thomas Strong and Jan Ericsson slowed down the efforts of their shoveling and then completely stopped and turned their heads toward Mikita as she continued to sing and stroke the strings of the mandolin. They looked on with astonished amazement as she continued to sing and play.

> *Swing low, sweet chariot,*
> *Coming for to carry me home.*
> *Swing low, sweet chariot,*

Coming for to carry me home.

"Oh my, Mikita!" uttered Thomas Strong in amazement.

A band of angels coming after me,
Coming for to carry me home.
Sometimes I'm up; sometimes I'm down,
Coming for to carry me home.

"Gentlemen, sing with me, for Charles Tarkenton!" urged Mikita, and everyone together.

Swing low, sweet chariot,
Coming for to carry me home.
Swing low, sweet chariot,
Coming for to carry me home.

Everyone chimed in on the last verse of the song that Mikita had taught so quickly. It was an easy hymn, it had a glorious sound, and it was a wonderful way to send Charles Tarkenton on his way to reconnect with his father and also meet his creator.

"Where did you learn that beautiful song, Mikita?" asked Jan Ericsson as we headed back toward the cabin.

"There was a man from Oklahoma that passed through Dawson City a couple of years back. I was tinkering around on the piano in between table settings at Mother McCreary's, and he sat down next to me and taught me the song."

"It was a great send-off for Charles Tarkenton," mourned Thomas Strong.

"The man that taught me the song told me his father was a preacher, and his father had written the song a long time ago. The song spread quickly in the middle states, so rapidly that many other people started claiming ownership to the song."

"That's not right," objected Jan Ericsson.

"The man didn't seem to mind who got credit for the song, and he just seemed happy it was spreading around."

"What was his name?" asked the author.

"His name was Jerome Johnson, but he liked to be called J. J."

"Well, that song was a wonderful way to usher Charles Tarkenton to God, and now it needs to be our theme song," urged my master. "It's time to go home."

I watched and listened as my master, Mikita, and Jan Ericsson discussed the best strategy for our return to Dawson City. At this point, there were three sled teams rested and ready to charge in any direction they were commanded.

The Pearson brothers' sled team was bored and anxious. Charles Tarkenton's team was in pretty good shape, considering the valiant effort they had made to bring their commander back here. Jan Ericsson's team was a well-oiled machine and ready to sled on instant command.

Jan Ericsson was doing most of the talking, and Thomas Strong and Mikita were smart enough to listen to the wise guide that had somehow managed to bring us all together. He described that the trip to Dawson City was a little over a half a day, around fourteen or fifteen hours, as long as there were no issues along the way. He explained that there was no need to make the trip in one stint, because he knew a great place to safely set a camp for one night. It was about eight or nine hours of sled travel, but he promised it would be a memorable last night in the north.

"We should leave two hours before nightfall," advised Jan Ericsson. "Dogs work better in the dark and the cold of the night, and the sleds will slide easier over the silver night snow, and with less weight on the sleds as we head downhill, it should be an easy trip."

"So we should get ready to go, Jan?" asked Thomas Strong.

"Yes, Thomas," respectfully responded Jan Ericsson. "Ideally, we should be on the sleds and heading south in two hours."

So there were just a couple of hours to spend collecting any belongings we might want to bring with us back to civilization. My master and Mikita were wandering around the cabin, thinking about what might be important to take on the journey south. Jan Ericsson continued to banter that if the timing of the trip was right, he knew of a beautiful place to set camp for one final night in the wilderness.

It soon became obvious that there wasn't too much to bring back on the trail south. The stories that were written by the great writer in the dwelling had already been delivered, as had most of Mikita's extraordinary drawings. I was thrilled to still have all four paws, shocked that I had suffered no major physical harm on this adventure. I was about to head home with a revitalized dad and an extraordinary new sister in Mikita, the new love of my life.

Quill pens, paper, and pencils had told the stories of what had happened in this cozy cabin, but they would be left behind in hopes that perhaps they would be used by future storytellers and artists. As we were collecting our bearings and gathering our final images of this cabin that made such a monumental impact on our lives, Jan Ericsson was hammering home the most important issues of packing and travel.

We all loved him for his concern and advice, but my master, Mikita, and I were lost in an effort to hear all the sounds, take in all the scents, and use our eyes to create the final images that had made this place our home.

We remembered the squeaks of the floorboards and the continuous crackle of the wood burning in the fireplace that sometimes had an occasional loud pop. We recalled the smell of the wood burning and the aromas of meals that were cooked with care. We could never forget the way the burning logs of the fire flickered so beautifully on the walls of this humble abode. We took it all in, but then it was time to go.

Thomas Strong, Mikita, and I exited the cabin, well prepared for the journey. We had enough clothing and food good to last for a journey three times as long. The only thing of real value that we brought with us was the mandolin that Mikita had found and entertained us with her amazing talent.

"Let's go, Thomas. Let's go, Thomas!" Jan Ericsson yelled as we exited the cabin for the last time.

"Yes, sir, Jan," responded my master with a relaxed laugh.

I was happy Jan Ericsson was taking control and hastening our departure. I hate long good-byes. He assured us that the sled teams were ready to move, and he ordered us to our sleds.

"Thomas, I have my dogs, and they need to be with me in front."

"Okay, Jan," responded Thomas Strong.

"Mikita and Stanley should ride home with Charles Tarkenton's dogs."

"That sounds good," responded Mikita as I bristled with pride because I was included in the sledding arrangements.

"And, Thomas, you bring home the Pearson brother's team. They are rested and ready to travel, and they should follow the other teams all the way."

"Okay, Jan, let's go."

Jan Ericsson mounted his sled quickly, and Thomas Strong was also swift to mount his sled. Mikita would have been just as fast and ready to go, but she spent a minute to find a flat spot on the sled for me and another minute to wrap me in a blanket. Mikita's efforts to keep me comfortable and warm for the trip delayed our departure briefly, but I noticed Thomas Strong and Jan Ericsson nodding in approval as Mikita cared for me.

"On to Dawson City!" yelled Jan Ericsson.

"Let's go, Stanley!" screeched Mikita, so loud that it made me howl like a wolf.

"Aaooooooooooohhhh."

"We're on our way!" yelled Thomas Strong. "We are on our way home," he yelled with an enthusiasm that he did not have before we had arrived in this cabin.

CHAPTER THIRTY-TWO

---·❄·---

Heading Back

We were organized as best as we could be, and everything seemed fine, but just a minute into our journey, we had a minor hiccup. I think we all wanted to speed as quickly as possible past the place where we had found Mikita and also where the Pearson brothers had been discarded. Jan Ericsson's sled team coasted right along, and despite the chill in our bones that Mikita and I felt, we passed with little issue. For some reason, the Pearson brothers' sled team that was now carrying Thomas Strong stopped short in the area of their former owners' final resting place.

My master went tumbling off the sled, and he rose, cursing and angry. He grabbed the lead dogs by their neck harnesses and slammed their faces into the snow. He headed back to mount the sled, and the dog's heads all turned to watch and follow him. Thomas Strong pointed his finger toward the trail, and all the dogs looked in the direction he was pointing.

"Onward, you mutts!" yelled my master, and I was amazed how he suddenly seemed like an accomplished sledder.

The beginning of our trip back toward Dawson City was so glorious and perfect. We watched the sun setting over snow-filled hills, and the pure whiteness of the slopes quickly turned into a flickering warm glow of so many shades of colors combining together. Then as the sun dropped out of sight, beneath the hills, the warm shades quickly turned into a chilly blue and then even a darker, almost black color.

As we continued to travel and the darkness of night settled upon us, it was easier to focus on the compelling sounds that were so unique to dog-sled travel. There was the thumping of the dogs' paws and the unity of the whistling of the sled team's synchronous breathing. The sloshing, slipping sound of the sled rails is very hard to describe. Sometimes the rails make a sharp squealing noise, but more often, it makes a gentle, whisking sound that can put most tired people to sleep. When our pace slowed down on an upgrade, the sounds of the paws became louder, and the rails went quiet. I liked it when we were able to hear the voices of the wind bustling through the trees.

The three sled teams had traveled through two hours of sunsetting daylight and then about six or seven hours in the calm and quiet of a most hospitable Alaskan night. It seemed so peaceful that I almost felt I was dreaming. Nobody was yapping unnecessarily or barking orders, so we just kept sledding easily on our way. Suddenly, Jan Ericsson raised his hand and yelled to everyone to prepare to stop.

"Here it is! Here is the campsite!" shouted Jan Ericsson. "Just a bit farther, just a bit farther, and you'll see."

As the echo of his shouting voice faded, he turned his sled around an enormous pine tree and disappeared down a sharp slope. As the sled teams led by Mikita and my master followed Jan Ericsson around that tree and down the slippery grade, a picturesque scene was revealed, unveiling what is most glorious about nature.

"I told you, Thomas, I told you, Thomas!" howled Jan Ericsson. "We had a great trip to get here, and this is the best place for us to spend our last night in the northland together!"

"Wow," mumbled Thomas Strong. "This place is so majestic, so overwhelming."

"It's astonishing," whispered Mikita as she hugged me and gazed in amazement at the beautiful scene surrounding us. She immediately began rummaging through the baggage on the sled for a pencil and paper.

"I have to draw this scene."

"Mikita," quipped my master in order to earn the enthused artist's attention. "We will set up camp, and you just relax and draw what you see. I have a feeling it will be special."

As we settled in for the night, the beauty of the landscape that surrounded us not only compelled an emotional response but also was a safe place to set up camp. At the bottom of the grade that we had swiftly glided down, we came to a flat area of open ground. In the rear of this level terrain, there was a large rock structure that had a significant overhang. With this natural wall of stone at our backs and the rock covering us from above, we had impeccable natural protection from dangerous wildlife and bad weather. On this night, the sky was astonishingly clear, so we set up camp and absorbed the beauty of our environment.

About one hundred yards in front of us, a small snow-covered lake shimmered and sparkled under the moon and stars. On the opposite side of the lake, enormous pine trees bent slowly back and forth in a surprisingly gentle wind. As the snow-filled branches of the pines moved to and fro, a sparkling silver dust floated into the night sky, casually meandering through the air as it headed to earth.

It was a glorious night in an unforgettable scene. As Thomas Strong and Jan Ericsson set up camp and tended to the three sled teams, I sat behind Mikita so I could see what she was looking at and also watch her as she made a drawing come to life. I kept looking up at the majestic scene she was drawing and then back again down to her artwork. It was exciting to watch Mikita as she composed something that looked so realistic with just a pencil scratching on a piece of paper, and her artistic talents amazed me. I loved her so much.

The camp was set, there was wood snapping with the crackle of a new fire, and Mikita had finished her drawing. Now we all settled near the fire for one last night of togetherness. Jan Ericsson put a bunch of mystery ingredients into a pot and tended to it occasionally. The aroma wafted throughout our campsite, and as we all waited for the meal to finish cooking, the attention turned to Mikita's artwork.

We had all been continuously amazed at Mikita's ability to surprise us with her talents. Her drawings and her music had always managed to bring a sense of happiness. As Thomas Strong and Jan Ericsson first began to take in Mikita's latest drawing of the scene that surrounded us, they appeared to be dumfounded and yet inspired all at once. The two men took turns holding the drawing in their hands and looking up from the page to compare it to the natural landscape. I had watched Mikita create this drawing, and I was in full agreement with both men when they exclaimed that this was Mikita's best work of all.

"I have set camp here many times, Mikita," started Jan Ericsson. "I have never been able to describe the beauty of all of this, all that is around us. What words can't describe, you somehow managed to capture with your drawing."

"You are too kind, Mr. Ericsson," said a humble Mikita.

"No, Mikita, he is not being too kind," said a choked-up Thomas Strong. "He is being honest, as honest as a man humbled by greatness can be."

"Well, thank you, gentlemen, for your compliments, but Stanley and I are hungry, and I think dinner is ready."

Jan Ericsson chuckled and then rushed to a smoking pot that he had left unattended a bit too long. He had been distracted by the art, but he managed to arrive just in time to his smoldering pot of food, similarly as he had arrived so many times in a timely fashion at our cabin to provide aid and advice. We ate Jan Ericsson's hearty stew without knowing exactly what was in it but enjoying it nonetheless.

"What's in this, Jan?" inquired Thomas Strong.

"This and that." The chef chuckled.

"It is really good," chimed Mikita. "What is the recipe?"

"Thomas, you write, and, Mikita, you play music and draw, and I don't ask you how you do it." Jan Ericsson laughed. "I happen to make a great campfire stew. I just hope you enjoy the stew as much as I have enjoyed your stories, music, and artwork."

It was obvious that there was such mutual respect and admiration between everyone that surrounded the fire. I watched as my master, Mikita, and Jan Ericsson settled down into a relaxed night of camping in the wilderness. I worked my way to my usual position of maximum comfort, which was snuggling as tightly and closely to Mikita as I could. I nudged her and motioned my head toward a satchel that I knew contained books.

"Do you want me to read to you, Stanley?" asked Mikita, knowing all too well that is exactly what I wanted.

Mikita read a few chapters from an obscure book that told a tale of a lonesome traveler. All of us listened intently as Mikita read the words from the old pages. We all looked at one another and were so happy to be traveling with such great and trusted friends. None of us was a lonesome traveler. The comforting sound of Mikita's voice slowly blended with the whispering winds of the trees surrounding the silver lake. We were all tired, and Jan Ericsson stacked a big pile of wood on our campfire. Soon, we all dozed off into the comfort of dreams.

The most memorable evening and glorious night of slumber ended abruptly with the sound of two pans being clanked together by Jan Ericsson.

"Wake up, and let's move."

Jan Ericsson and Mikita had already tended to the sled teams and packed up most of the campsite. It was typical of both of them to be so organized and efficient, but it still amazed me, and I could tell my master felt the same way. We were about to start a day of sledding that would bring us into Dawson City. We would probably have a smooth ride back into a place that had many people bustling about and doing things that people do in a civilized community.

As the sleds pulled us toward Dawson City, I felt confused by a mixture of emotions. I was thrilled to be heading back toward the home that Thomas Strong and I had once before shared with such happiness. Yet as I rode with Mikita on the sled toward Dawson City, I felt sad because I wasn't sure if we would ever be this close again. Our time in the cabin was so special and had drawn us so tightly together. I remembered all our special moments and prayed that there would be more in the future.

As we headed toward Dawson City, I listened to the noises around us as Jan Ericsson was guiding his sled team and all of us closer to humanity. The sounds of paws pounding in the snow were louder than the commands of Jan Ericsson's voice. There was an incredible rhythm to the working strides of the dogs, and I felt bad because I realized I would never hear that sound again.

So much had happened since our journey north with Jan Ericsson's sled team, but I had never forgotten the will and strength of these dogs. Again, just like I felt on the trip north to our cabin, I felt guilty to be spending most of our travels snuggled under a blanket on top of a sled.

I felt Mikita's gloved hand rubbing my head every now and then, which made me feel secure and confident that our journey was progressing safely. I also was comforted by the sounds of my master steering his sled team closely behind us, and I was filled with a feeling of contentment as Mikita and I continued to travel on together.

The sounds of the sleds sliding in the snow, for some reason, provided me with a sense of comfort and security. It reminded me of the feeling I had when a storm would blow in swiftly over Thomas Strong's estate in California. I would snuggle close to the man I loved so much, and listen to the sounds of rain spanking the roof and the wind howling and rustling through the trees. The inclement weather outside somehow made me feel more secure and safe inside.

I remember falling into deep sleeps to the sound of rain tapping the windows at my master's home, and the swishing sounds of the sleds had the same effect on me. Soon, our three sled teams pulled into Dawson City, and Mikita had to rustle me pretty hard to wake me up for our arrival.

Chapter Thirty-Three

I Am a Celebrity

As we pulled into Dawson City, Jan Ericsson guided our three sled teams toward people he knew and trusted. They would care for the dogs and look after our belongings on the sleds.

My master needed to secure lodging, and Jan Ericsson, Mikita, and I were hungry. We headed straight to Mother McCreary's, because with Jan Ericsson's connections, we could easily get a room and a good meal. As we entered, everyone in the room yelled a greeting to Jan Ericsson.

"Hey, Jan, welcome back!"

"Another safe trip."

"Glad you are back."

Suddenly the excitement in the welcoming room turned to silence, and everyone was looking right at me. People actually started to stand up and move closer toward me to get a closer look. I was getting a bit nervous and not even sure how to respond.

"Oh my!" someone screamed.

"It's him!"

"It's Stanley!"

"Get a good look at him!"

"Who is going to win the contest?"

Somehow, everyone recognized me, but it was more than that, because they were all urging the bartender to get "the drawings." Some of the local people remembered me from when I had first passed through and were wondering if a dog like me would survive up north.

When Bullman, Loser, and Kituk had arrived a few days earlier, they spoke of their journey and mentioned how Stanley, the French Bulldog, was thriving and enjoying the northland. They told fake stories of crazy things I had done and spent a drunken night turning me into a mythical legend. Some people really did remember me, and some just said they did. Bullman and Loser wanted to see who really remembered me, and for fun, they started a contest.

"DRAW A SKETCH OF STANLEY! BEST PICTURE GETS ONE HUNDRED DOLLARS!"

"Stanley will be here soon," said Bullman.

"And when he gets here, you can judge the contest," stated Loser.

When we arrived in Dawson City, our friends had already continued the journey south to Thomas Strong's estate, but before leaving, they had left the prize money that everyone was now hoping to procure. I was a little embarrassed by all the attention, especially when Mother McCreary herself made me decide the winner from the three finalists that had been selected by the excited roomful of voters. All three drawings were excellent, but I was attracted to the flowery perfume and big breasts of one of the artists, and I scratched my paw on her work to indicate she was the winner. The winner was so thrilled that she picked me up and pulled me into her bountiful bosoms and made my face the middle of a breast sandwich. Trust me, I wasn't about to complain.

I was so happy to see my master and Jan Ericsson laughing away throughout the festivities, but during the excitement, I had lost track of Mikita. I looked quickly and thoroughly around the room and did not see her. I began to panic, and I bolted toward the door. I sensed Mikita was outside, and I needed to get to her. Thankfully, someone was entering Mother's and opened the door just as I approached it, and I whipped outside.

I immediately saw Mikita hunched over on her knees in the middle of the wide-open courtyard area in the center of Dawson City. I raced toward her, not knowing what might be wrong. My adrenaline kicked in, and I am quite sure I was running faster than I had ever run before. I was sprinting so fast that when I reached Mikita and tried to stop, I slid on the icy snow about fifteen feet past her.

As I gathered myself and turned around, I was happy to hear the sound of Mikita laughing, and also there was another little voice making giggling sounds. When I collected my bearings and returned to approach Mikita, I found her embracing a young girl. I guess my arrival on the scene looked kind of goofy and awkward, and the little girl was chuckling at me.

"Teka, this is my friend, Stanley." Mikita laughed.

"Is he a good boy?" asked Teka.

"Yes, Teka," assured Mikita, and as she began to explain my best good-natured qualities, I had already begun to lick the face of this innocent little girl. Suddenly, I heard the concerned voice of my master as he approached.

"Is everything okay? Stanley? Mikita? Is everything all right?" yelled a worried Thomas Strong.

"Yes, yes," assured Mikita.

"The both of you," barked the concerned father, "don't ever leave my sight like that again!"

"I am sorry, I didn't mean to upset you," whispered Mikita, and at the same time, Thomas Strong instantly became aware of the little girl being held in his new daughter's arms.

"And who is this?" asked the writer.

"This is Teka. She is an orphan that I used to help take care of before . . ."

"Well," interjected the concerned father, "Teka seems very happy to have you back, Mikita."

I was about to be so lucky again. I could sense it! Another wonderful moment was about to happen. I knew what Mikita was about to ask, and I was certain of the answer my master would provide.

"Daddy?" asked Mikita in a childish voice that belied her toughness, strength, and will, "can we please bring Teka with us?"

A man whose broken heart had already been mended on this adventure north, dropped to his knees, and opened his heart even wider to accept more love and joy into his once-desolate life.

"My dear daughter, Mikita, please help me get to know my newest daughter."

The father and his two new daughters hugged and laughed and cried for a few minutes. I just excitedly ran circles around them until I realized my paws were freezing. Mikita sensed my discomfort, picked me up, and carried me toward Mother McCreary's. Thomas Strong held Teka's hand and walked with her, following right behind us.

"Let's get something to eat," offered a happy Thomas Strong.

As we entered Mother's, Jan Ericsson had already secured a table, and when he saw his friend Thomas Strong holding young Teka's hand and ushering her toward him, he quickly found a blanket and rolled it up to help prop the little girl up on a chair.

"And who is this special guest?" asked Jan Ericsson.

"This is Teka," said Mikita.

"And Teka will be traveling south with us," added a beaming Thomas Strong.

"Oh, Teka, you are a very lucky girl." Jan Ericsson smiled.

"Mr. Strong seems so nice, and that dog Stanley is sooooo cute, but I am most happy to be with my friend Mikita again," stated a surprisingly eloquent six-year-old girl.

It was such a joyous evening. Everyone at the table feasted on a glorious meal, and somehow I managed to share a good portion of it from beneath the table and between the chairs. Even Mother McCreary herself sat down to join everyone, and I noticed the tough business owner unwillingly shedding a tear as she hugged Mikita. It was obvious that she had been so worried about what had happened to this young girl, who had been such a friendly and reliable employee.

Old Mother McCreary must have been getting soft in her old age, because after she expressed her feelings to Mikita, she moved around the table to embrace Thomas Strong.

"Thank God for you," whispered "The Mother into "The Father's" ear.

"Don't thank me, thank him." My master laughed as he pointed at me.

"I know what you did, Stanley," barked Mother McCreary as she rushed toward me and swooped me off the floor. "And I have something special for you."

The owner of this renowned establishment carried me into the kitchen and dropped me to the floor in front a huge piece of elk meat. It smelled so good and was still steaming warm, so I lunged at it quickly in an attempt to devour it. Mother McCreary stopped me, and this busy, hardworking woman actually sat on the floor next to me and cut the elk meat into small pieces and then hand-fed them to me. Damn, my life just kept getting better and better!

"Thank you for helping Mikita. Always take care of her," she said to me, "and I know she will take care of you."

When I had devoured the last piece of meat from Mother McCreary's hand, we headed back into the dining area toward our table. Jan Ericsson and Teka seemed about ready for a good night of sleep, and Mikita and Thomas Strong looked to be not too far behind.

Jan Ericsson rose, excused himself, and headed toward the door. His humble abode was a modest cabin just behind the resting place of all the hardworking sled dogs. He promised to meet with us the next morning to bid farewell.

"I'll see you tomorrow morning, Thomas," said Jan Ericsson as he hugged the writer that had made his life more interesting during the last year.

"I think you are forgetting something, my good friend," quipped Thomas Strong.

"I beg your pardon, Thomas."

"Mother McCreary has your gold. I instructed my great and trustworthy friends Bullman and Loser to leave half of all the gold with her. I knew she could keep a secret and be trusted. Didn't you wonder how she knew about what happened to Mikita?"

"Well, yeah, I guess . . . wait a minute . . . half?

"You deserve it, Jan, and I didn't come up here looking to strike the riches of gold."

"Thomas . . . really?"

"Yes, Jan. The amount of gold waiting for me in California will be just enough to put together a business venture I have been thinking about. And I know you will spend the riches of your gold wisely."

"You are a good man, Thomas, truly the best kind of man, and I feel so fortunate to have met you. I can assure you that I will use my newly found wealth to help build a better and safer community here in Dawson City."

"I'm glad to hear that, Jan, and I regard you as the best of the best."

Thomas Strong reached out and began a hearty handshake with Jan Ericsson. The clasping of hands quickly turned into a sturdy bear hug between two men that had deep respect and admiration for each other.

"I'll see you tomorrow morning," was all the scratchy voice of Thomas Strong could muster.

As Jan Ericsson departed, Mikita was essentially carrying a half-awake Teka toward the door. She approached her new father with her index finger over her mouth in the customary gesture that expresses the desire of someone to be quiet.

"Shooooosh," whispered Mikita.

"Where are you going?"

"I am going to spend the night with Teka in the orphanage where she has been living," said Mikita ever so quietly. "I will pack her few belongings and meet up with you and Stanley here tomorrow morning."

"That's a good plan."

"I am still trying to get used to saying this, but thank you, Daddy," was Mikita's very shy expression of gratitude.

Thomas Strong was also just getting used to being called daddy, and the fact that he was a tired traveler made it even harder to hold back his emotions. He hugged Mikita and fought back tears. I know he was thinking that he had already cried enough for one day. My master opened the door for Mikita, and she carried Teka outside.

"Well, my boy, Stanley, it looks like it's just me and you tonight," huffed my master.

I loved all the great people I had met and traveled with throughout this past year, but I was remarkably happy with the thought of having my master all to myself for this one night. Thomas Strong turned to look for Mother McCreary, and even before he actually located her with his eyes, the amazing hostess tossed a room key, and it landed right in his hand.

We had room number 8 for the night. I always liked the number 8 because it was such a smooth digit with no sharp angles. Also, if you turn the numeral 8 on its side, it becomes the symbol for infinity. Hey, I am pretty smart for a dog and infinitely happy as well.

I had hoped to spend some quality time with my master, but that wasn't to be the case. He stumbled while trying to remove his boots and flopped onto the bed. He was instantly out cold and snoring like a bison with a bad cold. I was soon to follow his lead.

CHAPTER THIRTY-FOUR

---·❀·---

A Warm California Welcome

We did not have any interruption of our blissful slumber throughout the night, and the new day was quickly upon us. I couldn't remember the last time I slept that well. I guess being inside a locked hotel room allowed my senses and instincts to relax. From the looks of the contorted morning body stretching of my master, I gathered he had also slept quite well.

It didn't take long for us to gather ourselves and then head downstairs. It definitely wasn't that late in the morning, and it was surprising how much of a bustle was already alive inside Mother McCreary's.

As always, Jan Ericsson was the reliable caretaker. He had already garnered a table large enough for a hungry family. Thomas Strong had barely even planted his backside on the chair when Mother McCreary herself plopped down two plates full of scrambled eggs, sausage, bacon, and flapjacks.

"I expect your two daughters will be eating as well, Mr. Strong?"

"Yes, I expect so, ma'am."

"Don't call me ma'am. Just eat your food, and you better take good care of those girls."

"I will do everything I can for them, Mother," assured Thomas Strong as Mikita and Teka arrived at the table.

I remembered how my master and I had watched Mikita when she first arrived in our cabin. We observed her every move as she

---

began to heal and get stronger. Now, watching Mikita eating her breakfast and helping Teka with her food gave me the same feeling. Just as I knew my master and I would do anything to take care of Mikita, I knew that Mikita would do the same for Teka. My new sisters finished their breakfast, and both of them gave me a piece of bacon and sausage. I couldn't help but think that having two sisters is twice as good as having one.

"It's time to go, Tom," stated Jan Ericsson. "All your luggage is on the coach already."

"You are the best," boasted Thomas Strong as he hugged the man that had made the past year so much easier. "I am going to miss you."

I jumped up and yanked on our great friend's coat. He bent down and picked me up. He squeezed me tightly and rustled his hand over my head.

"I was worried about you from the start, Stanley, but you proved to be one tough little son of a gun. You take care of your dad and your new sisters."

We had a group hug, and we said our final good-byes. Mother McCreary had returned to being the tough lady she was known to be and waved us out the door. We were soon on a large carriage drawn by horses for what was only a short trip to a port just outside the Dawson City limits, on the bank of the Yukon River. We boarded a steamship that was large enough to provide comfortable travel but not too large to prevent the vessel from navigating some of the tricky twists and curves of the river.

The trip down the Yukon River provided some gorgeous scenery. Over the long history of the river, the constant fluctuation in the northern temperatures combined with the power of the flowing water had sliced through ancient bedrock and worked to create artistic masterpieces of natural rock sculpture. My master, Mikita, Teka, and I relaxed and enjoyed the steamship ride, absorbed the scenery that surrounded us, and wallowed in the joy of our togetherness.

We disembarked the steamship in the port of Yakutat. There was an enormous ship ready to head south but was still waiting for as many people as possible to fill empty cabins. Thomas Strong secured two cabins, one for the girls and one for the boys. The accommodations were quite luxurious, and we ended up spending one evening on the ship before heading home. I slept in the cabin that night while Thomas Strong took his two daughters to dinner.

The next morning, my master had a breakfast delivered to our cabin, and Mikita and Teka soon joined us. We were all enjoying a hearty breakfast and taking turns looking out through the porthole window at the scenery. Then the glasses and silverware on the table began to rattle as the boat began to slowly pull away from the dock and head toward the Bay of Alaska and then into the enormity of the Pacific Ocean.

The cruise on this huge ship lasted four days, with stops outside of Seattle and San Francisco, before finally pulling into Stern's Wharf, just outside of Santa Barbara. We spent a night of luxury in an extravagant hotel before beginning the last leg of our journey back to Thomas Strong's estate outside of Los Angeles.

I woke to the sounds of silverware on plates and glasses clinking as Mikita and Teka were smiling and having a happy breakfast together. Thomas Strong entered the room shortly after I was awake, and soon the breakfast was finished.

"It's time to go, everyone. It's time to go home," whooped Thomas Strong. "And I have a surprise for you."

Our father had already packed and secured our luggage, and as we exited the hotel, we gazed at something right in front of us that seemed both unique and remarkable. It looked like a big wagon that a team of four horses would be needed to pull it and get it moving forward, but there were no horses in sight.

"This is an automobile!" yelled my master. "It is the wave of the future, and it will be taking us home."

The interesting vehicle looked mighty heavy, and it had huge wagon wheels with the front ones being just a bit larger than the wheels in the back. There was room enough on board for all of us, and our luggage had room to spare as well. I just hoped it wouldn't start raining, because there was no roof. This was apparently state of the art transportation, so it was obvious that Thomas Strong had kept a little nest egg of gold for our travels.

"This is called the Best Wagon Automobile, and it should get us back home in three or four hours."

"This is going to be so much fun!" yelped Mikita.

"Just wait until Bullman and Loser see us pulling up in this thing," cracked Thomas Strong.

It was as much fun as Mikita had expected, but it was a bumpy ride over dirt trails normally used by horse-pulled wagons. It was late in the afternoon when Thomas Strong turned our Best Wagon Automobile into the long path that entered his estate, our home. We all began to whoop and holler, and soon Bullman, Loser, and Kituk bolted out of the house and raced to welcome us.

Suddenly, a strange but magnificent emotional sensation came over me. I was overflowing with a spiritual joy that I was having difficulty deciphering. I realized that I had never before experienced the incredible feeling of being welcomed home after being away for such a long time. The thought of people waiting for us and expressing happiness upon our return gave me such inner warmth that no wood-burning fire could ever equal.

I will always remember that blissful moment. There weren't any Welcome Home banners or a band playing music. It was just the sight of three people that we deeply cared about rushing to greet us. It's a welcome-home moment, and in my mind, I began hoping that everyone I had welcomed into our cabin had felt the same way that I was feeling right now.

"What the hell are you driving, Writer Boy?" screamed Bullman.

"Where are the horses?" asked Loser as we all began to huddle and hug in front of our Best Wagon. I was so excited to be home I sprinted circles around the house until I ran out of gas. Everyone was laughing at my antics while they also began to get acquainted with Teka.

"Mikita, who is your cute little friend?" inquired Bullman.

"What a cutey," added Loser.

"Actually, gentlemen, Teka is my little sister," declared Mikita, and Thomas Strong smiled and nodded in approval.

"Well, this house just keeps getting fuller and fuller." Bullman laughed.

"I guess we have to make more renovations," said Loser as we all began to enter our home.

"More renovations?" asked the curious owner of his home as he entered it for the first time in over a year.

"Tom, remember, you told us to do a few things," reminded Bullman.

"I think we did well, Tom," assured Loser.

As we entered the comfort of our old domain, there was an immediate and powerful contrast to the struggles and difficulty of the remote existence in the northland. I had grown up accustomed to the luxuries of this wonderful home, and now I had a new appreciation for all its amenities. I glanced at Mikita and Teka as we began to settle inside, and they both had dumbfounded looks on their faces. Neither of them had ever been in a residence like this, and I think they were in disbelief that this was now going to be their home.

"I don't think Writer Boy and Stanley need a tour of the house." Bullman chuckled.

"So let's just show Mikita her brand-new room," continued Loser.

"And after that, Stanley can show the girls around the rest of the place." Bullman laughed.

As we headed up the big staircase in the middle of the house, I had a new appreciation for just how large and spacious this house was, and perhaps that is why it felt so dark and empty before we journeyed north. Right now, under the security that the roof this home had always provided, all I could feel was warmth and happiness. Soon, we entered a large room that had previously been a dumping ground for anything my master was not quite sure whether to keep or discard. It was now Mikita's room, and even a dog like me can grasp that irony.

"I hope you like your new room," wished Bullman.

"We wanted to make it special for you, Mikita," chimed Loser.

"Oh my goodness!" barked a stunned Thomas Strong.

"Oh dear," whispered a choked-up Mikita.

In just the week that Bullman, Loser, and Kituk had been here, they had transformed a room full of discardable items into a sanctuary for a most precious person. There was an enormous new window on the wall that faced toward the west, which would be perfect to provide views of inspirational California sunsets. Under the left side of the window, there was a newly constructed desk that was perfect for Mikita to create more wonderful drawings. Next to that was a bench and music stand for Mikita, so she could easily develop her musical mandolin skills. There was a big bed and newly built armor and bookshelves with a hanging lantern and a rocking chair underneath.

"Unbelievable!" exclaimed Thomas Strong, as he remembered what this room had looked like before we left.

"This is my room?" screeched Mikita, because she could not believe this was her new home.

"So how did we do, Writer Boy?" asked Bullman.

"Yes, yes, yes," was Mikita's response. One yes for each man that had worked to provide a wonderful welcome.

Bullman, Loser, and Kituk had given her something she never could have asked for or expected. Mikita had worked so hard in her life for whatever she needed to survive, and she was not accustomed to this type of generosity. As her emotions began to overcome her, she slowly moved toward the three men that had done this for her and gave each of them a loving hug. As she hugged the men that had constructed her room, Mikita turned toward her father and smiled.

"I know I am going to be happy here," said Mikita. "But I will never be happier in this room than I am right now."

"So, boys, what improvements did you make to my room?" asked my master in a jocular attempt to keep Mikita from crying tears of joy.

"You didn't ask for that, Thomas," responded Bullman.

"But I guess we will need to fix up a room for Teka," observed Loser.

"For now, Teka should share this beautiful room with me," advised Mikita. "This is a big transition for all of us, and I want to keep Teka as close to me as possible."

"That sounds like a smart idea, Mikita," beamed the new father of these two lovely girls.

"Wait until you see what we have going on behind the house, Writer Boy!" whipped Bullman.

"Yeah, you're going to love this, Thomas," cracked Loser.

CHAPTER THIRTY-FIVE

Family Fun

I was deliriously happy to be back in the home that I had grown up in, and even more enthused to have more people to enjoy it with. It was a large and spacious residence that had many rooms, and now Bullman, Loser, and Kituk had settled into their own quarters and established them as their own. My instincts told me that this home was going to be busier and louder than it had ever been.

Mikita and Teka were spending the first day here, settling into their new room. Bullman, Loser, and Kituk showed Thomas Strong the once-empty rooms that they now had established as their own and now looked to be permanent residences.

"Hey, Thomas, we want to show you the project we started outside," started Loser.

"Wait until you see what we have going on behind the house, Writer Boy!" whipped Bullman.

"Yeah, you're going to love this, Thomas," cracked Loser.

"But before we do, we want to talk to you about something," said Bullman.

"Sounds serious, boys. What's wrong?" inquired Writer Boy.

"Nothing is wrong, Thomas. In fact, everything couldn't be more right," responded Bullman.

"We kind of like it here, Writer Boy," chipped in Loser.

"During the last week, hanging around here and waiting for your return, we took a few deep breaths and realized something," offered Bullman.

"What are you two philosophers trying to say?" asked Thomas Strong.

"Loser and I want to retire, Thomas," stated Bullman.

"And we would like to enjoy the rest of our lives here, with you, Writer Boy," finished Loser.

It was hard to describe the initial response of my master. As a dog with great instincts and a thorough familiarity with all his facial expressions, I did not have a clue what he was thinking. He seemed a bit bewildered but also pensive in thought.

"I left here a year ago so lonely and depressed that I could tell that even my boy, Stanley, was concerned about me," was Thomas Strong's initial response. "Now I return to a house that is filled with friends and loved ones. I was already planning to ask you guys to stay, so thanks for saving me the trouble." Thomas Strong laughed.

I was running around and jumping up and down with excitement. Everyone seemed so happy, and I sensed our lives were going to be filled with wonderful moments that would make cherished memories. My master found a dusty old bottle of scotch, and the four men in the room toasted to old friends, new friends, and a wonderful life.

"Hey, guys," were the first words that soft-spoken Kituk had uttered since our return. "Let's go show Mr. Strong what we have started to work on out back."

"What have you guys been up to?" asked Writer Boy as we all headed out the door.

Behind the house, there was a small structure in the earliest stages of construction, but somehow I recognized something familiar, and I began enthusiastically running around the new project. The size and shape seemed a spot on match to someplace we were all familiar with, and when my master saw a huge pile of logs not too far away, he started to figure out what his friends had planned.

"You guys have been busy!" exclaimed Thomas Strong.

"We wanted to do something special, something to help remember a place that was so important to all of us," offered Bullman.

"We loved that cabin up north, Thomas, and all the experiences we shared there, but it's a very long trip from here," added Loser.

"So we figured we would build that cabin on the grounds of your estate, just in case it ever got below fifty degrees here, and we need to have a place to build a fire," finished Bullman.

"You crazy lunatics!" yelled Thomas Strong. "I love it."

Everyone was smiling and laughing and began heading back toward the house. Mikita and Teka were curious about all the boisterous noise coming from outside the house and went to investigate.

Everyone met in a large patch of green grass right in front of the house. A moment like this is hard to describe. It seemed surreal and almost too good to be true. Everyone was celebrating the moment. There were no thoughts about the pain of the past, and nobody was worrying about the future. All our thoughts were about the present. It was an instant in time that we all knew would be secured forever in our memories. The glorious late-afternoon California sunshine toasted those lasting images with warmth, which helped to truly represent the feelings we all had for one another.

For the next two months, Thomas Strong's California estate was like a family vacation that didn't want to come to a conclusion. Mikita was doing an amazing job helping Teka get acclimated to her new surroundings. They went on long walks that tired me out if I went along with them. One day, Mikita taught Teka how to fly a kite, and I will always remember the sound of the young girl's laughter as she ran as fast as she could while looking up toward her kite sailing in the sky.

Kituk was enjoying the life he had in California, but he also was the only one that seemed to be working. He had taken control of the cabin project, and because of his diligence, things were moving along nicely. The combined efforts of Bullman, Loser, and Writer Boy barely totaled what Kituk was doing each day. Soon, the replica cabin was completed, and on the first night there was a chill in the air, we christened the fireplace with its first burning logs. All of us spent the evening on a glorified camping trip just fifty yards outside our home.

For the most part, Mikita ran the operation of the kitchen the same way Kituk ran the cabin project. She was always in charge, but everyone else took turns chipping in to help. I always enjoyed watching the creation of the evening meal and the coming together of everyone to eat it.

Just as it was in the cabin up north, Mikita was usually the provider of our evening entertainment. Sometimes she read aloud to us from a classic novel, and sometimes she played songs on the mandolin, and she was also regaining her piano skills on the dusty old instrument in the sitting room that had rarely been played.

After a few months, Kituk was ready to head back to his roots up north, but when he returned home, it would not be as a guide, but as an aspiring author. Thomas Strong had set up a deal for him with *American* magazine. Kituk's writing samples had been impressive, and he was expected to write some tales similar to those that his mentor had provided the magazine the previous year. The editors also hoped that Kituk's natural skills in the frigid wilderness might also provide unique adventure tales and some interesting reading.

Thomas Strong drove Kituk to the port just outside of Santa Barbara, watched him board a steamship, and waved good-bye to him as the ship left the dock. The mentor watched the aspiring writer head off into a promising future and then began the long drive home. While the great writer was sentimental about the departure of Kituk, as he traveled home, he realized that soon he would have to deal with a much more emotional departure.

Mikita was incredibly happy living in the warm sunshine of her new daddy's California estate. She loved to keep busy, and there were plenty of things to keep her sufficiently occupied. She catered to every need of the three retired wise men. Mikita also did everything she could to educate and entertain Teka and even managed to spend some quality time with me.

One day, after a couple of glorious years of family togetherness, Thomas Strong grabbed Loser, the best financial mind in the United States, and they took a drive into the growing city of Los Angeles. Bullman was left behind to babysit the girls and me. He didn't mind. The old cattle rancher didn't like riding in cars anyway. The two men did not return until the afternoon of the next day, because they had been very busy doing a lot of business. Thomas Strong had taken the gold that he had saved and some of his own money and created a unique opportunity for his multitalented daughter.

As they returned, Thomas Strong beckoned everyone to the dining room table, where we had enjoyed so many family meals. He sat down next to Mikita, grasped her hand, and began to explain the business he had been conducting with Loser in Los Angeles.

"Mikita, I love you so very much. You have brought so much joy to my life and happiness to everyone in this room," started this very emotional man.

"Yes, Daddy, I love you and everyone here too," responded a curious Mikita.

"I never want to say good-bye to you, Mikita, but you are too talented and have too much potential for great success to be spending most of your time taking care of three gray beards."

"I love being here with everyone," implored Mikita.

"I know you do, my lovely daughter, but it is time for the old men to look after Teka while you make a name for yourself in the real world."

Thomas Strong and Loser had spent the last two days establishing a new magazine that would feature the work of blossoming new artists. They had purchased a three-story building that had two floors of office space, and the top floor had some spacious apartments. *American* magazine's renowned writer reached out to talented people he knew from his experiences and recruited four quality individuals to get the magazine up and running.

There was a photo editor, an art editor, a copyeditor, and an advertising manager. These people were expected to do their jobs while also teaching everything they knew to Mikita, the future editor in chief of a brand-new publication, *Art and Images* magazine.

I watched Mikita closely as she listened to everything my master and Loser were explaining to her. At first she seemed a bit overwhelmed, and then she was somewhat stunned. Soon, she appeared to be in a state of shock almost as deeply as when we found her frozen and broken body in the snow.

"Mikita, do you understand what I am telling you?" asked the father, who was struggling with creating the opportunity that eventually would have him saying good-bye to his cherished daughter.

"I don't know what to say. I think you are doing too much for me, Daddy," whispered a talented girl who was turning into a young woman. She was struggling to comprehend the generous opportunity being provided to her. Mikita also knew it would be difficult to say good-bye.

"I could never do too much for you, Mikita. I might be a good writer, but I will never be able to find the words to describe what you have meant to me, and for Stanley too."

"I love you, Daddy."

"I love you too. Now just promise you will learn something new every day and make the most of all your talents."

"Thank you so much. I promise to do my very best!"

"I know you will, Mikita," encouraged Thomas Strong.

CHAPTER THIRTY-SIX

Get Busy Living

Soon the day came when it was time for Mikita to leave and move toward the promise of her professional career in the magazine business. I thought it was strange that there was someone heading off in pursuit of such a wonderful and exciting opportunity, and yet everyone seemed so sad. I guess it is a type of despair that can only be caused by the departure of a loved one.

Bullman, Loser, and Teka all carried some of Mikita's belongings and loaded the luggage into the Best Wagon Automobile, which had become a trusted form of transportation over the last couple of years. Mikita was now enthusiastic and excited about the new life she was about to experience, but she had concerns about leaving Teka. Her worries were certainly unwarranted.

Teka had grown so comfortable with her life on my master's estate, and she had grown so close with all the friendly old men that helped take care of her. Bullman taught her how to ride a horse, Loser taught her math, Writer Boy taught her how to read, and I was always happy to run and play with her at any time.

There was a lengthy hugging session on the front porch of the house as Mikita began her departure. Bullman and Loser acted like old crying ladies. I was trying to be stronger. Teka rushed to Mikita and grabbed her with all the strength of her young girl's arms, but Teka wasn't crying.

"Mikita, don't worry about me," began Teka as she pulled Mikita to her knees. "You have done enough for me. Go do something for yourself."

"Teka, sweetheart, I know everyone here will take care of you, but I am going to miss you very much."

"And I will miss you too, Mikita."

"You have to promise me one thing, Teka," said a choked-up Mikita.

"Sure, what is it, Mikita?"

"I want to make sure you take good care of my best friend, Stanley. Promise that you will make him smile every day."

"I will, Mikita, I will."

"No matter how far away I am, I will know when Stanley is smiling, so make him smile a lot!"

"I promise!"

I was taking all the emotions of Mikita's departure deep into my memory. I was overcome with so many thoughts and feelings, and I became confused. I just sprinted toward the automobile and ran in circles around it. As always, Mikita knew exactly what to do. She knelt down and calmly called my name, and when I settled in her arms, she said the words that always brought me joy.

"I love you, Stanley!" were the words spoken with the sound of Mikita's voice that always made me most happy.

"You have to say good-bye, Stanley," urged my master.

"You will always be my hero, Stanley, and I promise I will be back here as often as I can to visit. Make sure to look after Teka, our daddy, Bullman, and Loser," were the last words Mikita said to me before she left.

I kissed Mikita to make sure she knew I understood what she had just requested of me, and my tongue licking her face was an obvious expression of the love I had for my special friend. I followed her to the door of the automobile, and after she patted me on my head, she got into the Best Wagon. My master climbed into the driver's seat and started the motor, and they were on their way.

The next day, Thomas Strong returned just as the light of the California sun was vanishing and was quickly being replaced by sparkling darkness. As he parked the automobile and strode toward the front door of his home, he was surprised by the complete darkness inside the large house and also curious that nobody was there to welcome him. He stood there perplexed for a moment, just long enough for me to surprise him. I bolted from around the back of the house and leaped into his arms.

"Hey, my boy, Stanley, where is everyone?"

I wanted so badly to usher my master to the surprise welcome we had all planned, but I spent a minute jumping up and down in front of him, licking his face, and scratching at his legs in a private moment to show how much I loved him. After I had expressed my love and admiration, I led him around the house, toward the welcoming party.

The cabin that had been built as a replica of the special dwelling up north was now about to have a very special moment. There was smoke pluming from the chimney, and something was cooking that smelled really tasty. At the front of the cabin, Bullman, Loser, and Teka stood waiting with enormous smiles.

"Welcome back, Writer Boy." Bullman chuckled.

"I hope you had a nice trip," chimed Loser.

"Daddy," started Teka, "I hope it is okay with you. We wanted to camp in the cabin."

"Oh, darling Teka, I think that was a great idea!"

We spent a wonderful night in the cabin. There was a fine dinner, from which I managed to procure some tasty leftover morsels. Teka and I played together in front of the fire, and the three good friends drank fine single malt scotch and told tall tales all night long.

The late hours of evening were turning into the early hours of morning, when I noticed that the only person moving around was my master. He had positioned himself in a place that was always most comfortable. The familiar sound of his quill pen scratching paper meant he was at his writing desk and most likely telling the story of this memorable evening of his family camping in the cabin.

After that night, we all had so many more wonderful times together, and I enjoyed getting to know Bullman and Loser much more deeply and felt closer to them each day. I also think that the more time they spent with me, they liked me even more as well.

Naturally, a young girl and a dog would spend a lot of time together. Teka and I became such close pals, and we did so many things together. Most days, we would find a new adventure on our sprawling California estate. At ten years old, we were both the same age, so we were meant to be friends. But soon I started to notice that while Teka was getting bigger, stronger, and faster, I was getting slower and more tired at the end of each day.

As she had promised, Mikita came back home to visit quite often, almost every month. My master had purchased a Breer Steam Runabout automobile for her to drive on her trips back and forth from Los Angeles to our home. It was a sturdy, big-wheeled wagon with two large padded seats. I sensed the sound of that Runabout approaching before anyone else, and I always raced two hundred feet, halfway up the path leading to our home, to greet my beloved friend.

After a couple of years, Mikita was becoming much more responsible for the development and success of *Arts and Images* magazine, and her trips back home became more and more infrequent. She was developing all her skills and talents, and the sky was the limit for anything Mikita wanted to achieve.

I was getting older, and each time Mikita came home for a visit, the distance from the front door to where I greeted her got shorter and shorter.

In the thirteenth year of my life, I heard Mikita's Breer Steam Runabout approaching. I was sore and tired and struggled to my feet.

"Are you okay, Stanley?" asked my beloved master as he opened the door for me.

I had some excitement and enthusiasm and tried to rush and greet Mikita. I moved too quickly through the door and stumbled and fell on the steps. I landed hard on the ground and felt pain, and my instincts told me I was a goner.

I heard my master yell "Stanleeeeey!" and it made me smile through the pain, because it reminded me of when he used to screech my name when I was a puppy.

"Stanley, my Stanley, are you okay?" Mikita was frantically asking as she rushed to my side.

"I love you, Stanley. I love you, Stanley," were the words Mikita kept repeating over and over.

Those lovely words were the last words I ever heard, and as my eyes slowly closed, the final image I saw was Mikita's eyes looking at me with love. I was on my way to the Happy Hunting Ground for Dogs, and my last thought was that I was the luckiest dog that ever lived.

EPILOGUE

---·❋·---

T he Fahrun twins, Wolfgang and Dietmar, returned to San
Francisco to work with their parents at Fahrun Furniture. They
helped build the business to its fullest capacity, but when power tools
arrived on the scene in 1915, the brothers saw an opportunity for
increased productivity and expansion. Fahrun Furniture began to
spread all throughout California. The Fahrun brothers worked so
hard they burned out many of the power drills and saws that they
used. Wolfgang and Dietmar eventually designed a lubricant that
helped keep the motors of the tools from failing. They invented this
lubricant in the fortieth year of their lives, so they called it WD40.
That lubricant is still, to this day, a household brand.

Payuk, the guide that had delivered Wolfgang and Dietmar
Fahrun to and from the treacherous northland, continued to build
on his reputation of being a great guide. He later tired of babysitting
people he hardly knew, and he devoted his attention to a new concept
in the north. In the year of 1908, in Nome, Alaska, Payuk began
to organize sled dog races that would measure the skills of the best
sledders. In 1973, many years after Payuk had passed away, the
first Iditarod sled race was run. It was the truest test of will and
determination of both dogs and sledder, and when they had the
opening ceremonies of the inaugural race, they acknowledged the
work of Payuk early in the twentieth century.

Maureen Winston and Mandy Bagley had gone on an adventure
with their husbands. They returned without them, but they forged
on in pursuit of success and happiness. The hotel they established,
Strong Manor, was an enormous success. The little chocolate treats

---

with the little *M* were a great touch, but sometimes the chocolate melted on the pillow. Maureen and Mandy designed a crisp coating that surrounded the chocolate, and they printed the letter *M* on that shell. Strong Manor was a great success, but the little chocolates with the shells and *M* printed on them became one of the most recognizable products in the United States.

Francis Krausse returned to his parents' cabin near Lake Michigan. He took Maruk with him, and they established a hunting and fishing guide service that became a model for so many other such businesses in the future.

Kituk returned to the cabin where he had met Thomas Strong. The simple dwelling had provided a spectacular revival for one old writer that had lost his way, and it would also provide the birth of a new writing talent. Kituk picked up where Thomas Strong left off, telling the stories of northland travelers. Jan Ericsson continued his role as the worthy provider of sustenance and the courier of the stories back to civilization. With the approval of Thomas Strong, Kituk and Jan Ericsson continued to work the mine with great success. Both Kituk and Jan Ericsson became wealthy from their efforts in the mine. Kituk used his wealth to travel the world and write stories about his experiences. Jan Ericsson used most of the riches from his gold to help make Dawson City a better place. He built a town hall, a courthouse, and two hospitals, one for people and one for animals. Kituk became a world-renowned writer, and Jan Ericsson ended up being mayor of Dawson City.

Teka loved living on the California estate with Thomas Strong and enjoyed all that Bullman and Loser taught her about life. She followed Mikita to work at *Art and Images* magazine. She was a fast learner and good worker, but she had a different calling that only Mikita could completely understand. Teka wanted to help orphans the way she had been salvaged by Thomas Strong and Mikita. She began bringing orphans from the city of Los Angeles back to the estate of Thomas Strong. Usually she brought two or three children with her per week. Mikita had given the Breer Steam Runabout to Teka, and the children loved the bouncy ride to the California estate of Thomas Strong. The orphans were treated to a week of cabin camping, horse-riding lessons from Bullman, math and history lessons from Loser, and some quality storytelling from a famous author.

Writer Boy, Bullman, and Loser lived the rest of their lives in complete happiness. They were true friends that had all helped one another in times of need, and they appreciated every day that they got to spend with one another.

Mikita went on to great success as the editor in chief of *Arts and Images* magazine. The notoriety from the magazine gave her an opportunity to open an art gallery next to the offices of the magazine. Many artists became famous from their exhibits in the gallery, especially with the help of the publicity from the coverage in *Art and Images*.

Mikita was encouraged by many people to present an exhibit of her own drawings, especially the ones from her days in the northland. She agreed to the exhibit but stipulated that all the work be auctioned off, with all proceeds going to help Teka and her efforts to help orphans.

Thomas Strong, Bullman, Loser, and Teka all attended the showing. It was a great success, both artistically and financially. There was only one piece of art that Mikita refused to display or sell at the auction. It was a drawing of me sleeping in front of the fire in our cabin. I had never seen it before, but when Mikita brought it home and hung it on a nail over her fireplace, she knew I had never left her.